"We took vows, Jayne.

"This may be a marriage in name only, but I intend to protect you. You'll be safer here than anywhere else."

Danger had heightened her senses, making her aware of the taut cords in Ethan's neck and the heat of his skin. She'd lost so much—her home, her business, her dream of loving a good man. Tears welled and spilled from her eyes.

Ethan brushed them aside with his knuckles. "It'll be all right. I promise."

But she couldn't stop the throbbing in her chest. More tears spilled, thicker than the first ones, until Ethan tipped his head downward and kissed them away, trailing his lips from her temple to her cheek.

Did he feel it, too, this yearning for comfort? She couldn't be Laura for him, not ever. But just for tonight she could meet a need, both his and hers...!

* * *

West of Heaven
Harlequin Historical #714—July 2004

West
—of—
Heaven

VICTORIA BYLIN

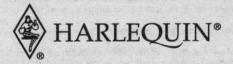

HARLEQUIN®

TORONTO • NEW YORK • LONDON
AMSTERDAM • PARIS • SYDNEY • HAMBURG
STOCKHOLM • ATHENS • TOKYO • MILAN • MADRID
PRAGUE • WARSAW • BUDAPEST • AUCKLAND

ISBN 0-373-29314-3

WEST OF HEAVEN

This edition published by arrangement with Harlequin Books S.A.

® and TM are trademarks of the publisher. Trademarks indicated with ® are registered in the United States Patent and Trademark Office, the Canadian Trade Marks Office and in other countries.

www.eHarlequin.com

Printed in U.S.A.

Available from Harlequin Historicals and
VICTORIA BYLIN

Of Men and Angels #664
West of Heaven #714

Please address questions and book requests to:
Harlequin Reader Service
U.S.: 3010 Walden Ave., P.O. Box 1325, Buffalo, NY 14269
Canadian: P.O. Box 609, Fort Erie, Ont. L2A 5X3

To Mom and George,
for having the courage to love twice.

I also want to thank my editor, Kim Nadelson, and
executive editor Tracy Farrell for their guidance.
They made this book possible.

As always, hugs to my husband and sons,
who make life…good.

Prologue

Midas, New Mexico
April 1885

"What in God's name is all that racket?"

Her husband's voice rasped in Jayne Dawson's ear. She and Hank had been married less than a week and were sharing a real bed for the second time. He'd been whispering that this time would be better than the first, when someone had started pounding on the door to their room in the Midas Hotel.

"Criminy," he muttered. "He's gotta be mixed up."

As Hank went back to nuzzling her neck, Jayne closed her eyes to block out the intrusion. When the man coughed again, she stiffened like a fence post. "Hank, maybe we should—"

Silencing her with a kiss, her husband stroked her breast. The rhythm was too quick for her. She needed time to catch up with him, maybe a little sweet talk, anything to take her mind off the stranger standing just outside their door. With a determined moan, Hank slid a wet kiss down her neck.

Rap. Rap. Rap.

Jayne turned her head against the pillow. "Hank, I can't do this with someone standing in the hall."

"He'll go away. Just relax."

Knock. Knock. Knock.

"I know you're in there, Jesse."

"Shit!" Hank leaped off her as if he'd been struck by a bullet. Moonlight turned his body bone-white as he snatched his pants off the chair and hurried into them. He put on a shirt, then pulled his Peacemaker out of the gunbelt and cocked the hammer.

"Hide, Jayney," he ordered. "Get under the covers and don't move a muscle."

"Who's Jesse?"

He shook his head. "Just do what I say."

It wasn't in Jayne's nature to obey anyone, but being stark naked put her at a distinct disadvantage. She scooted lower on the bed, flattened herself against the mattress and listened as her husband stepped into the hallway and closed the door behind him.

She strained to hear through the thick oak, but the tinny music from a nearby saloon masked the voices in the hall. She lowered the sheet an inch and peeked over the hem. The oil lamp flickered against the ivory wall, casting shadows through the gloom as a sinister chortle reached her ears. Her gaze narrowed to the doorknob just as it began to turn.

Was it Hank? Or the stranger with the rasping cough? She would have given a month of Sundays to have been wearing her best dress, or any dress for that matter, but she settled for leaping out of bed and shoving her arms into the cotton wrapper Hank had tossed on the floor. There hadn't been time for a fancy trousseau like the ones she had stitched for the Lexington well-to-do. A week ago she'd been disappointed. Now she was just glad to be covered.

Clutching the flaps of the garment around her middle, she dropped to a crouch in front of her trunk and rummaged for her mother's sewing shears. If the stranger came at her, she'd fight with her last breath before she'd let him touch her. And she had a few things to say to Hank, too. He owed her an explanation.

As her fingers gripped the scissors, Hank slipped back into the room, turned the lock and braced both hands high against the door. With his wheat-colored hair and slim build, he reminded her of the little Dutch boy with his finger in the dike.

Still clutching the scissors, she pushed up from the crouch. "Who was that man?"

Her husband raised his face to the plaster ceiling, blew out a breath, then dropped his arms to his sides and faced her squarely. "Do you remember when I told you I had a past?"

How could she forget? They'd been alone in the tiny sitting room above her mother's dress shop. He'd told her she was the best thing that had ever happened to him and that he wanted a fresh start in life. That's when he had revealed that he'd been a lawman in Wyoming and that he'd killed a good man by mistake.

"There are things I can't tell you," he had said. "But if you can see fit to forgive me for my secrets, I'll love you forever."

Forgiveness sprung from her soul as easily as water from an abundant well. She'd met him in church just two months earlier on Christmas Eve, and never before had she seen a man with such soulful eyes. His sun-bleached hair had been tipped with gold, like the ornamental angels hanging in the snow-crusted windows of the sanctuary.

"God can forgive anything," she'd said. "And so can I."

Until tonight, not once had it occurred to her that the *past* might not be ready to forgive *him*. How naive she'd been. But thoughts of California had stirred her blood. She had wanted to see more of the world than the streets of Lexington, and so she had trusted Hank with her dreams. At least until now. Tying a knot in the belt to her robe, she made her voice firm. "You have to tell me everything, Hank. Right now."

His shoulders rounded as he blew out a breath and faced her. "I will, Jayney, as soon as I get back. But I have to go with this man. I've got something he wants, and that means I'm going to be gone for a few days."

"A few *days?* This is crazy. We should go to the sheriff right now. He'll help us."

He shook his head. "Going to the locals will just make things worse."

"Are you sure?"

"I'm positive. We'll talk as soon as I get back,

but until then, stay in the hotel. If I'm not here in three days, that's when you need to go to the law.''

She watched as he slipped into his old brown duster. A week ago she had stitched a packet of money into a secret pocket for safekeeping. ''Hank, our savings—''

''Trust me, Jayney. I'll be back, but I might need something that's in that pouch.''

She understood how it felt to be poor and friend-less. She wanted to grab her scissors and cut out the money, but his eyes were pleading with her to be-lieve in him. Besides, she'd spoken her wedding vows from the heart and she believed in keeping promises.

''All right,'' she said. ''But hurry. I'll be wor-ried.''

After he lifted his hat off the bedpost, Hank brushed his lips against hers, a soft kiss that tasted like goodbye.

Which is exactly what it turned out to be.

Chapter One

"Lady, face it. Your husband's dead and you've got to go."

Jayne pushed to her feet from the crouch she had assumed next to Hank's body and scowled at the rancher blocking the light from the barn door. The day was as gray as pewter and just as hard. She was standing in a falling-down barn on a ranch in the middle of nowhere with a filthy man glaring at her as if she'd just spit in his face.

Where were his manners, not to mention his compassion? Granted, he'd found a dead man in his barn and he had a right to be upset, but couldn't he show a bit of sympathy for a new widow? Almost anyone else would have offered a kind word, even a cup of hot tea to take off the chill, but not this man. He was looming in the doorway with his arms crossed over his chest and one dirty boot draped over the other, staring at her as if she were vermin.

She'd eat dirt for a week before she would let him intimidate her. A wife had duties, and she intended to fulfill them. She also needed the greenbacks in Hank's duster.

The sheriff was standing just inside the barn door, tapping his boot as if she were wasting his precious time. "I'm sorry, Mrs. Dawson, but Mr. Trent is right. We've got to leave."

"Surely we can wait a few minutes. I'd like to be alone with my husband."

The rancher huffed like a bull getting ready to charge. "You don't *have* a few minutes. A storm's coming, and I want you and Handley out of here."

"It's April," she said reasonably. "A little rain is nothing. I need some time—"

"It won't be rain, dammit. It's going to snow like hell and if you don't leave now, you'll be stuck here for a week. I want you *gone.*"

The sheriff grunted. "Settle down, Trent. You've got no call to yell like that."

"Like hell I don't." The rancher narrowed his gaze to her face. Gold flecks burned like a campfire at dusk and his lips thinned to a bitter sneer. "Do you understand, ma'am? You *cannot* stay here."

With the silvery sky at his back, he was more of a shadow than flesh and blood, but she'd gotten a good look at Ethan Trent earlier in the day. His face was lean to the point of gauntness, and he was wearing the most ragged clothes she'd ever seen. He needed a bath and a shave, not to mention a few good meals, but it wasn't her place to march him down to the creek with a scrub brush and a cake of soap. Hank had left her with a mess of her own to clean up.

Rising to her full height, she glared at the man blocking the light. "My apologies for the *inconvenience,* Mr. Trent. We'll leave right now. If you'll loan us a horse for my husband's body—"

"I don't have a horse to spare. I'll bury him myself."

"Thank you, but no. I want to take Hank back to town."

"You can't."

But she had to. She wanted the comfort of standing in a church and singing hymns as she'd done a year ago for her mother, though she doubted Ethan Trent would understand that sentiment. He was staring at her with the angriest brown eyes she had ever seen. They were liquid and hard at the same time, like water frozen across a slick of mud.

"I have to see my husband properly buried, Mr. Trent. I have to say goodbye."

He huffed as if she had told a joke. "Don't waste your time. He won't hear a goddamned word."

Her mouth gaped. "That's a cruel thing to say."

"It's the truth."

Shaking his head, he paced across the barn, picked up a shovel with a rusty blade and glowered at her. "The wind's picking up. You and Handley need to hit the trail."

She shook her head. "I'm not leaving without my husband. Not like this."

Who else in the world knew that Hank was afraid of the dark? That he slept with a lamp turned low and that he feared death? The one time he'd accompanied her to her mother's grave, he'd stood several feet away, whistling to himself as if that would make a difference.

I don't ever wanna die, Jayney. It's just too damn dark.

And it was. Especially today with the hard sky pressing through the splintery walls of the barn and a wild-eyed rancher gripping the shovel, scowling at her as if she'd committed a crime.

Sheriff Handley strode through the doorway, not bothering to take off his hat. The man had no respect for the dead, or for her.

"Are you finished, ma'am?" he asked forcefully.

Jayne glared at him as he glanced down at Hank with marked disgust. Why hadn't the man thought to bring an extra horse to carry the body? He was both stupid and rude. He didn't deserve to carry the badge.

She cleared her throat. "Sheriff, would you please tell Mr. Trent that we need to borrow a horse."

The rancher shrugged. "Like I said, I don't have one to lend. I ride the roan, and the gelding's not going anywhere."

The sheriff dipped his chin at her and arched his eyebrows as if she were a child. "I'm sorry for your loss, Mrs. Dawson, but circumstances can't be changed. Mr. Trent has kindly offered to give your husband a decent burial. You need to take him up on that offer."

Kindly wasn't how she would have described the man clutching the shovel as if it were a weapon. He resembled a half-crazed grizzly more than he did a human being. And maybe something even more dangerous—an animal wounded beyond caring about himself or anyone else.

She'd heard tales of trapped animals gnawing off their own paws to escape from steel traps. As she looked into Ethan Trent's hard brown eyes, she knew those stories were true. She didn't want her husband to be buried by this bitter man.

"All right, Sheriff," she said, standing straighter. "You and I will leave as soon as Hank is buried, but I need a few minutes alone with him."

The rancher huffed, grabbed a pickax to go with the shovel and stormed out of the barn. "*You* deal with her," he said, glancing back at Handley.

The sheriff put his hands on his hips. "Ma'am, Mr. Trent is right. That storm could turn to a blizzard in the blink of an eye, and it's gonna get mighty cold. I'm partial to sleeping in my own bed, and for you, young lady, I recommend the comfort of the hotel."

But the hotel held nothing but bad memories of the night Hank walked out on her, and of the three foolish days she had waited for him. She wasn't ready to go back to that emptiness. She had to make Handley understand. "Are you married, Sheriff?"

His eyes stayed as hard as rock. "For thirty years."

"Then you understand why I have to stay."

"No, ma'am. I understand why you have to leave. Your husband would want you to be safe."

The sheriff had a point. Hank would have been annoyed with her for riding out here in the first place, but she had taken a vow, "Until death us do part."

Though death had come, they weren't quite parted, and they wouldn't be until Hank was buried.

"Please, Sheriff, ride back to town without me. If the rain gets worse, I'll sleep in the barn and go back to town tomorrow. I'm a good rider, and I'm sure Mr. Trent will loan me a blanket."

"I wouldn't count on it." He chuffed like a mule and Jayne knew she had lost the argument.

If she couldn't win with logic, she would have to find another way to see her husband laid to rest, but no matter what else happened today, she had to retrieve the money hidden in his duster.

"I understand, Sheriff." Steepling her fingers at her waist, she glanced down at Hank. "I won't take more than a few minutes."

Handley gave a curt nod and paced out the door.

As soon as he was gone Jayne dropped to her knees, looked at the frozen mask of her husband's face and broke into sobs. She had given him her heart and trusted him with her future. How could he have done this to her? Who was "Jesse," and why had Hank gone off with a stranger? What secrets had he kept from her?

A moan tore from her throat as she made a fist and pressed it into his belly. His duster had gaped wide, revealing the denim shirt she'd mended for him in Lexington. The sight of it shot her back in time to their first kiss, the brief marriage ceremony and the wedding night that had been a disaster from start to finish. She couldn't bear to think about that night, the grimy train ride that followed or their last moments in the Midas Hotel.

Tears as thick as oil spilled from her eyes. Would Hank still be alive if she'd gone to the sheriff sooner? She had followed his orders to a tee, waiting for three full days before she told the story to Handley.

The balding sheriff had been skeptical and rude. "Your husband's probably off with an old drinkin' buddy, ma'am. He'll be back when he's sobered up."

But Hank never drank. When she had told the sheriff, he'd shrugged it off. She had searched on her own, but no one had given her the time of day, except for Reverend John Leaf. He'd asked a dozen questions, none of which she could answer, and then promised to keep his ears open. Not until a rancher reported finding the body of a U.S. Marshal had the sheriff paid her a visit.

In spite of his objections, she had insisted on riding with him to the Trent ranch today. She had to see the facts for herself, and yet this moment wasn't quite real. She had expected to feel a connection to Hank that bridged the gap between life and death, but she sensed only a terrible stillness. She wanted something to hold, a memory that wouldn't fade with time, but she had no keepsakes. Hank hadn't given her a wedding ring, and with their one pitiful night of coupling, she doubted she'd conceived a child.

Her gaze locked on the badge pinned to his duster. She had never seen it before and she couldn't imagine why he'd put it on. Sucking in a breath, she unpinned the silver star and put it in her pocket. Like it or not, she had her keepsake, and it was time to get down to the business of living.

Her fingers shook as she turned back the bottom flap of his duster in search of the secret pocket. Her stomach lurched at the thought of being penniless. She had been too small to fully understand poverty when her father died, but her mother had kept her own memories alive.

Always save for a rainy day, Jayne. You never know when a storm will strike.

What had Hank been thinking when he'd walked off with their nest egg? She should have stopped him, or at least demanded that he leave the money. She'd let love get in the way of practicality, and that was a mistake she wouldn't repeat. It was only by God's grace that she hadn't ended up flat broke.

She picked at the seam of the pocket until she managed to make a small hole, then she ripped the stitches, took out the envelope and broke the wax seal. It tore the paper like a scab that wasn't ready to fall off. Feeling the wax tight under her nails, she slid the contents of the envelope into the light. Instead of greenbacks she saw a collection of papers covered with several kinds of writing.

"Oh, God," she whispered. "This isn't right."

Her stomach lurched as she focused on the first sheet of paper, a crinkled advertisement for land in Los Angeles. Across the top Hank had written the name of a bank. As she set the handbill on the dirty floor, she saw a sheet of stationery bearing the name of a Lexington attorney. Beneath the letterhead she saw typewritten words that made her gasp. Franklin Henry Dawson had written out his Last Will and Testament the day before they had married. In stiff, formal language, he had bequeathed to her all his worldly possessions.

What worldly possessions? They had nothing but hope, and now that was gone.

"Hank, how could you?" she whispered.

As she turned to the next page, she saw another formal letter, this one from a bank confirming the receipt of Mr. Dawson's wire deposit. It didn't make sense. Hank wasn't a wealthy man. They'd used the money from the sale of her dress shop to buy train tickets.

Confused, Jayne scanned the next sheet of paper where she saw Hank's blockish printing. As if reaching down from heaven, he started to answer her question.

Dear Janey,
If you're reading this, it means I'm dead. I love you, girl. I wanted to give you that "always" we talked about, but—

"Ma'am? It's time."

The sheriff's bellow rumbled through the barn as he paced in her direction. She suspected that he'd drag her out by her hair if she didn't come willingly, but she couldn't leave Hank to be buried alone. Not with his final "always" echoing in her heart.

She couldn't stand unfinished business or ragged seams of any kind. She needed a last goodbye, but if Handley wasn't willing to give it to her, she'd take it. The trail back to Midas wove through the hills like a tangled thread. Her livery mare was surefooted.

She would lag behind and then race back to the Trent ranch. The sooner she left with the sheriff, the sooner she'd be back.

Slipping Hank's letter into her pocket, she pushed to her feet. "I'm ready, Sheriff."

As he marched out the door, she hunched against the cold, following him to the pine tree where their horses were tethered. A distant thump drew her gaze to a grassy slope about fifty feet from the barn. There she saw the rancher in profile as he raised the pickax high above his head. The blade sliced through the air with a whoosh, then struck the hard earth with a thud.

She winced.

The sheriff gripped her arm. "Ma'am? Come along now."

"I'm all right." Shaking off his grasp, she pulled herself into the saddle. Handley mounted his bay and led the way down a path that cut across the meadow near Hank's gravesite. As they rode past the brown gash in the grass, Ethan Trent pushed back his filthy hat and looked at her with eyes as unyielding as petrified wood.

The remnants of a life lurked in that hardness and her heart pulsed with understanding. She knew how it felt to be alone and in pain. But she also knew how it felt to drag herself out of bed in the morning and face each day. She'd done it when her mother died and she'd do it again tomorrow, without Hank.

She believed in herself and in God, and no matter what difficulties came her way, she'd find a way to survive. She always did.

Trust God and stay strong.

Louisa McKinney had used those words to stitch her way to success. In spite of being a twenty-year-old widow without family or resources, she had established herself as Lexington's leading dressmaker. Jayne vowed to follow in her footsteps.

Today she would bury her husband. Tomorrow she'd find work in Midas and put every penny aside for the train fare back to Lexington. She'd cry for Hank, but it wouldn't stop her from cleaning up the mess he'd left, nor from helping the authorities find his murderer. His letter chafed in her pocket. She would show it to Handley in the morning, but tonight she wanted to be alone with her husband's last words.

Her mare followed the sheriff's bay into the forest without being nudged. Silent minutes passed as the temperature dropped with the coming storm. The path wound through thick pines, then dipped into a ravine and climbed up a slope littered with pine needles.

Handley had almost reached the top of the hill when his horse lost its footing. Righting the animal took all his attention, and Jayne saw her chance. She turned the mare, dug in her heels and took off for the Trent ranch at a gallop.

Chapter Two

"*Mrs. D-a-a-a-w-s-o-n!*"

Jayne sat tight in the saddle and gave the mare full rein. The hood of her cloak slipped from her head and her hair collapsed in a tangle. When a shower of sleet burst from the sky, icy needles crackled through the trees and stung her face. The wind howled, masking the mare's hoofbeats as they rounded the first curve. In another minute the road would be slick with mud, but for now it was safe for the mare to gallop.

"*Mrs. D-a-a-a-w-s-o-n!*"

The shout was fainter now. Surely the comfort of a warm bed and a hot meal would draw the sheriff home to Midas. The trail steepened and then veered east. Listening for Handley, she heard nothing but the storm and slowed the mare to a fast walk.

As suddenly as the sleet had started, it stopped. She raised her face to the sky where snowflakes as big as teacups were collecting on the trees. In front of her eyes, the pines were changing from towering sentries to lacy white angels.

Taking the greeting as a sign that coming back to bury Hank was right, she nudged the mare into a trot and rode straight into Ethan Trent's meadow.

The rancher was nowhere in sight, but the grave was deep and surrounded on three sides by freshly turned earth. Snow mottled the brown mounds, and a loamy fragrance drifted to her nose on the stiffening wind. The scrape of canvas against dirt drew her eyes down the slope where she saw the rancher dragging a burlap sack past the splintery wall of the barn.

He could have been pulling a child's sled, but she knew the sack held Hank's body. She reined the mare to a halt, sat straight in the saddle and watched as Ethan Trent dragged his burden up the hill. His steps were slow and measured, his back rounded and his gloved hands knotted in the frayed weave of the burlap. When he reached the grave, he aligned the body with the long edge of the rectangular hole, paused for breath and bowed his head.

He was probably avoiding the snow, but she wanted to think he was showing respect for the act he was about to commit, if not for the man he was laying to rest.

She was grateful for that small comfort, but then he knotted his fists at his heaving sides, stared straight into the heavens and shouted a curse she would never repeat. With his oath ringing in the air, he dropped to his knees and rolled the corpse into the grave.

Jayne stared in horror. The veil of snow erased all color from her world except for the red flush burning across the rancher's cheeks. Through the mist, she watched as he crossed one arm over his chest, rested his elbow on his forearm and pinched the bridge of his nose. His wide shoulders started to shake, and a low groan cut through the air as he raised both hands to his face and pressed them against his eyes, as if to hold in tears.

Stunned by a grief that matched her own, Jayne climbed off the mare and walked in his direction. As the horse clopped to the barn, the rancher's gaze drifted to her face. Rising slowly to his feet, he blinked as if he couldn't quite believe his eyes. Golden hope flickered in his irises like a candle in an empty window, but it died as suddenly as it had appeared. In place of that hope, she saw a loathing as deep and lasting as the grave at his feet. Sneering, he picked up the shovel and hurled more dirt into the hole.

Fresh tears scalded her cheeks. "I've come to help you bury my husband."

"*Help* me? God Almighty," he said, heaving more dirt into the grave. "Where the *hell* is Handley?"

"On his way to Midas. We parted ways at the ravine."

From beneath the brim of his hat, he assessed her with a cold stare. "You're stubborn, aren't you?"

"No, I'm strong-minded."

"What the hell's the difference?"

"A stubborn person just wants her own way. Someone who's strong-minded has principles and lives by them."

He looked down at the dirt thumping into the hole, lifted another load and sent it flying. His gaze shifted back to hers. "So what damn principle gives you the right to invade my privacy?"

If he wanted an apology, he wasn't going to get it. "Common decency is what gives me the right, Mr. Trent. How would you feel in my shoes? What if this were *your* wife?"

As soon as the words left her mouth, Jayne realized that she had made a terrible mistake. The shovel stopped in midswing, hanging over the grave as the rancher stared blindly into the hole. She'd once seen ice break apart on the Ohio River. The fractured planes of his face were no less treacherous.

"I'm sorry," she said. "I don't know you. I shouldn't have presumed—"

"Damn right." He slowly turned the blade of the shovel so that dirt and snow fell together in a tarnished mist.

Trying to be respectful, she said, "I should have realized—"

"You should've gone with Handley."

"But—"

"Dammit, lady. Mind your own business."

"I'm trying to apologize."

"Don't."

Taking a step back, she bowed her head and kept quiet. She owed him that much for burying Hank, but every instinct told her that silence was the last thing this man needed. He was a kettle boiling in an empty kitchen, one that had long since gone dry and was ready to explode. She'd be wise to keep her distance.

Closing her eyes, she prayed for strength as the rancher worked. The rhythm of the shovel became a dirge, a wordless goodbye that lasted for a small eternity. The snow was blowing sideways by the time he finished.

Tamping the mound with the shovel blade, he said, "I'm done. You can sleep in the barn or freeze on the trail. I don't give a damn either way."

Jayne believed him, but it didn't matter. She'd come back to say goodbye to Hank and that's what she intended to do. She had a warm cloak and would make a bed in the barn out of straw. She didn't need the rancher's help. She felt nothing but relief as he stormed off, put away the tools and marched across the yard to the tiny cabin.

The door slapped shut. In the sudden silence and absence of all things human, she surrendered to the tears she'd been fighting for a week. She sang her favorite hymns. She recited the Shepherd's psalm and walked through the valley of the shadow of death, over and over, until the words were a jumble.

Exhausted, she dropped to her knees and squeezed a fistful of dirt. Someday she and Hank would be together again, but not for a very long time. On one hand, life was uncertain and eternity was a breath away. On the other hand, that gap spanned thousands of days.

Rising to her feet, Jayne turned her back on the grave and looked across the meadow to the rancher's cabin. An L-shaped sliver of light marked a small window covered with a sheet of boards. Next to it a vertical line gave shape to the door. She smelled wood burning in the hearth and saw a plume of white smoke rising from the chimney.

As the adrenaline drained from her body, so did her natural warmth. Shivering, she imagined sipping hot coffee and the heat of a fire thawing her toes. She also imagined the rancher's gaunt frame and his filthy clothes. He smelled like the bottom of a barn. The horses were better company, and that was a fact.

Holding her skirt above the snow, she trudged back to the splintery shell of the outbuilding. The cold and the dark didn't scare her in the least. She would make it through the night an hour and a prayer at a time.

Ethan let go of the sheet of boards covering the window. The flat wood dropped back into place and pinched his finger.

"Dammit," he muttered, shaking his hand to get the blood moving again. He had been standing at the sill for close to an hour, and the crazy woman was still singing hymns. He hated that sound. It brought back memories of Laura humming lullabies to their children and singing in church.

The widow had to be frozen half to death, but nothing on God's green earth could bring her husband back. Ethan knew that for a fact.

Damn him for a fool, but the window drew him like a magnet attracting iron ore. After downing the dregs in the coffeepot, he slid the plywood open again. The widow had dropped to her knees and bowed her head.

He could still taste the acid coffee in the back of his throat and his stomach was burning. He needed to eat something, but the thought of this morning's charred biscuits didn't appeal to him. Neither did another can of beans or canned meat or canned anything. Laura had been a good cook, even better than his mother, and Ethan steeled himself against the memory of real food even as the widow's singing tugged at him.

Be Thou my vision, oh, Lord of my heart.
Naught be of else to me, save that Thou art.

God damn him to hell. The widow was singing Laura's favorite hymn. Did she have regrets for words left unsaid and things left undone? Was she as alone as she seemed? As brave and daring as it appeared? She must have been crying, but the melody didn't waver. Her shoulders stayed still and her arms remained stiff at her sides, as if by not moving she could make time stop.

Everything about this woman's grief was familiar to him except the need to see her husband buried. He wished to God he'd never seen the casket holding Laura's body with the baby on her chest, nor the pine boxes holding his two sons, nailed shut, one on top of the other in the grave next to hers.

His stomach rumbled with hunger, a defiant echo of life in the face of so much death. Hating himself for feeling that need, Ethan covered the window, slopped a can of beans on a plate and ate them cold. He washed the mess down with more bad coffee.

The hymn stopped just as he took the last swallow. Holding the empty cup, he pulled back the wood and looked for the widow. The sky had turned from gray to royal blue, a sign of twilight and colder temperatures, but the widow hadn't budged. If she had a lick of sense, she'd get settled in the barn before nightfall.

Ethan felt a niggle of worry low in his belly. He knew how it felt to be numb with grief and, for an awful minute, wondered if she intended to freeze to death. He couldn't let her stand outside much longer, but the thought of having her in his house was unbearable. Closing his eyes, he counted to ten and then to twenty, praying she'd be gone.

When he found the courage to look, he saw her walking down the hill through the ankle-deep snow. Heavy flakes dotted the shoulders of her cloak and he worried that her feet were wet. Even wrapped in heavy wool, she had to be shivering. When she reached the barn, she looked back at the cabin. Her eyes, he remembered, were bright blue, but in the dim light they were hollow and dark. He slammed his fist against the wall. He didn't want her here. With a defiant tilt of her chin, she walked into the barn and closed the door.

He wondered if she'd find the matches and lantern he'd put on the shelf for her, and if she'd burrow in the fresh straw for warmth. The temperature would plummet before dawn, and the walls had holes the size of his fist. He'd made them in fits of rage.

She had to be hungry. The thought unnerved him, but he refused to give in to the small voice urging him to invite her inside. Loneliness was the price he paid for the worst decision of his life.

His shoulders sagged with a familiar guilt as he tossed two logs on the fire, stripped down to his long johns and rolled under the comforter covering the wide bed. In the silence of the night, echoes of the hymn she had sung drifted into his usual thoughts of Laura and the children. He considered going out to check on the widow, but he didn't want to see her clear blue eyes. Besides, he reasoned, even a dog had the sense to get out of a storm. If Mrs. Dawson wanted to come in out of the cold, she could knock on his door. He might not like it, but he wasn't quite heartless enough to turn her away.

Ethan knew how cold it could be at night. His ranch was situated on a high plateau in the shadow of the Sangre de Cristo Mountains. Some winters were as dry as the southwestern desert. In other years his land endured as much snow as the Rockies. This winter had been mild and the spring storm would have been welcome, except for the woman in his barn.

Curled against the rough wall, he wrapped the blanket around his feet. The fire had burned down to embers and the cabin was nearly black. Sleep came slowly, bringing with it vivid pictures of his family. But instead of recalling happier times as he usually did, he relived the day they died. Vivid and harsh, the memories followed him into an exhausted sleep until the gray light of dawn filled the cabin.

Waking up with a jolt, he thought of the widow.

Boiling mad, he tossed back the blanket and pulled

on his clothes. Just as he did every morning, he stood straight and stared at himself in the heart-shaped mirror hanging over the bed, trying to remember the man he had once been. It was a hopeless cause, and today it was worse because of the woman in his barn.

Guilt burned in his belly like a banked fire as he hunched into his coat and tugged on the gloves Laura had knitted back in Missouri. Pushing down on his hat, Ethan opened the door and groaned at the sight of knee-high snow. His gaze rose to the barn. Half buried in the drifts, it looked like a sinking ship, and his heart sank with it. The trail to Midas would be impassable for days and muddy for weeks.

The thought of having Mrs. Dawson on his property for another minute, let alone a week, turned his mood from sour to rancid. Fighting his temper, he stomped across the yard and stormed into the barn. He expected to see the widow wrapped in her heavy cloak in the pile of fresh straw, but she wasn't there.

"Mrs. Dawson?"

The silence accused him of being a coldhearted son of a bitch. Had she wandered into the storm to die? He knew how it felt to fight that temptation. Only his pride and a sincere fear of hell had kept him from eating a bullet when Laura and the children had died. If Jayne Dawson had chosen that path, the decision was hers. They would both have to live with the choices they had made.

The thought gave Ethan no comfort. He made his voice louder. "Mrs. Dawson!"

A low moan drew him to the back of the barn. Peering into an empty stall, he saw a filthy horse blanket and the bottom edge of the widow's navy-blue cloak.

"Lady, get up."

She stirred beneath the blanket, then bolted upright as a chest-deep cough erupted from her throat. She covered her mouth with both hands, but the air still shook with the ferociousness of the coughing spell. Fever burned in her cheeks.

Ethan wanted to look away, but he couldn't. Her eyes were the color of the sky at high noon, and her straw-blond hair had frozen into a tangle. Remorse burned from his heart to his head. He treated his two horses better than he had treated this woman. What if it had been Laura in need, or his daughter?

He cleared his throat to soften his gravelly voice. "Ma'am, you need help."

Struggling to breathe, she clutched at the blanket. "I am so sorry...to do this to you...I shouldn't have—"

"Don't waste your breath." He couldn't bear that high-pitched wheeze. "Can you wait while I do chores?"

Nodding, she struggled to her feet and stood while he filled the feed bins and used an old broom handle to poke through the ice covering the water buckets. He needed to muck out the stalls, but it would have to wait. Mrs. Dawson looked ready to faint.

He leaned the stick against the wall. "We need to get inside."

Instinctively he held the door for her, just as he had done a thousand times for his wife. The widow's skirt brushed across his boots, then she waited for him to take the lead. Her eyes barely reached his shoulder. She'd never be able to match his stride, and so he swung his boot from side to side to kick a path for her.

He couldn't hear her footsteps, only a light wheezing and the swish of her skirt. When she fainted, he barely heard the thump of her body sinking into the drift.

"Oh, hell," he muttered.

Dropping to his knees, he yanked off one glove and touched her cheek with the back of his hand. Feverish heat burned straight through to his bones, and he saw that the collar of her shirtwaist was wet with perspiration. He shook her shoulder and called her name, but she didn't make a sound.

The last thing in the world he wanted to do was to carry her, but what choice did he have? Sliding one arm beneath her shoulders and the other under her knees, he rocked back on his heels and lifted her from the snow.

As her face rolled against his chest, he saw bits of straw stuck in her hair and sleep creases on her cheeks. He wanted to scream at the heavens as he trudged to the cabin, pried the door open with his elbow and carried her to his bed. The unwashed sheets still bore the mark of his body and the torment of his dreams. It seemed wrong to set her down in such a private place, but he did it anyway.

She moaned and muttered how sorry she was, whispered Hank's name and called for her mother. He had to get her into dry clothes, but the cabin was barely warmer than the barn, and it made sense to leave her in the cloak until he had a fire roaring in the hearth.

He poked the coals and added two handfuls of kindling so it would catch fast and burn hot. The scrap box he kept by the rock fireplace held next to nothing and he kicked himself for being lazy about filling it. Hunching in his coat, he made a quick trip to the woodpile behind the cabin, stacked the logs on the hearth and laid a piece of dry pine on the embers. It caught with a whoosh, pushing heat into the room as Ethan looked at the woman on his bed.

She hadn't moved a muscle, and he honestly didn't know which would be worse—undressing a live woman or burying a dead one. All he knew was that he didn't want to touch her, and he would have to do just that if she didn't wake up. "Mrs. Dawson?"

No answer.

Ethan took off his coat and rested his palm on her forehead as if she were a child. Her fever shamed him. He imagined burying her next to her husband and waiting for the spring grass to wipe out the graves so that he could forget this moment, but he knew he would never forget.

He couldn't see her chest moving beneath the cloak, so he touched her throat in search of a pulse. He found it in an instant, a strong beat that told him she wasn't a quitter. "Lady, wake up," he said.

Moaning, she struggled to open her eyes.

"Your clothes are wet from the fever. Can you get undressed?"

"This can't be happening," she said, almost whimpering.

"Here, let me help you, love."

Love. His pet name for Laura. Horrified, Ethan shot to his feet, snatched his nightshirt off a nail and tossed it on the bed. "Wake up now. You've got to get out of those damp things."

"I'll try." She raised her head and tugged on her cloak, but she didn't have the strength to pull it free. Weaker than before, she fell flat against the mattress.

Steeling himself against the heat emanating from her body, Ethan wrapped his arm around her shoulders, removed the cloak and dropped it on the floor. "We have to get your shoes off, too."

Nodding, she pulled her feet to the side of the bed. Her soles brushed his thigh, and he stepped aside as he unbuttoned the fancy boots and slid them over her ankles. Gritting his teeth, he rolled her stockings down her slender calves and tugged the cotton over her toes. They were small and pink and pretty. His stomach clenched, but he touched them anyway, just to be sure they were warm.

The woman was shivering now, struggling to undo the front of her jacket with her half-frozen fingers.

"Here, let me," he said.

"I can do it—" But a racking cough stole her breath.

Forcing himself to look down, he slid his fingers beneath hers and undid the buttons. He pulled at the jacket sleeves until her arms broke free, revealing a white silk shirtwaist blotched with perspiration. Bravely, he worked those buttons, too, this time discovering rosy-gold skin and a chemise made transparent by a feverish sheen.

He tried not to look directly at the widow's breasts, but he couldn't stop himself from taking in the differences between her body and Laura's. His wife was the only woman he had ever known in that way. She had been soft and round, a dark-eyed beauty with a complexion like cream. Mrs. Dawson's skin made him think of the summer sun. On its own, his gaze roamed downward, where he saw her firm breasts and the shadow of brown nipples beneath the cotton.

A rush of desire made Ethan hard and angry. That ache belonged to Laura, and he didn't want to feel it ever again, especially not now. He wanted to get the widow undressed, in bed and out of his head as fast as he could.

Her damp underthings needed to come off, but a man had his limits. He'd help her with the skirt, but that was all he could manage. Growling, he said, "Raise up your hips."

Strangling on a cough, the widow did as he ordered, though she failed miserably to work the button at the waist. Ethan took over, looking at the ceiling as he maneuvered the skirt down her thighs and past her knees. As she curled into a tight ball, he dropped the garment on the floor, covered her legs with his quilt and shoved an old nightshirt in her face. "You can finish without me."

Turning his back, he added a log to the fire and poked the coals. Only when the bed stopped creaking did he dare turn around.

What he saw shattered his lonely world like a splitting maul in a round of pine. The woman sleeping in his bed was beautiful. Wrapped in his blanket with her gold hair tangled on his pillow, she didn't look to be much more than twenty years old. Ethan had a good ten years on her, and the past two had turned him into an old man.

He strode into the kitchen, poured himself a cup of coffee and sat near the fire to muddle through his thoughts. He had a woman in his bed burning with fever and coughing like a lunger. He didn't want her here, but Mrs. Dawson hadn't given him a choice or even a say in the matter.

Guilt sluiced over him. *Laura, I'm so sorry for taking you away...*

Laura had been content in Missouri, but he had wanted a change. She had supported his dream of owning land because she loved him, but deep down he knew she would have been happier to spend their lives in the same small town where they had grown up. He'd promised her a bigger house and a good life for the kids, but he had failed them all. They hadn't made it past Raton.

Ethan didn't want to think about that lost part of his life. The immediate problem at hand was Mrs. Dawson. As much as he hated having her in his house, he was stuck with her until the trail cleared and she recovered enough to ride.

Staring at the fire, he listened to the thud of snow falling from the trees. It was a lonely sound, but one he welcomed in his silent world. Today, though, other sounds filtered to his ears. Mrs. Dawson whimpered like a kitten in her sleep, and her cough rasped like sandpaper on fresh-cut wood. When she rolled to her side, the bed creaked and he thought of Laura filling the spot next to him.

Gulping the last of his coffee, Ethan rose and walked to the kitchen. As he passed the bed, the widow moaned and flung the blanket aside, muttering something about missing a train and calling to her mother. Sweat beaded on her forehead and he saw half moons of dampness on the nightshirt just below her breasts.

He picked up the blanket intending to cover her, but common sense told him her body needed to cool as the fever spiked. Not knowing what to do scared him, but what scared him even more was not wanting to look away.

Disgusted with himself, Ethan tugged the quilt up to her chin and turned to the kitchen. His boot caught on the clothing he'd dropped on the floor, and he caught a whiff of the barn. Bending low, he picked up the riding skirt, the jacket and the blouse. She'd have to wear them again. Hoping it would be soon, he hung the suit on the nail where his nightshirt had been and shook out the blouse.

Her scent filled him with a hunger that was both unwelcome and sharp. Closing his eyes, he buried his nose in the silk where he smelled honeysuckle and a woman's skin. He ached for Laura, and yet this wasn't her scent. She preferred lilacs and the feel of his clean-shaven face. Clutching at the fine silk, Ethan touched it to his cheek until his stubbled whiskers snagged it, hurling him back to his senses.

What kind of a man sniffed at a woman's clothing? Appalled at his behavior, he draped the blouse over the suit and hung her cloak by the door. Stooping down, he picked up her shoes and set them on the hearth to dry.

Scouring his memory for home remedies for fever, he surveyed his stock of canned goods. Laura had given the children soup when they were ill, but his own mother dosed him with whiskey to settle a cough. He decided he would try both when Mrs. Dawson woke up.

She needed to rest and recover, but Ethan vowed to get her out of his house just as soon as she could ride. She had already taken everything he had to give.

Chapter Three

Jayne woke up with whiskey on her breath. Tasting the pungent sweetness, she remembered the rancher ordering her to swallow. It was the same remedy her mother had used, and she had downed the cure without arguing.

The whiskey helped her sleep, but she had lost track of time. Days and nights had blurred together in waves of prickly fever followed by violent chills. Had she been here a day? A week? She didn't know, and the gloomy cabin offered no clues.

She needed to look out the window to see if the snow had melted, but before she could stand, a ferocious cough nearly cracked a rib. Pressing a rag to her mouth, she gasped for breath until the coughing stopped.

The feel of the rough muslin against her lips filled her with memories. In the mix of lantern light and shadows, she had imagined her mother at her side, but then the dream had faded and she'd recognized the rancher's rough fingers and the smell of snow that clung to him. In near silence, he'd brought her clean rags for her cough, emptied her chamber pot and fed her hot soup for strength.

For strength…

She almost laughed out loud. Pneumonia had made her as burdensome as a baby. It was the most demeaning circumstance she could imagine, and Ethan Trent's cabin was the last place in the world she wanted to be.

The rancher had taken good care of her, but he didn't have a kind bone in his body. Lying in his bed, she wondered if he shouted at children and kicked dogs who didn't get out of his way fast enough.

And yet he could be gentle, too. A plug of mucus had lodged in her throat last night. Close to suffocating, she had raised her hands over her head. The rancher had hurried to her side, braced her chest with his muscular forearm and thumped on her back. When she croaked for water, he'd brought it to her in a tin cup small enough for a child.

The distant ring of an ax and the smell of burned coffee gave the room a distinctly male air. Had a woman ever put wildflowers in a jug just to make the place pretty? Jayne doubted it. A square of rough logs, the cabin had a corner kitchen with a dry sink, a rock fireplace and two small windows, each covered with a sheet of boards instead of glass.

With the exception of the bed, the furniture was roughly made, and there wasn't much of it. She saw a small table, two chairs, a rocker and a long shelf holding books and a cigar box. Work shirts and dungarees hung from nails on the wall, and he'd left a roll of wire and a pair of leather gloves on the hearth.

Curious, she twisted in the bed and peered into the kitchen where she saw a cookstove and a long-handled spoon dangling from a hook. Jayne's heart clenched at the picture of the rancher standing at the stove and eating straight out of the pot.

As she turned her head, a heart-shaped mirror hanging above the washbowl caught a ray of sun. The feminine glass shone bright, as if he wiped it every day. The bed troubled her, too. The carved oak frame belonged in a Midwestern farmhouse rather than a mountain cabin.

Had Ethan Trent made love to a wife in this bed? It seemed more than likely, and her cheeks reddened with embarrassment. She had invaded this man's privacy in the worst possible way.

Beyond the cabin walls, a log groaned as it split in two. Her bones ached with a similar misery and it hurt to breathe. She wanted to curl up into a ball and grieve for Hank and all she had lost, but she had to think about her future.

When she returned to the hotel, she would retrieve her trunk and the tools of her trade. She'd also have the ten silver dollars she'd stitched into the hem of a skirt. The money would be enough for a room in a boardinghouse. She'd find a job, save for a train ticket and go back to the life she'd always lived. It wouldn't be hard. Her mother had given Jayne the skills to support herself and she had earned a reputation of her own.

"All women like pretty dresses," her mother used

to say. "As long as you can sew, you can take care of yourself."

Jayne didn't want to think about her mother's store and the sweet memories it held. Her father had died in a riding accident, leaving his wife alone to support their baby daughter. It hadn't been easy, but by the time Jayne was old enough to ask questions, her mother had made a name for herself and their simple needs were met.

Jayne closed her eyes and hugged her knees. She ached to be standing behind the familiar counter, but instead she was in Ethan Trent's lonely cabin with more questions than answers. Every muscle in her body tensed. The time had come to read Hank's letter. Still wobbly from illness, she shuffled to the wall where her cloak was hanging. Plunging her hand into the pocket, she found Hank's papers and turned to go back to bed.

As she took a feeble step, an ominous tickle swelled in her throat. Too weak to cough and stand at the same time, she lurched toward the bed, but her lungs exploded before she reached the mattress. As she collapsed to her hands and knees, Hank's letter fluttered to the floor, just out of reach.

She heard the door fly open.

"Dammit!" The rancher wrapped his muscular forearm around her waist and brought her upright so that his chest was pressed against her back. As the coughing eased, she smelled pine shavings and male perspiration. His hands shook as he spun her around.

"What the *hell* are you doing out of bed?"

''I just—'' Her chest shuddered again. She couldn't breathe, much less talk.

Holding her arms, he sat her down on the bed and held her steady as she hacked up something vile. With a growl of disgust, he handed her the rag she'd been using for a hankie and then stepped back from the bed. ''Don't push yourself. I want you well enough to leave.''

She wiped her mouth. ''We agree completely.''

He pointed to the envelope on the floor with the muddy toe of his boot. ''What's that?''

''A letter from my husband.''

His eyes turned to agate as he picked up the letter and handed it to her. Their fingers brushed, and on the envelope she noticed a smudge from his warm hands. Wondering if she would see Hank's fingerprints as clearly, she took the letter and slid it under her pillow.

After he took off his coat, the rancher poured coffee for them both and dropped into the rocker by the hearth. Steam misted the air as he lifted the cup to his lips, giving a damp shine to the whiskers hiding his face. She wondered what he would look like clean-shaven, whether his jaw was square or curved, and what his chin looked like. She suspected it was as hard as the rest of him and just as stubborn.

Stretching his neck and shoulders, he took a deep breath, causing the shirt to gape where a button was missing. He'd also torn the sleeve, probably months ago judging by the ragged hole.

Aside from being in need of mending, his clothes were just plain dirty. He could have passed for the town drunk, but she had never seen him indulge in the whiskey he'd used for her cough. He read dime novels at night, or else he browsed catalogs, making notes on scraps of paper he tucked between the pages. Sober and silent, he spent the evenings ignoring her, just as he was doing now. Except this morning she felt human again, and she needed answers.

Folding her hands in her lap, she asked, "What day is it?"

The rancher shrugged. "What difference does it make?"

It made a big difference. Back in Lexington she had kept a calendar by her bed, marking off the days. Time mattered, even if Ethan Trent didn't think so. "I need to know how long I've been here."

"Too long," he said with a huff. Rocking forward, he jabbed at the fire with a broken broom handle. The logs crackled to life and embers plumed up the chimney.

"You must have some idea," she insisted.

"As a matter of fact, I do. It's been eight days, nineteen hours and twelve minutes since you showed up uninvited. Is that enough detail for you?"

She would have given five dollars to be wearing her riding costume, complete with boots, leather gloves and a riding crop. She had a good mind to tan this man's hide.

"Is my horse still here?" she asked.

Nodding, he said, "She's fit and ready to go."

"Then I'll leave tomorrow."

Midas was less than two hours away. She'd tie herself to the saddle if she had to. She'd manage, just as she always did. Except Ethan Trent had risen from the chair, laced his arms over his chest and was glowering like a man on the wrong end of a bad joke.

"Mrs. Dawson, I want to be *very* clear. I want you out of here even more than you want to go, but it has to be for good. You're in no condition to ride, and I won't fish you out of another snowbank."

He cocked one hip and glared some more. "You're so thin you could fall through a crack. You can't take a full breath without coughing, and we both know you haven't eaten enough to keep a bird alive."

"I'll manage." Except she could barely use the chamber pot herself, and the coffee cup in her hand weighed ten pounds. "I can take care of myself."

"Like hell you can," he said, scratching his neck. "But I'll make you a deal. As soon as you can walk to the barn and back without gasping like a broken-down nag, I'll ride with you to Midas."

She bristled at being compared to a sorry excuse for a horse, but she held her tongue. "I know the way. You don't have to go with me."

"I'm not that kind of man."

"And I'm not that kind of woman. I don't want your help."

"But you need it. I've buried enough bodies. I don't want to find your bones picked clean by buzzards next time I go to town."

"Really, I can—" A wet cough rose in her throat like cream in a butter churn. She tried to be discreet, but there was nothing dainty about the hack coming from her chest. Facing facts, she coughed as hard as she could while Ethan Trent poured a cup of water.

"Here," he said, shoving it in her face.

It tasted fresh, giving her hope that tomorrow would be a better day. Putting the cup on the nightstand, she met his gaze. "I suppose you're right. I'll leave as soon as I'm well, but there's something I have to say."

"Don't bother."

"Do you read minds, or are you just plain rude?"

"You're going to thank me for saving your life. I didn't do it for you, Mrs. Dawson. I wish you had never come here."

"That may be true," she said. "But you've been considerate, except for the first night."

"You should have asked for help."

"You should have offered."

The rancher walked to the window and slid the wood cover an inch to let in a bit of fresh air. A shaft of sunshine hit his eyes and he squinted against it. Through the whiskers, she saw his jaw clench in a wolflike snarl.

She had seen that look once before on a dog that had been run over by a wagon. Too young to know better, she had tried to pet it. The mutt had nipped her hand, drawing blood and leaving two small puncture marks. Louisa McKinney made sure her daughter never made that mistake again.

"You can't trust an animal when it's in pain," she had said. "They don't know what they're doing and they don't care who they hurt."

Jayne still had a scar from the dog's fangs, and

she had never forgotten its eyes, watery and glazed with suffering.

The rancher snatched his hat from the nail. "I'm going back to work."

As the door slapped shut, Jayne sagged with relief—until she remembered Hank's letter waiting under her pillow. Her fingers trembled as she slid a half dozen sheets of paper out of the envelope. She riffled through them, catching words that made her stomach flip.

Dear Janey,

If you're reading this, it means I'm dead. I love you, girl. I wanted to give you that "always" we talked about, but I can't. I hope you can forgive me for what I've done. I've lied to you about so many things.

I never was a marshal. In fact, I've never had a thing I didn't lie, cheat or steal to get. The past is ugly, but here it is. I met Timonius LeFarge a year ago in Wyoming and we started robbing banks together. We were good at it, but the last job went bad. A marshal named Franklin Henry Dawson chased us into the badlands.

I'll never know if my bullet killed the man or if it was Tim's, but it doesn't matter. I saw his last breath as if it were my own and knew I had to change. Tim got drunk that night and passed out, so I took the money and the marshal's badge and ran for my life.

A month later I found you in church, all sunlight and hope. I wanted you, girl—enough to turn into someone else, a deputy named Hank Dawson. I hope I gave you some happiness, because deep down I know I stole you, too.

If you're reading this, I'm dead and Tim is alive. He wants the money, but it's the only way I can give you that future I promised. I wired three thousand dollars to the First Bank of Los Angeles. All you have to do is show the manager our marriage certificate and the will.

Tim doesn't know about you, but keep your eyes open. He's older than me, a skinny fellow with red hair, light eyes and a scar on his left cheek. If you see him, go the other way. I've seen him do awful things to men and women alike.

I'm praying to God that Tim never finds us. And if he does, I'll be praying I can end things right. That's why I'm carrying the marshal's badge. It's a reminder that a man has choices.

No matter what happens, Jayney-girl, know that I love you. You gave me a second chance I didn't deserve. Be safe.

Love,
Hank

P.S. Dawson was the marshal's name. It's a better name than mine and the only one I want you to remember me by.

One by one, she squared the pages into a neat pile. Tears welled for her losses, but anger burned even brighter. She didn't even know her husband's real name, and that was the cruelest lie of all.

Propped against a pillow in Ethan Trent's bed, she wondered what had possessed her to marry a man she had known for just a few months, except she knew the answer. She'd been alone, had a thirst for adventure and was curious about a man's company. She wanted to hate Hank for what he'd done, but the choice to marry him had been hers.

Right or wrong, she had to live with her decision. She would go to the sheriff as soon as she could ride and tell him the truth. Somewhere in this world, the real Mrs. Dawson was grieving for her husband. And somewhere in New Mexico a man named Timonius LeFarge was looking for his money, which meant he would be looking for her.

The steady pounding of a hammer broke through her thoughts. Warning the rancher about LeFarge was the right thing to do, but she hesitated. If he wouldn't let her ride to Midas alone, what would he do if he found out she was being pursued by an outlaw? She didn't want to find out. LeFarge was her problem, and she'd solve it herself.

Fresh anger welled as she thought about her five short days with her husband. He should have come clean with the law. If he'd given her a choice, she would have stood by him. Instead he had trespassed on her future without so much as a please or a thank-you. Nothing killed love faster than lies.

Tugging at the bedsheet, Jayne thought of the rancher sleeping on the hard floor while she slept in his bed. She'd stolen a piece of his life just as surely as Hank had stolen her future. Rolling onto her side, she vowed to leave just as soon as she could ride.

Chapter Four

Ethan took Mrs. Dawson's cloak off the nail, saw a bit of straw on the sleeve and gave the garment a good shake. Her letter fell out of the pocket and landed next to his boot. He wasn't a snoop by nature, but with the widow taking care of private matters outside, he was sorely tempted to read it.

Almost every night she had slipped it out from her pillow as soon as she thought he was asleep. With the hard floor digging into his shoulder blades, he would watch her eyes glitter in the firelight. He envied her those final words from her husband. Laura's last words to him had been so ordinary he couldn't remember them.

Ethan studied Dawson's thin writing and the ugliness of the words "In the event of my death." He hated the need for such a letter, but he respected the man for writing it. Not once had Ethan written a letter to his wife. They'd grown up together and there had been no need. Now he wished he'd given her that small pleasure.

He didn't know if it was nosiness or thoughts of

Laura that made him open the envelope. Being careful of the dog-eared flap, he took out the sheets. Curiosity got the better of him and he started to read.

I lied…stole…Timonius LeFarge…second chances… Love, Hank.

The punk fool didn't know a damn thing about love. He'd left his wife in the middle of nowhere without a friend or an honest dollar to her name. He didn't deserve the widow's tears or the devotion that drove her to see him buried. If Dawson had walked through the door at that moment, Ethan would have bloodied his nose on general principle.

He didn't want to look too closely at those feelings. Over a month had passed since she had come to his ranch, and yesterday she had marched to the barn and back without coughing once.

"I'm well enough to leave," she had announced at supper last night.

They had taken to sitting together at the tiny table, eating in silence. Ethan had just scraped the last bite off his plate. "I can see that. Where will you go?"

"Home to Kentucky."

"Do you have family there?"

"No, but I'll be fine."

He believed her. If the widow could put up with him, she could put up with anything. Yesterday she'd scrubbed the floor and he'd tracked in mud. She tossed him a rag and told him to wipe it up. The mud had stared at him for a good hour before he wiped up the mess and told her to mind her own damn business.

There wasn't much of a chance of that, though.

For one thing, she'd helped herself to his books, reading everything from his dime novels to Laura's volumes of poetry to the Bible verses their sons had circled for Sunday school. A few times he had glanced up and caught her staring at him. He stared back, daring her to ask him what had happened to his family, which she did but only with her eyes.

Ethan put the letter back in her pocket. She insisted she was well enough to travel, but he wasn't so sure. Twice he'd heard her retching in the garden, and in spite of long afternoon naps, she looked exhausted.

Reminding himself that he wanted her to leave, he walked to the barn, hitched up the workhorse and tied the livery mare to the back of the wagon. As he led the horses through the yard, he looked at the privy. The door was ajar, and he didn't hear her in the cabin. Where the hell was she? "Mrs. Dawson?"

"Just a minute." Her reedy voice had come from the garden.

Irritated, Ethan strode around the corner of the cabin just in time to see Mrs. Dawson toss up her breakfast.

It was a familiar sight to a man who had fathered three children, and his heart squeezed at the realization that the widow was expecting a baby. Memories of Laura carrying their first child washed over him. It had been a glorious time. It should have been a wonderful time for the widow, but knowing what she had ahead of her, Ethan couldn't swallow.

She was standing in the shade with one hand

braced on the cabin wall and the other holding her abdomen. "Please don't watch me, Mr. Trent."

Nodding, he went to the water pump, filled the bucket and brought it to her with a ladle. She rinsed her mouth and grimaced as she spat on the ground. "Is the wagon ready?" she asked.

"It's ready, but you're not."

"I'm fine. The bacon didn't agree with me, that's all."

Her eyes glazed at the thought of the grease and Ethan almost smiled. "I think it's more than that."

She shook her head. "It can't be. I have to leave."

He knew she felt both guilty for taking advantage of him and fearful of LeFarge. He wanted to tell her he understood, but he didn't want her to know that he had read her letter. "Look, I know I've been a little—"

"It's not that. I have to get settled, that's all."

Lifting her skirt, she stepped over a patch of mud and rounded the corner of the cabin. Ethan was two steps behind her when she suddenly swayed on her feet. Grabbing the wall for support, she leaned against the logs and slid to the ground. "I've never been this nauseous in my life," she said.

The sight of her took him back to the day of the storm. His breath caught in his chest and he knew that he couldn't let her leave. Dropping to a crouch, he touched her shoulder. "Looks like I'm stuck with you."

"But I need to go home."

He gave her the hardest look he knew how to give a woman. "What you need is rest."

"There's nothing wrong with me. It's just that—"

"You're going to have a baby."

The joy in her eyes was mixed with sadness, making her seem older than her years. Understanding flashed across her face, as well, and Ethan felt cold and exposed.

"It seems you know about these things," she said.

"I do." His gaze held hers. Was that relief he saw in her eyes, or fear? She would be in danger if she left, but he'd made it clear that he didn't want her to stay. Without giving his motives a thought, he made a decision. "You're staying here while I go to town."

"I was better yesterday," she said. "Maybe we could go tomorrow."

"Trust me. The sickness won't go away for a while, and I'm low on everything from beans to bacon."

Her face knotted and he wondered what he'd said wrong until he heard a sound that reminded him of a stream bubbling over smooth stones. When she tilted her face up to the sun, he realized she was laughing. How long had it been since he'd taken pleasure in a woman's good humor? "What's so funny?" he asked.

The widow tilted her face to his and poked him in the chest. "Don't *ever* say *bacon* to me again. Just the thought turns my stomach."

Ethan grinned. "So we'll eat sausage instead."

The widow got the giggles, and the next thing he knew, the spot she'd touched on his chest was burning, but he was laughing at the same time. The joke hadn't been that funny, but she had tears streaming down her face, and so did he. Laura used to say that a belly laugh was good for the soul. Except he didn't have a soul. He'd lost it in Raton. As quickly as it started, his laughter faded into a grunt. "Come on, let's get you inside."

She looked confused, as if he'd blown out a lantern and left her in the dark. "Mr. Trent?"

Ethan stared straight ahead. "What is it?"

"Will you tell the sheriff I need to speak with him?"

She wanted to tell the sheriff about Dawson, but she didn't want to share that problem with Ethan. Given his foul mood, he could understand her reluctance. "I'll do that," he replied.

"There's one more thing."

Ethan flinched. "What?"

"You are going to *pay* for that bacon remark."

God help him, he smiled. "Am I now?"

"Definitely. When you least expect it. I'll sew up your sleeves. Or—"

"Put salt in the sugar jar?"

She shook her head. "You don't use sugar in anything."

It was true. He hadn't eaten so much as a cookie in two years, but this morning his mouth watered at the thought of something sweet—maple syrup on cornbread or a stick of peppermint candy.

With the widow leaning on his arm, he steered her to the cabin and left her by the door with her back pressed against the coarse wood. Then he climbed into the wagon, picked up the reins and doffed his hat.

"I'll be back around dusk." Thinking of Dawson's letter, he added, "There's a pistol in the cigar box on the mantel."

Her eyes flickered with curiosity, then in the way of mothers-to-be, she touched her belly. "I'll have supper waiting for you."

He gave the reins a shake and took off down the trail. How would it feel to come home to a hot meal and a woman's company? Probably good, and that was a problem for a man who couldn't be happy.

Aside from his quick trip to report Dawson's body, Ethan hadn't been to town in weeks, but it hadn't changed. A train in the station was working up a boiler full of steam, and the rattle of wagons filled his ears as he drove to the livery stable.

Glancing at the sky, he saw that it was close to noon. He'd had a hell of a time getting here. The wagon had gotten mired three times and he and his horses were covered with mud. If he had been alone, he would have ridden the roan and just filled up his saddlebags. Yet with a pregnant woman in his care, he needed more than a few bags of flour, coffee and beans.

But no bacon. He could still hear that laughter. It had charmed him, and his own chuckle had been a shock. So was the pressing need in his gut to get back before nightfall. Leaving her alone with a man like LeFarge on the prowl made his skin crawl.

Ethan stopped the gelding in front of the livery

stable. He'd thought about keeping the widow's mare until she was ready to ride, but he'd decided against it. The man who ran the livery had an ailing wife and six children to feed. The mare was income he wasn't taking in. As he untied the horse, Ethan glanced around for the stable boy. The kid wasn't around so he left the horse tied to a post. Not answering questions suited him just fine.

Next he visited the Midas Emporium. All two hundred pounds of Mrs. Wingate loomed behind the counter. "Mr. Trent! How are you today?"

Ethan ignored the question. He'd been studiously unfriendly to the town busybody, but in addition to everything else in her cluttered store, she sold books. She'd been the one to shove the dime novels into his hands, so Ethan put up with the chatter.

"Here's my list," he said.

He handed her the paper and browsed through the store as she put the order together. The shelves were full of trinkets meant to catch a woman's eye and he stiffened at the sight of ribbons and fancy buttons. He thought of Laura's box of doodads, but then a bolt of sky-blue gingham caught his eye.

The widow had one outfit to her name. He had no business noticing, but she'd look pretty in blue. Cautiously fingering the fabric, he wondered what Mrs. Wingate would do if he plopped it on the counter. She would probably bust a gusset with curiosity, but this wasn't the time to make mischief, not with LeFarge looking for Dawson's widow.

That meant he couldn't fetch her trunk, either, so he settled for a plain wooden hairbrush, some white ribbon that could be used for anything, and a pair of trousers and a shirt that were too small for him. He didn't want to think about her unmentionables, but that had to be an issue, so he picked up a bolt of white cotton. If Mrs. Wingate asked about it, he'd growl at her.

The clerk met him at the counter. "Can I get you anything else?"

Ethan glanced down at the small stockpile. It was enough to support a single man for a couple of months, but a pregnant woman had different needs. Gossip aside, he had another mouth to feed, or two if he counted the baby.

Pulling out his billfold, he said, "I want another twenty-five-pound sack of flour, three more cans of Arbuckle's, a ten-pound bag of sugar, cornmeal, whatever tins of vegetables you have, dried apples, three dozen cans of milk and a bag of lemon drops."

"Did you say three *dozen* cans of milk?"

"Yes, I did." He slapped a few more greenbacks on the counter. "I've had a craving lately."

Mrs. Wingate arched her eyebrows, but she didn't say another word as she piled boxes on the floor. Then she glanced at the cotton and stared down her nose. "How many yards of *this* would you like?"

"All of it," he said, scowling. He had no idea how much material it took to make a pair of ladies drawers, but it was clear Mrs. Wingate wasn't going to back down. "I'm reseeding the garden. This is to keep off the frost."

As if that made any sense. Any sane person would use old flour sacks, but Mrs. Wingate didn't say another word as he loaded the boxes into the wagon and rode away.

The sheriff's office was four blocks to the north. A flat-roofed adobe set apart from the storefronts, it was the oldest building in town. Ethan tied the gelding to the rail, hopped down from the seat and walked through the door. His gaze locked on Sheriff Handley who was sitting at his desk reading the *Midas Gazette*. As the hinges creaked, Handley lowered the newspaper and scowled.

"I've been wondering about you, Trent. Did that damn fool woman make it back to your ranch?"

Ethan had planned to tell him that the widow was alive, but Mrs. Dawson wasn't some "damn fool woman," and the sheriff had a spiteful glint in his eye. It seemed wise to find out more about LeFarge and the circumstances before he revealed the widow's whereabouts, so Ethan frowned. "She was a pain that day."

As Handley rocked forward in his chair, the front door opened again, stirring the air as Ethan looked over his shoulder. A stranger in a gray duster and a fussy black bowler stepped over the threshold, covering his mouth as he coughed. At the sight of wispy orange hair curling over the man's neck, Ethan felt his blood chill.

The stranger removed his hat and scanned the room, glancing briefly at Ethan before locking his gaze on Handley. "Good afternoon," he said. "Am I interrupting you two gentlemen?"

"That depends," Handley replied. "What can I do for you?"

Ethan wasn't about to politely excuse himself.

"My name is Timonius LeFarge," the outlaw said. "I'm a detective with Pinkerton's, and I'd like to ask you a few questions about a missing woman."

Handley pushed to his feet. "You wouldn't be looking for Jayne Dawson by any chance?"

LeFarge's eyes narrowed. "Yes, I am."

"Then we're on the same side of the law." Handley stood and extended his hand as LeFarge approached the desk. When the two men shook like old friends, Ethan's doubts about Handley's judgment turned into the certainty that the man couldn't be trusted.

Handley nodded in Ethan's direction. "Detective, this is Ethan Trent. He's the man who found Dawson's body."

"I see," said LeFarge. "How far away is your place?"

Ethan's mind snapped into action. No matter what else happened today, he had to prevent the two men from riding out to his ranch together. Handley knew Ethan lived alone, but LeFarge didn't. If Ethan could keep the sheriff from blabbing that he was a widower, he and Mrs. Dawson could pass for husband and wife if the outlaw decided to pay a call. Given the circumstances, Ethan doubted that LeFarge would invite Handley along for the ride.

The plan would work as long as the outlaw didn't already know what Jayne looked like. Determined to glean all the information he could from LeFarge, Ethan forced himself to be cordial. "My place is a ways from here, and the road's full of mud. We can talk here just as well.''

Handley nodded. ''That suits me fine. Have a seat, detective. Ethan can fill us in at the same time. I was escorting the widow back to town when she made a beeline to his ranch.''

''Is that so?'' LeFarge lowered his angular body into the chair. ''Where is she now?''

''She's dead,'' Ethan replied.

After staring for a good three seconds, LeFarge settled into the chair across from Handley. ''Please, sit down, Mr. Trent. It sounds like you have a story to tell.''

Handley pursed his lips. ''Why exactly are you looking for her?''

As Ethan pulled up a third chair, LeFarge leaned back like a judge holding court. ''It goes back to her husband. The fellow you buried was named Jesse Fowler. Back in Wyoming, he robbed nine banks, shot a woman and killed the real Hank Dawson. When the Feds failed to arrest him, the marshal's family hired me. It seems Fowler's been using the man's good name.''

''The man sounds like trouble,'' Handley replied.

''That he is, Sheriff. He got away with a lot of money from those robberies.''

LeFarge sounded grim, but Ethan wasn't fooled. Greed was burning in the stranger's glassy eyes as he cocked his head to the side. ''I trust we can count on your help, Mr. Trent. I have reason to believe that Jayne Dawson was in possession of the money from the bank robberies. That makes her an accomplice to Dawson's crimes.''

The man was the smoothest liar Ethan had ever met, but two could play that game, especially if it meant protecting a woman and an unborn child. ''She never made it back to the ranch. I found her remains in the middle of nowhere and buried the body where I found it. I figure she froze to death in that blizzard.''

The outlaw blinked like a bobcat waiting for its prey. ''Did you check her pockets? Was there anything to indicate where she might have been headed?''

''Not a thing.'' Ethan shrugged. ''I wish I could help you, but I just came by to tell Sheriff Handley about the body.''

The sheriff rocked back in his chair. ''I almost forgot. The hotel sent her trunk over a few weeks ago.''

LeFarge shot up from his chair. ''Where is it?''

Handley pointed to the back of the room. ''It's right there. Help yourself.''

The outlaw pried the lock with a knife and opened the lid. The scent of honeysuckle wafted through the air as he tossed dresses and petticoats onto the floor. Lingering over a satin nightgown, he smirked. ''I bet she's a whore.''

Handley shook his head. ''I talked to her a bit. That's not too likely.''

Damn right, Ethan thought. He'd bet his ranch that she had worn that satin on her wedding night.

LeFarge kept riffling through the garments. ''Can

you gentlemen give me a description of Mrs. Dawson? I haven't had the pleasure of seeing her for myself.''

Handley pursed his lips as if he were straining to think. ''As I recall, she had light hair and came up to my nose. She was pretty but nothing special.''

Wrong. She was very special. Ethan had never met such an iron-willed woman, but he wasn't about to argue.

''Eye color?'' LeFarge asked.

Handley shrugged. ''I don't know.''

Ethan did. Her eyes changed color with her moods, from blue ice when she was angry to a soft shade of aqua when she laughed. ''I think they were brown,'' he said.

''What was she wearing?'' LeFarge asked.

Handley sat straighter in the chair. ''I can help you there. She was wearing a dark cloak when we rode out. It was black, or maybe gray.''

No, it was navy-blue with large brass buttons. Ethan nodded. ''That's right. It was gray.''

Shoving the widow's things aside, LeFarge tore into Hank Dawson's clothing, snapping his shirts like a dog shaking a rabbit. Next he dumped out the drawers located in the sides of the trunk. A pair of scissors clattered to the floor and ribbons swirled on the planking like a posy of spring flowers. LeFarge kicked everything aside, took a knife from his belt and slashed the lining.

At the rasp of tearing silk, Ethan imagined skinning the outlaw an inch at a time.

Handley stood and ambled to the pile of clothing.

"I'll give you a hand," he said. "Are you looking for anything in particular?"

"Just being thorough. I'm looking for a letter, train tickets, anything."

Handley kicked at a skirt with his toe. "If it's any help, she and her husband were headed to Los Angeles."

God bless you, Sheriff Handley.

"Then it looks like I'm on my way to California." Rising from his knees, LeFarge coughed viciously, wiped his hands on his thighs and straightened his hat. "Gentlemen, thank you for your help. If Los Angeles doesn't pan out, I may be back. Where exactly is your place, Mr. Trent?"

"About ten miles east," Handley offered to Ethan's chagrin.

"If you remember anything else, I'll be at the hotel." LeFarge extended his hand. The sheriff shook it as if he'd just met Wyatt Earp. Ethan shook it because he had no choice.

"It's been a pleasure." The outlaw tipped his hat and paced out the door.

Handley dropped to a crouch and stuffed the clothing back in the trunk. "Someone could use these things. Did you bring the wagon today?"

"It's out front."

"Would you mind dropping the trunk at the church? You can leave it on the steps. I'm sure Reverend Leaf will find it."

"I'd be happy to help, Sheriff." And even happier to have the widow's possessions.

Handley put the last garment in the trunk, stood

upright and shook his head with disgust. "That Dawson woman made me look like a fool when she ran off. The world's better off without her kind."

Ethan fought a powerful urge to set Handley straight about Mrs. Dawson's character, but he didn't trust the man. LeFarge had played his part well, and even with the letter from her husband, the sheriff was apt to lock her up. Ethan's jaw tensed. He and the widow needed a new plan.

He picked up the trunk and followed the sheriff to the wagon. The lawman unlatched the tailgate and surveyed the supplies. "It looks like you're stocking up."

Ethan grunted. "I am. I hate coming to town."

When the sheriff nodded and walked away, Ethan silently thanked Mrs. Wingate for wrapping the white cotton in brown paper to protect it from the dust in spite of his stupid explanation. He unwrapped the reins from the hitching post, climbed onto the seat and drove to the edge of town.

With its white clapboard sides and shake roof, the First Church of Midas resembled a New England farmhouse. He had been there once, exactly a year after he'd lost his family, but Reverend Leaf's words about the seasons in a man's life hadn't done much good.

A time to weep, a time to laugh.

A time to mourn, a time to dance.

Ethan had left in the middle of the service and never went back, but that hadn't stopped the Reverend from visiting his ranch every so often. Once he'd shown up with fresh-baked bread. They'd eaten it together, dry because they had no butter, and that night Ethan had cried himself to sleep. Sitting on the wagon, he wondered if maybe the preacher had been right.

A time to give birth, a time to die.

A time to tear apart, a time to sew together.

Clicking his tongue at the gelding, he drove past the empty churchyard with Mrs. Dawson's trunk snug in his wagon. Only she wasn't Mrs. Dawson anymore. She was just Jayne, and she needed his help. If the outlaw showed up, they needed to be prepared.

The thought of pretending to be married made Ethan's heart thud with misery, but what choice did he have? To protect Jayne and her baby, he'd put up with just about anything.

Instead of finding his way back to the hotel, Timonius LeFarge took a window table at the restaurant across the street and watched as the rancher drove to the church. It made sense to donate a dead woman's things to charity, but the rancher didn't stop. Perhaps Ethan Trent had a wife…but the outlaw's instincts told him otherwise.

LeFarge walked out of the restaurant without ordering and strode to the railroad depot while considering the events that had led to Jesse Fowler turning into Hank Dawson. Their last meeting had left Tim in a fury.

After discovering his ex-partner's ruse in Lexington, Timonius had caught up with him in Midas where he'd learned that Mr. and Mrs. Hank Dawson were registered at the hotel. He'd gone to their room and told Jesse he had two choices: he could turn over the money or watch his wife die—right after Timonius took his pleasure.

To his credit, the kid had seen the wisdom of handing over the money. He'd told Tim that he'd gone straight and had deposited the cash in a bank in Albuquerque under his new name. They had taken off that night, but just before dawn the kid had gone for his gun. He'd missed, but Timonius hadn't. Jesse had taken a bullet before galloping into the dark.

Tim hadn't minded all that much. He'd learned to be all things to all people, and conning a bank manager sounded like child's play. Except the fellow in Albuquerque had never heard of either Hank Dawson or Jesse Fowler. Timonius had been duped. He'd made his way back to Midas, asking questions along the way, but the widow had vanished into thin air.

The money had to be somewhere. The rancher might have taken it. Or maybe the widow and the rancher had formed an alliance...

Timonius thought about asking the sheriff if Ethan Trent was a married man, but if the answer was no, Handley would insist on riding with him to the Trent ranch.

As Timonius walked to the railroad depot, he weighed the possibilities. Either the widow was really dead and the money was waiting in Los Angeles, or the rancher had made it up as a ruse to throw him off track while she was near Midas waiting for the right time to go after it herself.

At the ticket window, a clerk peered at Timonius through his round spectacles. "Can I help you, sir?"

"When is the next train to Los Angeles?"

"Not for three days. We have a problem on the track down near Las Vegas."

"One ticket, please," LeFarge said.

The timing suited him perfectly. Three days was just enough time to pay a personal call on Ethan Trent.

Chapter Five

When she heard the rattle of the rancher's wagon, Jayne climbed out of the warm bed, lit the lantern on the nightstand and peeked out the window. She saw him in the moonlight, sitting with his knees wide and his shoulders bent with fatigue, guiding the horse through the meadow.

It had been a hard day. The morning sickness had churned in her stomach until noon, and she had spent the afternoon wondering if being pregnant had sharpened her senses. She heard pine needles rustle and imagined LeFarge coming after her. When she pumped water, she recalled Ethan Trent's rusty laughter. His smile had shocked her down to her toes. Behind that scruffy beard, she saw the hint of a handsome man.

The clatter of the wagon was louder now, so she went to the stove and stirred their supper. In spite of his meager supplies, she'd managed a batch of biscuits and a hearty stew from tinned meat and vegetables. It smelled good, and she wondered if the

rancher liked to eat his food piping hot or if he preferred to let it cool a bit.

His wife would have known. Jayne could almost
feel her fingerprints on the worn handle of the frying
pan. The heart-shaped mirror must have been hers,
too, but the rest of the cabin was untouched by a
woman's hands. Had Mrs. Trent died in childbirth or
from an illness? Or perhaps she'd lost her life in an
accident.

Jayne was certain that she hadn't left her husband
willingly. The woman had drawn stars next to the
love sonnets in a well-thumbed volume of poetry.
The Bible on the shelf held a mystery as well. Someone had written dates and initials by the simple
verses taught in a child's Sunday School class.

As the wagon rattled to a stop, Jayne picked up
the lantern and opened the door. Light spilled into
the yard, circling the rancher as he climbed down
from the seat. Her gaze traveled from his muddy
boots to his thighs to the hard line of his whiskered
jaw. He was spattered with mud from head to foot.

Peering through the golden light, she said, "It
must have been a terrible trip."

"I got stuck a few times, but that's the way of it."
He gave the horse a quick scratch on the neck. "Old
Buck's even dirtier than I am."

She hung the lantern on a nail and walked to the
back of the wagon. "I'll help you unload. You must
be starved."

"I am."

"I've got stew and—" Her fingers grazed var-
nished wood. "My trunk! How did you get it?" Her

mother's scissors. Her clothing. Letters and keepsakes. Trailing her fingers across the dark walnut, she said, "I can't thank you enough, Mr. Trent."

"There's no need. You can look through it while I get the horse settled."

He hoisted it from the wagon and headed for the door. Jayne grabbed a sack of cornmeal and followed him into the cabin. "I can't believe you brought my things. Did you go to the hotel?"

The rancher set the trunk down and stepped back. Her gaze narrowed to the broken latch and then shot to a dress sleeve dangling over the side. Someone had searched her belongings. "What happened?" she asked.

He rocked back on his heels and stared straight into her eyes. "Jayne, we have to talk."

He had used her given name, and she wondered why. "Yes, we do. You're entitled to the truth."

"So are you." Using the toe of his muddy boot, he nudged the trunk closer to the bed. "We'll talk when I'm done with chores."

Together they carried in cans and packages, stacking everything on the counter until she was worried it would tumble to the floor. He'd bought enough flour to last six months and enough milk for an entire family.

As soon as he left for the barn, she knelt in front of the trunk and opened the lid. Everything from her best dresses to her unmentionables had been jumbled together, and someone had rabbit-eared all of Hank's pockets.

Who had riffled through her things and why? Shivering at the implications, she lifted the tangled clothing from the trunk and set it on the bed. Her mother's scissors clattered to the floor. Bending low, she scooped them up and slipped her fingers through the loops.

You're strong, Jayne. As long as you can sew, you can earn a living.

She heard Louisa McKinney's voice in her heart and knew the words were true. She'd find a way to start over, but first she had to tell the rancher the truth. If LeFarge had found her, Ethan Trent was in more danger than she thought.

Leaving the clothing on the bed, she went to the kitchen to dish up his supper. Just as she ladled stew onto a plate, he opened the door. For the first time in a month, he left his muddy boots on the porch. Glancing at her, he stepped inside, reached into the pocket of his coat and handed her a small brown bag.

"These are for you," he said.

His rough fingers brushed her palm as she took it. She peeked inside and then arched her eyebrows at him. "Lemon drops?"

"Sour things might settle your stomach."

"That would be a blessed relief," she said with heartfelt gratitude.

"I have some other things for you, too." He picked up the new trousers and shirt she'd thought were his, a bolt of fabric and a plain wooden hairbrush. He shoved it all into her arms and stepped back.

"What's all this?" she asked.

"I bought it before I got the trunk. I figured you

could make do with the trousers and the shirt, and the bolt of cotton is for woman stuff.''

Jayne bit her lip. She didn't want the rancher taking care of her, especially not if it led to thoughts of ''woman stuff.'' Frowning, she said, ''I owe you money.''

''Consider it a gift. An apology for the way I treated you that first day.''

The lemon drops were a taste of heaven and the clothing was purely practical. She could accept all of it with a gracious smile, except the brush. It meant he'd been watching her, that he'd noticed her hair and probably more.

''I accept your apology, but I want to pay you back,'' she insisted. ''A gift is too personal.''

The rancher scowled. ''So is emptying your chamber pot.''

He had a point. A humbling one. ''All right,'' she said, setting everything on the bed. ''I accept. Thank you.''

He skimmed by her and reached for an almost-clean shirt hanging on the wall as she walked to the stove to dish up their meal.

''What's for supper?'' he said. ''It smells good.''

''I made a—'' She turned around and nearly dropped the plate. Ethan Trent was naked from the waist up. Until now he'd been careful to change clothes in private, and she wasn't prepared for the sight of his chest, well-muscled and covered with a smattering of dark silken hair.

''I made a stew,'' she finished lamely.

''Supper sounds good. Do I smell biscuits?''

With his shaggy hair and unshaven face, he reminded her of a bear waking up from a long winter's nap. He looked ravenous, and she put another dollop of meat and gravy on his plate. "I took a chance on the yeast, but I baked bread today."

He tucked his shirt into his trousers, strode to the table and pulled up a chair just as she set down his plate. She sat across from him, unwrapped the fresh bread and cut two slices for him and one for herself. Her stomach wouldn't tolerate a heavy meal, but the bread tasted good.

Judging by the rancher's appetite, the stew tasted even better. He downed the first serving, helped himself to seconds and wiped the plate clean with two more slices of bread. When they'd finished eating, he carried their dishes to the scrub bucket, poured coffee for them both and returned to the table.

Jayne took the letter out of her pocket and slid it across the table. "I have to tell you the truth about my husband. This explains everything."

"I already know what it says. I read it this morning."

"You read my letter?"

"It fell on the floor, and it's a good thing it did. LeFarge is in Midas. I met him at the sheriff's office today."

Jayne sat straighter in the chair. "Does he know where I am?"

"I told him you were dead." In slow sentences he described LeFarge's masquerade as a detective, his search of the trunk and the sheriff's tip that Hank Dawson had been headed for California. Leaning back in the chair, he said, "I think it's most likely he'll head for Los Angeles."

"And if he doesn't? Mr. Trent, I—"

His eyes burned into hers. "Call me Ethan."

Every instinct told her to stick to the formalities, but how could she? She was living in his house and she had nowhere else to go.

"Ethan it is," she said, breathing his name. "I can't endanger you any more than I already have. I need to get word to the authorities, and then I'll go home to Lexington."

"What about money?"

"I wouldn't touch a dime of what Hank stole, even if my life depended on it." She thought of the heavy coins sewn into the hem of her traveling suit. "I've got ten dollars and a bit of cash in my reticule. I'll get by."

He shook his head. "That won't pay for a train ticket to Kentucky."

"No, but it'll pay for a ticket to Raton and a room in a boardinghouse. The city's getting bigger every day. I'll find work."

"What about the baby? It'll change things for you."

"My mother managed just fine, and so will I. I'm not even going to use Hank's last name."

Ethan looked mad enough to spit. "You don't even know what it is."

"That's true, but it doesn't matter."

"It might someday. Your son might want to know who his father was."

The statement hit a nerve. *Mama, where's my*

daddy? Her child was entitled to the same answers Jayne had wanted when she saw little girls with big men they called "papa." Clutching her coffee cup, she said, "You're right. Tell me everything."

"His real name was Jesse Fowler. According to LeFarge, he robbed banks in Wyoming and killed at least two people, including a woman."

Jayne knotted her hands in her lap. "I don't know if that's true or not, but I do know that Hank had changed. He had a good heart." And secrets, she reminded herself.

"You can believe what you want about your husband, but the fact is that he left you flat broke and with child." He huffed with disgust. "My cattle take better care of their young."

"I'll manage just fine," she said evenly. "I'm a good seamstress. I'll reopen my mother's shop."

He arched one eyebrow. "What will you do for rent and materials?"

"I'll borrow."

He huffed at her. "Believe me. Bankers are heartless. People who need loans can't get them."

Jayne looked down her nose. She had no time for doubt. "Do you have a better idea? If you do, I'd like to hear it, but frankly, you're not one to talk. You live like an animal, your ranch is falling apart and you're ill-tempered."

Ethan's eyes narrowed to slits, but he wasn't the only person who knew how to stare. Jayne glared back until he blinked, then she spoke her mind. "I can see that you've suffered from a tragedy. I can understand the pain, but I can't quit living the way you have.''

Flecks of gold burned in his irises, but the flames died as quickly as a match in the darkness. Looking away, he said, "Don't let anyone take away your hope, Jayne. Especially not someone like me.''

"Someone like you? That's ridiculous.'' She huffed, then softened the criticism with a smile. "You haven't been particularly friendly, and you could use a bath—''

He glared at her.

"Yes, a bath,'' she said pointedly. "But other than that, you've taken good care of me.''

He shook his head. "No, I haven't. I've been a selfish son of a bitch. I should never have left you in the barn. You had a right to a little respect.''

"So did you. I came back uninvited, and the storm was worse than I thought.''

Rising from her chair, she walked to the hearth and jabbed at the fire with the charred broom handle. A log shifted with a clunk and sparks shot up the chimney as she spoke. "I think we both proved our points, for better or for worse.''

For richer, for poorer,
In sickness and in health…

She hadn't meant to imitate the wedding vows, but they both knew them by heart.

He looked at her with glassy eyes, and his lips had parted as if he wanted to say something but couldn't find the words. She understood how that felt, to have feelings trapped inside. She didn't want to care about this man, but she did.

Still, it was a dangerous mistake. As she stared into his eyes, she glimpsed the mirrored heart just over his shoulder and imagined his pretty wife brushing her hair. Louisa McKinney had taught her daughter that true love came just once in a woman's life and that a wise woman trusted herself and no one else. Jayne had to remember those simple truths.

She laced her fingers together at her waist and faced Ethan. "Your wife was a very lucky woman."

"You can trust me, Jayne. Stay here for a while."

"I can't. I leaned on Hank and look where it got me. If LeFarge is gone, this may be my only chance to leave."

"You fainted this morning, and you just ate a slice of bread for supper. You're not well enough to travel."

She shrugged. "Where there's a will, there's a way."

A mischievous gleam lit Ethan's eyes as he leaned back in the chair and laced his fingers behind his head. "So let's see you fly. We'll climb up to the roof, you can make a wish, flap your arms like an eagle and jump. If you make it all the way to the barn, I'll eat my words and buy your train ticket."

"You're being ridiculous."

"No, you're being stubborn. You've got to face facts. The baby's going to change your life. It's going to tell you when to eat and sleep and even when to toss up your breakfast. All the willpower in the world won't change its mind."

He had a point. Dipping her chin, she touched her

belly, low where the baby was warm and snug. "I have a lot to learn," she said.

His gaze softened. "It's your first, isn't it?"

"Yes, it is," she said, feeling shy. "We were only married a few days."

"Then you aren't very far along." He looked from her face to the fire, then rose from his chair and walked to the nightstand. He opened the drawer, took out a wooden box adorned with a carved rose and brought it to her.

"Take it," he said. "Look inside."

As she wrapped her fingers around the burnished wood, Ethan dragged a chair from the table to the hearth for her. She sat down, watching him as he lowered his tall body down to the rocker, lit his pipe with a twig and propped his feet on the hearth. His cheeks puffed as air hissed through the bowl and she caught a whiff of vanilla-scented tobacco.

Until this moment she hadn't seen him indulge in pleasure of any kind. It made her heart ache for him, and she looked down at the box, knowing it held his most precious memories. Carefully she lifted the lid, peered inside and saw three photographs. She recognized Ethan immediately. Younger, clean-shaven and dressed in a suit with a black string tie, he was standing behind a pretty brunette seated in a Queen Anne chair with his hands resting proudly on her shoulders.

In the second picture she saw two boys standing on either side of a lacy bassinet. The oldest was about eight years old. He had his father's cheekbones and a mischievous streak the camera failed to hide.

Ethan's second son had his mother's bow-shaped mouth and dark hair. The baby's face was a blur, as if it had been crying.

The final shot showed the entire family. Flanked by his sons, Ethan stood behind his wife who was seated and cradling the baby in her arms. They stared straight-faced into the camera, and yet Jayne saw pride in Ethan's eyes, a mother's tenderness for a new baby and two well-loved sons.

Fighting tears, she laid the photographs gently in the box. "You had a lovely family," she said tenderly.

He took a drag on the pipe, tilted his head up to the ceiling and blew out four rings of smoke, one for each person he'd lost. "Laura and I were married for more than nine years. We grew up together in Missouri. That life was everything a boy becoming a man could want."

His voice scraped like a pine bough breaking beneath the weight of snow. Jayne clenched her fingers together in a silent prayer that God would heal this man's grief.

He puffed again on the pipe, clenching it between his teeth, then lowering it as he blew more smoke. "We went to school together, whispered in church and spooned in the hayloft on summer afternoons. It was pure heaven, though I didn't know it at the time. We got married in June. Josh came a year later and then William two years after that. Katie was—Katie came later."

He picked up the poker, leaned closer to the flames

and jabbed at the burning wood. "Are you sure you want to hear the whole story?"

He meant how they died. "I think you need to tell it," she said.

"I haven't talked to anyone, Jayne. Not for a long time. What I hate the most is that I failed my wife. It was my dream we were chasing—not hers—but she never said so. Instead she talked about how exciting it would be to see real mountains."

He jammed the pipe stem between his lips and sucked hard. After curling his lips into a tight O, he blew two more rings of smoke. "They died in a fire in Raton. My whole family. Everyone but me."

His eyes stayed on the two rings until they broke apart and vanished into the murky haze.

"I wanted a change," he continued. "I wanted to own land and raise cattle and quarter horses. I sure as hell didn't want to be working for her father in that damn bank of his. That had been the plan when we first got married. I'd work and we'd save every penny, and then someday we'd go west. Only time kept slipping by. When William came along, we used our savings to buy a bigger house in the center of town, but it never felt like home to me. I grew up on a farm, but even if my brother hadn't taken it over, I wouldn't have stayed in Missouri. I wanted a place of my own."

"I can't quite see you working in a bank," she said tentatively, wanting to encourage him but afraid of treading on sacred ground.

"I hated every minute of it, and to make matters worse, her old man was mean and cheap. Laura took after her mother, thank God. Only a saint could have put up with that bitter old man, and I was starting to think just like him. Turning down neighbors for loans made me sick to my stomach.''

''It must have been hard for you.''

''Oh, yeah,'' he drawled sarcastically. ''I thought it was hell on earth, but the truth is that I was just plain selfish.''

Every story had two sides, but Ethan had lost that perspective. Jayne traced the rounded edges of the wooden box in her lap. ''You wanted to give your family a good life.''

''Don't fool yourself, Jayne. I wanted to give *me* a good life.''

''But—''

''But nothing,'' he said with disgust. ''My wife and kids were happy with things just as they were. Laura tried to be excited about the move, but I knew she was hurting. She put on a smile, because she was that kind of woman, but it hurt like hell to leave her mother and sisters.''

Lowering the pipe, he cupped the bowl in his palm and stared into the flames crackling in the hearth.

''We got as far as Raton,'' he said quietly. ''It's odd what you remember. The hotel was four stories tall with a bright red roof. It stood out like a palace, and I remember thinking that Laura deserved a night in a soft bed. I remember thinking—all sorts of things.'' His voice cracked.

''Oh, Ethan,'' she whispered.

''I got them settled in the rooms and went out to get a newspaper. It felt good to walk after being cramped on the train, and so I took my time finding a store. I was buying licorice for the boys when the fire wagon raced by. I remember it as plain as day. I stood there like a fool and breathed a prayer for those in harm's way, not once thinking of my own family.''

But how could he possibly have known? Jayne wanted to fight that demon of guilt, but he had to finish his story.

He tugged on the frayed neckline of his shirt, as if the room had heated by twenty degrees. "I was just about to leave when that mirror shaped like a heart caught my eye. Laura would have loved it. She liked doodads, and I wanted to do something nice to make up for everything she'd lost. I walked all the way to the back of the store and waited a solid minute while the clerk counted out a lousy nine cents in change, one penny at a time.

"As soon as I walked out the door, I smelled smoke and then someone shouted, 'It's the hotel.' I ran like hell, but it was too late. By the time I got there, flames were shooting out the windows. I screamed Laura's name and called for the kids. I looked at every single face in the crowd, not knowing a soul until I found the desk clerk. He told me the stairs had caught first, and no one on the fourth floor had made it out.

"That's right where we were. The boys had never seen an elevator, and so I'd asked—" He wiped at the moisture glistening on his cheeks. "I'd asked for the fourth floor just so they could ride it."

Tears welled in Jayne's eyes. She longed to touch

him, but it was too soon. His grief was like an infection that had been lanced but still needed to drain.

He sucked in a lungful of air, then blew it out hard and fast. "I stood there praying that somehow they'd made it down the back stairs, but I knew otherwise. The fire marshal found their bodies pretty easily. He said the smoke got to them, but I didn't believe him. I still don't. I'd tell the same lie if it would spare a man that kind of pain."

She could imagine Ethan standing in front of the ruins, lost and grieving in a town full of strangers. Tears welled as she spoke. "Where did you go that night?"

"An old preacher took me to his house. He made up a bed, heated a bowl of soup I couldn't eat, and then he started reading from the Bible. I didn't hear a word until he got to 'a time to give birth, a time to die.' That's when it all turned real. I cried like a baby all night long, and the next day I buried my family. The day after that I saw an ad for a ranch near Midas and bought it sight unseen."

Lowering the pipe, he looked into her eyes. "You know the story of King Midas, don't you? He wanted more than he had, and he got his wish. Everything he touched turned to gold, including the people he loved."

Ethan held up his left hand so that firelight glinted off his wedding ring. "I know how he felt, because this gold band is all I have left of Laura and the kids."

Desperate for cool air, Jayne rose from the chair, set the memory box on the seat and uncovered the nearest window. In the moonlight she saw knee-high pampas grass rippling in silvery waves. The blades scraped together in a haunting whisper. The landscape was endless and consuming, a fitting place for a man who wanted to die but couldn't. She knew his grief in her own soul, but she didn't believe in self-pity, and his guilt was a lie she couldn't abide.

She took a breath of fresh air, then faced him. "You didn't set the fire, Ethan. You didn't do anything wrong."

He glared as if she'd just spit on his wife's grave. "It's not up to you to decide that."

"But it's true. You need to look at the facts."

Jayne walked across the room, planted her feet in front of him and got down to business. "You loved your wife very much, and that's more than some women ever have. Laura would have been happy there."

"You don't know that."

"Yes, I do, and I know something else." She took a breath to steady her pounding heart. "Guilt is a choice, and so is self-pity."

"A choice!" He shot to his feet. "Let me tell you about choices. I would have died with them in a heartbeat. I'd walk a thousand miles to see them for just five minutes. I'd put a bullet in my head right now if I thought it would bring them back. Where are the choices in that?"

Pivoting, he grabbed a revolver from the shelf and popped open the cylinder.

"Please don't do this," she whispered.

Glowering, he emptied the bullets into his left

hand and slapped them down on top of the box of pictures. "I know what it's like to make choices, Jayne. You can choose to live or you can choose to die. And that's about it."

Stark fear filled her with courage. "You're wrong, Ethan. You can live well or you can die like a coward. You might be walking on this earth, but you aren't living. It's an insult to your wife. Laura would have wanted you to be happy, and you owe it to your children to be the man they knew."

Huffing, he snapped the empty cylinder shut. "You don't know what the *hell* you're talking about."

"Yes, I do. I've lost everything in the past year. My mother, my business, my husband—first to death and then to his lies. I have plenty of reasons to feel sorry for myself, but I'm *not* going to do it."

"It's different. You have the baby."

The truth sucked the air right out of her lungs. He was right. She had a reason to fight for every breath, and he had nothing, not anymore.

Every instinct told her that this man needed to be touched, now and often. Stepping in front of him, she cupped her fingers against his whiskered jaw. His eyes burned into hers. Then slowly, he covered her hand with his, dipped his head and pressed his full lips against her palm.

She grazed the tender skin below his eye with her thumb, smoothing away the last of his tears.

With a terrible sweetness, he whispered, "God help me, I want to kiss you."

When she gave a tiny nod and raised her chin, he

drew her into his arms so that his breath echoed in her ear. He feathered his lips over her temple, then down her cheek to the corner of her mouth. She felt the tripping beat of his heart in that kiss, and when he covered her mouth with his, she tasted vanilla smoke.

She'd expected the kiss to be tentative, tinged with memories of Laura and a lifelong love, hesitant like a man finding his way across the thin ice of a frozen lake. But Ethan had no such reluctance. He spread her lips with his and kissed her with the confidence of an experienced man. The exploration was thorough, unending, and like nothing she'd ever known

Shocked by the need low in her belly, she pulled her lips away from his, but he didn't release her from his arms. Instead he cradled her head against his chest, pulling her close so that their hips were pressed together like the matching halves of an apple.

At the realization that he was fully aroused, her blood heated and rushed to her cheeks. She needed cool air. She needed to be sensible. She had to ignore the fact that she, too, was aching with desire. Easing her grip on his broad shoulders, she looked into his eyes.

"I won't—I can't." Her voice sounded like a hammer pinging against a nail in hard wood.

With the suddenness of lightning, Ethan jerked his arms away from her, stepped back and stared as if she were a stranger. Without a word he pivoted and hurried out the door, slamming it behind him. She heard a bump as he leaned against the wood, probably to pull on his boots. Heavy footsteps followed, echoing through the night.

In the dim light of the dying fire, she twisted the ends of her shawl into a knot. Tomorrow they would have to deal with this moment, but not tonight. Ethan needed to lick his wounds in private, and she had to stop shaking long enough to remember that he'd really been kissing his wife.

Never mind the ache in her breasts and the smoky taste of him on her lips. One kiss would have to be enough.

Chapter Six

The rhythm of her breath hung in the air like a newly spun thread. A comforting whisper, now as familiar as the silence of the past two years, it filled Ethan's dreams as he curled on his side in the bedroll by the hearth. With dawn pressing against the window covers, he was coming awake in the gloom, emerging from a vivid dream of last night's kiss.

When their tongues had touched, she had made a little squeak deep in her throat, then she'd clutched his shoulders and hung on for dear life. Ethan had only kissed a handful of girls before settling down with Laura, but he knew innocence when he tasted it. Married or not, Jayne wasn't accustomed to kissing for the sake of being close.

Unless he missed his guess, he'd given her something to think about. The thought made him feel ten feet tall—for about two seconds. Then his gut clenched with guilt and he wanted to be sick. He'd betrayed his wife last night, or at least her memory.

He didn't need anyone to tell him why. More than once, lust had driven him to kiss Laura awake just

to make love to her. Katie had been conceived in
such a union. Trying to conjure up that humid August night, he chewed on his bottom lip, imagining
Laura's small mouth. But it was Jayne's kiss that he
tasted.

His groin sprang to life and he winced at the need.
Old Faithful hadn't been this hard for two years,
maybe even longer. Maybe not since he was sixteen
when Laura had let him touch her breasts behind his
father's barn.

Staring blindly at the ceiling, Ethan heaved a sigh.
So what? He'd woken up horny this morning. It was
just part of nature. He didn't have to act on that desire. Nor did he have to lie here like an old dog,
thinking about Jayne's breasts pressing against his
chest.

To block the memory he started counting down
from a hundred, but when he got to ninety-three, he
remembered nuzzling her ear. It was small and tick-
lish, and she'd bent her neck and arched into him,
pressing herself tight. Ethan stifled a groan and tried
naming the books of the Bible to cure what ailed
him, but he didn't get past Genesis. His mind took a
turn through the Garden of Eden, where Eve had
blond hair and wasn't wearing fig leaves.

Annoyed with himself, he tossed aside the blankets, yanked on his clothes and strode into the yard
for a breath of air that didn't smell like honeysuckle.
Glancing eastward, he paused at the sight of sunlight
spreading across the sky like melting butter. It made
him think of other mornings when he'd buried his
face to escape the light, but it had never worked.

Dawn was inevitable. Some forces of nature couldn't be stopped.

But others could, particularly the one making his trousers two sizes too small. He needed a bath for more reasons than one, so he hiked over a hill to a creek filled with spring runoff, stripped off his clothes and splashed chilly water all over himself. With Old Faithful back in its proper place, Ethan thought about his wife. He could almost hear her singsong voice, the one she used when she lectured the boys about mucking out the stable behind their house.

Since when is being unhappy an excuse for being lazy? The chores won't do themselves, you know.

Ethan's throat swelled at the memory. At the same time a ray of sunshine hit his shoulder, as if Laura were looking down from heaven. *Now, Ethan—*

For just a moment he felt like a henpecked husband again. And as usual, his wife was right about what needed to be done. He'd neglected himself, and the ranch, too.

After scrubbing his skin with willow leaves, he climbed out of the creek, dressed and headed for the barn to survey the mess he'd left. As soon as he stepped through the door, he saw the holes he had punched with his fists. The splintery walls had hooks for tools, but they were all empty because he'd taken to tossing things in a pile just inside the door.

Across the yard, the cabin door groaned on its rusty hinges. Closing his eyes, he tried to picture Laura walking to the well, but the sense of her had left him. Peering through the gloom to the sunlit yard, he saw Jayne lift a bucket to the pump. He recognized the blue calico dress and white apron from the trunk, and she had brushed her hair until it shone. A blue ribbon held the strands in a long braid, but a tendril had already escaped and was curling behind her ear.

At the thought of seeing her hair loose around her shoulders, Ethan felt his belly tighten. He hated himself for that yearning. He wanted her to leave, but he'd hate himself even more if LeFarge hurt her in any way. Last night had ended in a kiss, but it had started with a terrible threat. He'd rather die than see a woman suffer because of his weakness. That meant he had to convince Jayne to stay until he was sure she'd be safe.

Hidden in the shadows, he watched as the door slapped shut behind her and then started his chores. As he fed the two horses, the morning air came alive with the smell of frying sausage. His stomach rumbled with hunger and his mouth watered at the thought of biscuits and gravy.

He wouldn't mind having a decent meal now and then. If he paid Jayne for chores, she'd have a reason to stay and she'd be nothing more than a housekeeper to him.

At the smell of fresh coffee, Ethan almost smiled. He'd been angry with God for two solid years, but this morning he felt a twinge of good humor. If the Almighty was going to torture him with the presence of a woman, at least he'd sent one who could cook.

* * *

Jayne wanted eggs for breakfast, but the rancher didn't keep chickens. He didn't even have a milk cow. It was no way for a man to live. She couldn't stand the darkness, the layers of grease, the memories stacked on shelves and hidden in drawers. Especially the memory of his arms around her and the hunger in that kiss.

What was she going to do? She cared about him, and under the circumstances, that was just plain foolish.

You can't depend on anyone but yourself, Jayne.

Louisa McKinney had given her daughter that lecture more times than Jayne could count, and Hank had driven the point home in spades. She had no intention of marrying again, but if she *did* lose her mind, she wanted to be first in her husband's heart. Not second to lies as she had been with Hank, nor second to a memory as she would be with Ethan. Like it or not, those were the facts of her situation.

Never mind that his kiss had been a taste of heaven, possessive and patient, a memory she'd cherish for the rest of her life. He'd come alive in her arms. And for the first time she'd understood the power of a woman's touch, the hunger in a man's answering need.

Heaving a sigh, she put four biscuits on Ethan's plate, covered them with gravy and added a hefty portion of the sausage he'd brought home last night. She had managed to cook breakfast without being sick, but she couldn't eat the meat. A scrambled egg would have been nice. For the second time that morning, she wondered how Ethan liked his eggs. Probably fried with lots of pepper. His wife would have known for sure.

He walked through the door just as she set Laura's frying pan down on the stove. "Good morning," she said calmly. "Are you hungry?"

"A little."

When he took off his hat, Jayne's stomach plummeted to her knees. His damp hair was curling around his ears, and she could see that he'd scrubbed his neck until it was pink. His clothes still smelled musty, but she caught the scent of willow leaves on his skin.

When he almost smiled at her, she knew last night's kiss had to be dealt with immediately. If he thought she was willing to step right into Laura's shoes, or her place in his bed, he was sorely mistaken. She had to make it clear that the kiss had been a one-time gift of comfort, nothing more.

As soon as she handed him a full plate and a mug of coffee, he seated himself at the table. She served herself a single biscuit, poured a cup of milk and sat across from him. "We need to talk," she said.

Intent on his meal, he dragged a bite of sausage through the gravy. "About what?"

Jayne held in a sigh. Were all men this dense? Perhaps she'd read too much into last night. She decided to change her tactics. "I need to report everything I know about Hank to the authorities. When can you take me to Midas?"

"Today if you'd like, but what about LeFarge? We can't trust Handley."

He was right. Her stomach flopped like a dying fish. "I have enough money for a ticket to Raton. I'll talk to the police chief and he can notify the district marshal. After that, I'll look for a job."

Ethan shook his head. "If LeFarge comes back, he'll find you in two seconds flat. You need to hide."

"I can't. I need to support myself."

Ethan sliced off another bite of biscuit, chewed thoughtfully and washed it down with coffee. "What would you say to working for me? I'll pay you for housework. You can stay here until LeFarge is dead or in jail."

It seemed like a good plan, but that kiss had to be considered. Her mother used to say, "You can't un-ring the bell," and Ethan had rung her bell so thoroughly that she quivered at the mere memory of his lips parting hers. He would be an easy man to love, which made staying almost as risky as leaving. Hank had broken her heart once, and she didn't want it to happen again.

Squaring her shoulders, she said, "I don't think that's a good idea."

"Why not?"

"You know why not." She made her voice firm. "You kissed me last night."

Ethan shifted his gaze from her face to the heart-shaped mirror on the wall. Drawing a breath so deep that it pulled at the buttons on his frayed shirt, he turned his head and looked straight into her eyes.

"Don't misunderstand me, Jayne. I appreciate what you did for me last night. That kiss was kind

and generous, but it will *not* happen again. I won't
let it.''

She should have been relieved, but instead she felt
like a dress left on the rack in favor of a prettier one.
Her chest ached as she laced her fingers together in
her lap. ''Then we understand each other.''

''Yes, we do.'' With a brusque nod, he tapped his
fingers on the table. ''I'll pay you five dollars a week
for cooking, laundry, whatever needs to be done.''

It was a generous sum. In a few months she'd have
enough money for train fare to Lexington. She could
be home before summer's end. The thought of dec-
orating a room for herself and the baby warmed her
toes, but she couldn't look at Ethan without seeing
his need. As long as she was staying, she might as
well do some good.

''I'll take it,'' she replied. ''But I have a requirement of my own.''

His eyes narrowed. ''What?''

''It's time you stopped living like an animal. That
beard has to go, and so does all that hair.''

''That's none of your business,'' he growled.

''If I have to look at you, it is. I'm sorry, Ethan,
but you look like the backside of a beaver.''

The unkempt beard hid his lips, but she saw a
twinkle in his eyes as he wrapped both hands around
his coffee cup. ''That good, huh?''

Jayne looked down her nose like the Sunday
School teacher she used to be. ''You have two options. You can ride into town and visit the barber, or
you can shave yourself and I'll trim your hair.''

Just like that, the twinkle in his eyes turned into a

painful gleam. "I can't leave you alone. It's not safe."

"Then get busy with that razor." Jayne pushed up from her chair and lifted his plate out from under his nose. He'd left the tin so clean that it looked as if he had licked it. "I'll wash the dishes while you shave. There's plenty of hot water in the reservoir."

As she walked to the scrub bucket, she listened for the scrape of his chair against the floor. Instead she heard him chuff like a mule. "This is silly," he said.

Maybe, but it needed to be done. She put a teasing lilt in her voice. "I think I know what the problem is. It's been so long that you've forgotten how to shave. All you have to do is—"

"All *you* have to do is be quiet." With a grimace, he pushed out of the chair and glowered at the hot water reservoir. Jayne hid a smile. Anger was a sure cure for constant sorrow.

"Would you like to use my scissors?" she offered.

He grunted. "I can manage."

While he filled the washbowl and prepared his shaving tools, Jayne puttered in the kitchen. Humming to herself, she stole glances as he chopped at his facial hair with a pair of squeaky scissors. The brown fluff fell to the floor in chunks, revealing a square jaw and a stubborn chin.

When he finished with the scissors, he dipped both hands in the hot water and raised them to his face to soften his whiskers. Water ran down his arms and soaked his shirt. The collar was in his way, too. Her good manners prodded Jayne to leave the cabin so he could finish the chore in private, but curiosity kept her polishing dishes that were already dry.

When Ethan globbed shaving soap onto his shirt, he gave up and stripped off the blue cotton. At the sight of the tanned skin stretched over his ribs, she dropped the plate with a clatter. Hard work had given him the muscles she had noticed last night, but the rest of him was as skinny as a starving coyote. She made up her mind to feed him double portions of everything, including dessert.

"Are you all right?" he demanded.

She bent at the knees to pick up the plate. "Just clumsy."

He watched until she pushed to her feet, putting them eye to eye. Her gaze dipped to his chest and then lower still, to the line of dark hair that disappeared into his dungarees.

Red heat flooded her cheeks and she averted her eyes. To fight the blush, she decided to think of him as a customer in her mother's shop. Except none of her customers had been over six feet tall and in need of a shave, except Mrs. Ashton who had terrible chin hair. But that was beside the point.

At the scrape of the razor against his skin, she took another peek. He was holding his nose out of the way and focusing on the mirror as he wielded the blade in short strokes. Jayne turned back to the kitchen and busied herself with shelving the clean dishes.

"Shit!"

She spun around just as a line of blood beaded on his jaw. He snatched a flour sack he'd been using for a towel and pressed it to the cut. "Excuse my language. I'm not used to company."

"You need soap," she said. "I have some in my trunk."

She opened the lid and handed him a small white bar scented with honeysuckle. He glared at the soap and then at her, but finally he took it, brushing her palm with his damp fingers. Sensing he'd endured all the attention he could stand, she retrieved her scissors and a mirror from the trunk. Dragging a chair to the door, she said, "I'll be outside."

She stood in the sun until Ethan strode out of the cabin. "Let's get this over with."

When he planted himself in the chair with his feet flat on the ground and his hands resting on his thighs, Jayne realized that he'd done this before. Laura had probably cut his hair once a month. Maybe she had lined up the children and made a game of it. A lump rose in her throat.

"I'm ready," Ethan said in a tight voice.

Gently she took a fingerful of hair and snipped away. As the last swatch fell to the ground, she positioned herself in front of him, tipped his chin upward and finger-combed his temples to be sure the sides were even. She wasn't the least bit surprised to discover that Ethan Trent was a very handsome man.

"Would you like a mirror?" she asked.

When he didn't reply, she took it for yes and handed him the silver glass. The sun glinted off the surface, sending a beam of light into his eyes. He blinked, then surveyed the face staring back at him. Was he seeing the man he used to be or someone new? Jayne didn't know, but at least she'd given him something to think about.

As she turned to leave, he grabbed her wrist and squeezed. "Thank you," he said. "For everything."

An uncommon silence spanned the gap between them. She had an urge to kiss his forehead, but she was sure he'd jerk away, so instead she smiled. "I'm just glad you look human again."

But he looked better than human. She saw a man who had everything to give and nothing left to lose. He was a warrior who would have gladly died to protect the woman he loved. A father who would have spilled blood to save his children.

Abruptly, Ethan released her wrist and pushed up from the chair. "I better get busy with chores."

"Me, too," she said. "It's laundry day. Where's the washtub?"

"In the barn."

At the same time, they heard the distant rumble of a galloping horse. The thunderous hoofbeats drew their gazes to the mountain trail, where a man dressed in black and mounted on a mare the color of midnight was racing toward them.

Chapter Seven

"Ah, hell," Ethan muttered. "It's the Reverend."

He'd had about all the attention he could stand for one day. If John Leaf made a smart remark about the haircut, he was going to get a lecture about minding his own business.

Standing at his side, Jayne waved a greeting to their visitor. "I like Reverend Leaf. He tried to help me find Hank."

At the mention of Dawson, Ethan's common sense kicked in. If the sheriff had asked the Reverend about the trunk, Handley could be headed to the ranch, too. He would discover that Jayne was alive and he'd insist on taking her to town. A chill slithered up Ethan's spine. He had to find out what had happened after he had left Midas.

The Reverend slowed his horse to a walk as he rode across the yard, taking in the details with a wry smile. "Hello, Ethan," he called. "I'm glad to see the rumor isn't true."

"What rumor?" Ethan demanded.

The Reverend dismounted and walked toward

them, casting a long shadow across the ruts in the yard. With his lanky build, John had a few inches on Ethan as well as a couple of years. At thirty-five, the man still had dark brown hair and the piercing eyes of a gunfighter.

He was also single and easy on a woman's eyes, a fact Ethan found irksome when he extended his hand to Jayne and smiled.

"Mrs. Dawson, it's nice to see you again."

Beaming, she took his hand. "It's a long story, but I go by Miss McKinney now. Please, call me Jayne."

"With pleasure," he said, smiling. "As for that story, that's why I'm here today."

Horrible pictures of an evil man doing violence to Jayne hurdled through Ethan's mind. His throat tightened with urgency. "What have you heard?"

The Reverend rocked back on one hip and raised an eyebrow at Ethan. "It seems a trunk belonging to a dead woman was supposed to show up at church. I never saw it. Rumor has it you've started wearing dresses. I tell you, Ethan, it took real courage for me to come out here today. Nice haircut, by the way."

Ethan was about to tell the Reverend to go to hell when Jayne's wind-chime laughter filled the air. "I think you two gentlemen should leave the dresses to me."

The Reverend grimaced with feigned relief. "I agree completely. Ethan? What do you think?"

Still feeling ornery, he replied, "I think you're a royal pain in the butt."

The preacher chuckled with pleasure, and so did Ethan. John Leaf was his only friend. Every now and then, he came to the ranch, bringing newspapers and tidbits of town gossip. He hadn't pushed Ethan to get to church. He had brought church to Ethan. During one of those times, he stayed late into the night telling tales from his life. Ethan wasn't the only man in Midas with regrets. The Reverend had been on a first-name basis with the devil himself, and that devil had been named John Leaf.

Reformed or not, it wouldn't hurt to have an ex-gunslinger on their side. "Tell us what happened," Ethan said to John.

"When Handley told me about Tim LeFarge, I knew you had trouble on your hands. I knew the man back in Laramie, so when the sheriff mentioned the trunk, I thanked him on behalf of the widows and orphans of Midas and decided to ride out here to check things out."

Relief sluiced through Ethan. "So he doesn't know Jayne's alive?"

"Handley doesn't suspect a thing, but he's not the problem. LeFarge won't go away until he has answers." The Reverend looked at Jayne. "I'm sorry to bring bad news, but you're in danger."

Rage rose in Ethan's throat. "If that bastard shows up here, he's dead."

Jayne clutched his sleeve. "Maybe I should leave."

"Like hell!" he roared. "If you think I'm going to let a pregnant woman get on a train with a killer chasing after her, you better think again."

"I'm not your responsibility."

"Yes, you are." Ethan shifted his gaze back to

John. At the sight of a Cupid-like gleam in the man's eyes, he had to bite his tongue to stay civil. "What do you suggest?"

The amusement drained from John's face. "I'll wire the authorities as soon as I get back to town, but that's not enough. Jayne Dawson needs to stay dead, and Jayne McKinney should turn into someone else."

"All right," Jayne said, standing straighter. "I'll change my last name to Smith or Brown, something ordinary he won't be able to trace."

But Ethan knew that LeFarge wouldn't be fooled by a fake name. He'd track every blond dressmaker west of the Mississippi until he found her. If she was going to take on a new identity, it had to be authentic.

Ethan had already reconciled himself to faking a marriage if LeFarge showed up. He'd never betray Laura's memory, but a legal name change offered Jayne even more protection, both now and in the future. The baby would bear the Trent name, too. Thoughts of the child filled Ethan with a shred of painful pleasure. Lord, he missed his kids. Bedtime stories and fishing on Sundays. Wrestling matches with Laura yelling at them all to stop. Even "chicken pops," as William had called the itches on his little-boy skin.

Coming back to the present, Ethan sucked in a breath. Jayne was wringing her apron, and the Reverend had wrinkled his brow into a thoughtful frown.

"I have an idea," he said to John. "I want Jayne

to use my name to hide from LeFarge. Will you file a marriage certificate for us?''

She gripped his arm. "That's too much to ask."

"I want to," he said. "You'll be safer and so will the baby."

The Reverend eyed them both. "I can manage the documents, but I have a requirement of my own. What goes on behind closed doors is between you two and God, but I won't falsify a marriage. You have to take real vows."

Ethan waved off the concern. "They're just words."

"Maybe so," John replied, "But I'm honor-bound to warn you. When I marry people, it sticks."

"This isn't *that* kind of wedding," Ethan countered.

"Maybe not. Only time will tell." The Reverend nodded in the direction of a knoll overlooking a vast meadow. "I'm going to walk to the top of that hill and have a smoke. Come on over after you've talked."

John strode away, leaving Ethan staring at his back with the hill slightly to the Reverend's right. That spot was special to Ethan. At night he'd stand there and stare at the stars because it was a bit closer to heaven and Laura and the children. Sometimes during the day he'd peer through the empty miles and imagine them coming home in a cloud of dust.

Forcing himself to blink, Ethan looked directly at Jayne. "You have my word that this will be a marriage in name only," he said. "We'll get an annulment when LeFarge is out of the picture."

She wrapped her arms around her waist. "It's all wrong, Ethan. People should marry because they love each other. I used to dream about weddings and white dresses with lots of lace. This just doesn't seem right."

"You can still dream," he said. "This is temporary."

She turned her back and spoke to the clouds. "I'm done dreaming. I'll never marry again."

"Don't say that," he said gently. "Someday you'll meet a man who's worthy of you. He'll love you because you're a good woman, and he'll want to be a father to your baby. Don't go slamming any doors."

She shook her head. "That door is shut and locked."

"It shouldn't be," Ethan insisted. "You're young enough to start over. Besides, what if you have a boy? Someone has to teach him how to ride and shoot, and how to fish. It's important."

She shrugged. "I'll manage. I always do."

"Take my word, Jayne. Life is easier with a partner." Ethan felt his throat swell. "I hurt every day for Laura, but I wouldn't trade a minute of the time we had for anything on this earth. Someday you'll have that joy. I *want* you to have it."

Her stark posture struck Ethan as oddly defiant. He had no idea what she was thinking. A marriage in name only followed by an annulment made sense to him, and he'd expected Jayne to see the practicality. Instead she'd turned stubborn and sworn off love completely, as if he'd broken her heart. Unsure of what to say, Ethan watched as she tilted her chin to the sky and took a deep breath. He heard the rush of air escaping from her lungs, and then she turned around.

"I don't know what to do," she said. "I have to think about the baby, but marriage should mean something. Hank betrayed our vows, but I still believe in promises."

Ethan felt hot blood racing to his head. "Dammit, Jayne. I *know* what those vows mean, but I also know that you're being chased by a killer and your baby's in danger. I'm going to do everything I can to keep you safe. It seems to me you could put your romantic notions aside, until LeFarge is gone and you can go home."

At the sharp inhalation of her breath, Ethan knew that he'd punctured the last of her excuses. Jayne had a mother's heart. She'd do anything to protect the baby, even it meant taking a man's name and nothing else. No white dress. No bouquet of roses. No tender wedding night.

Ethan felt his gut knot with pain and a longing for things he no longer had. He had to focus on the trouble of the day, and Jayne would be better off if she did the same. "Shall we get the show on the road?" he said.

She lowered her arms from her waist and managed a wry smile. "That has to be the most pitiful marriage proposal I've ever received."

It was also the most pitiful one Ethan had ever made. For Laura, he'd bought a ring and taken her for a buggy ride beneath a harvest moon. They had kissed under the stars, dreaming of children and a future bright with hope. His throat closed at the memory. "I just want things to be clear."

"We both understand the circumstances. Let's go see the Reverend."

Jayne pivoted on her heel and paced through the yard, giving Ethan a clear view of her straight back and narrow shoulders. With two strides, he caught up with her. Together they trudged up the hill to where the Reverend was grinding out a cigarette with his boot.

"Are you ready?" he asked.

"Yes," they said in unison.

John nodded. "Ethan, take Jayne's hand in yours."

The gesture seemed fitting, like a handshake to seal the deal, so he wrapped his fingers around hers.

"I usually say something about life's hardships to a new bride and groom, but you two have been down that road already. You know all about the disasters that come with time, and what it's like to start over, so today I want to talk about hope.

"Life isn't for the faint of heart. You've both lost people you love, but hope is what sustains us through dark nights and empty days. Hope is what gives us the promise of eternity and of seeing our loved ones again."

Ethan had to swallow hard. He knew all about heaven. He was dead sure it rang with Laura's laughter, and that Josh and Willie were playing kick-the-can. As for Katie, she'd be an angel with her mother's dark eyes.

A bold sympathy filled the Reverend's gaze. Ethan managed a nod, and the preacher continued. "A man I once knew said, 'Hope is a rope. Tie a knot and hang on.' That's what I'm telling you both to do today. Just hang on. Can you agree to that?"

"Yes," said Jayne almost whispering.

Ethan barely nodded, but it was enough.

"Then we're ready for the vows." John turned to Jayne first. "Do you, Jayne McKinney, take this man to be your husband, in sickness and in health, for richer and for poorer, until death do you part?"

"I do." Her voice rang clear and true.

The Reverend turned to Ethan with a challenge in his eyes. "And do you, Ethan Trent, take this woman to be your wife, in sickness and in health, for richer and for poorer, until death do you part?"

"I do."

The Reverend gave a final nod. "I now pronounce you man and wife. Ethan, you may kiss the bride."

The day he'd married Laura came alive in a torrent of light. The church had been overflowing with family and friends. He had kissed her until his spinster aunt huffed and little boys started to giggle. He could smell the white roses she had worn in her hair and taste the wedding cake she'd fed him with her fingers.

He looked straight at the Reverend, intending to say *I can't,* but the sympathy in the man's eyes had hardened into a command.

"It's an absolute law," John said. "A woman has to be kissed on her wedding day."

He felt Jayne's fingers squeezing the blood from

his hand. Glancing at her profile, he saw that she was pleading with the Reverend with her eyes and subtly shaking her head no. With a start, Ethan realized that *she* was protecting *him*. He felt as if he'd been kicked in the gut, or worse, like a scared kid running from his first fight.

The Reverend was still staring at him. "If you don't do it, I will."

"Like hell," Ethan muttered. He'd be damned before he'd let John Leaf get the best of him twice in one day. Reaching across his body, he raised his hand to Jayne's cheek and tilted her face to his. As he bent to kiss her, she avoided his mouth to shield him from the hurt and instead brushed her lips against his jaw.

The gesture touched Ethan to the core. He wanted to thank her and tell her he cared about her, at least as much as he could. So he kissed her back, tender, on the mouth. The kiss held none of last night's passion, but it was sincere and just between them. As he pulled back, he saw tears in her eyes.

After a determined sniff, she wiped away the moisture and managed a smile. "Just ignore me," she said to both men. "I always cry at weddings."

The Reverend chuckled. "Don't tell anyone, but I do, too."

Ethan just wanted to get the day over with. "Is there something we have to sign?"

"I'll write out a marriage certificate before I leave," John replied. "Let's head inside."

The three of them walked down the hill to the cabin where John opened his Bible and took out a sheet of paper. After Ethan supplied him with a stubby pencil, he sat down at the kitchen table and wrote out the words that made the marriage legal.

Looking up at Ethan, he said, "Sign here."

After scrawling his name, Ethan handed the pencil to Jayne. Next to his chicken scratch, she spelled out Jayne Elizabeth McKinney in a loopy cursive. She had pretty penmanship, exactly what he would have expected.

As soon as the ink dried, John tucked the paper back into his Bible. "I'll file the minister's return as soon as I get to town. It's official. You two are married."

The declaration should have called for joy, but Ethan couldn't muster even a faint smile. Jayne filled in the silence.

"Would you like a bite to eat? I can whip up a batch of corn muffins."

"No, but thank you. I'm headed to the Chandler place next. Do you know them, Ethan?"

The Reverend knew damn well that Ethan hadn't spoken to a soul by choice in two years. Jayne's secret made that isolation more necessary than ever. "Can't say that I do," he replied.

"Luther might have a milk cow for sale, and Priscilla would welcome company. They've got a passel of kids, too."

"Visiting isn't a good idea," Ethan said.

But Jayne's eyes were shining like the noon sky. "I'd *love* to talk with her. I have a million questions about babies."

"She's the person to ask," John offered. "Ethan,

I'll send that wire to the district marshal today. As soon as I hear something, I'll be back.''

''The sooner, the better,'' Ethan said. He had a woman to protect, and this time he'd succeed or die trying.

Timonius LeFarge had lost weight. He had never been comfortable in a saddle, and today his bony butt made the ride out to the Trent ranch unbearable. The starchy clothes he'd bought for his Pinkerton's ruse chafed in ways he wouldn't soon forget, and though his bowler gave him a sophisticated look, it didn't shade his eyes from the sun.

Over the years he'd grown to dislike the open range. He was fifty years old and too worn out to be stealing for a living. He wanted to retire and buy a saloon in a big city. He'd been considering Denver until Jesse had stolen his money.

The kid had deserved to die. Nor did Timonius have any sympathy for his widow. The circumstances stank, and the more he thought about Ethan Trent, the more suspicious he became of the man. Tim had spent hours at the local saloon talking with the barkeep and the regulars, but no one knew anything beyond the fact that Trent had bought his place two years ago and rarely came to town.

The church crowd might have known if the rancher had a wife, but Tim wasn't about to stick around until Sunday. Nor did he want to stir up gossip at the local businesses. If he asked too many questions, the whole town would be looking for the widow Dawson and her money. He wanted to keep his cards close to the vest, especially since his ruse as a detective was thin at best.

As he neared the crest of a hill, the trail turned east. The ranch had to be close, and LeFarge kicked his horse into a trot. His plan was simple. If the cabin was empty, he'd search the house for any sign of a woman. If he got lucky and found her alone, he'd introduce himself as a detective and watch her face. If she twitched, he'd take Jayne Dawson at gunpoint and force her to bargain for her life. If she stayed calm and claimed to be Mrs. Ethan Trent, he'd stay the night and study them both.

When he reached the edge of the forest, he spied the ranch, including a pile of rocks marking a grave. Using the trees for cover, he reined in his horse and watched a slender woman with mousy hair hanging laundry on a clothesline. A green skirt and jacket swayed in the breeze. Next to it he saw a man's shirt. She looked like an average ranch wife doing chores. Letting his eyes wander, he took in her sun-warmed skin and the round breasts straining against her dress.

Damn, but he wished he'd laid eyes on Jayne Dawson when he'd rousted Jesse at the hotel. He should have spied on them for a day, but he'd been eager to end the hunt. That impatience had been a mistake. Irritated, he nudged his horse into the meadow. He wanted to catch the woman by surprise, but his mount snorted. The woman looked right at him with no reaction at all.

''Hi, there,'' she said cheerfully.

He perused her body and saw she was wearing a blue dress he remembered from the trunk. The garment matched her height, but it was loose at the waist and tight across her breasts.

"Good afternoon," he said, reining his horse to a stop. "I'm Detective Timonius LeFarge. I'm looking for information concerning Jayne Dawson."

Chapter Eight

"The widow? I'm afraid she's dead, but you can speak to my husband," Jayne replied.

With one hand resting on the edge of the washtub and the other shielding her eyes from the sun, she studied the man who had murdered Hank. He was leaning back in the saddle with the casual air of an old man in a rocking chair, but his eyes were as hard as nickels.

Jayne reached into her pocket and took out the wire-rimmed spectacles Ethan had given her this morning and slipped them on her nose. After the Reverend had left, her new husband had insisted on talking about what to do in case LeFarge paid them a visit. He'd rummaged in a drawer for the glasses she was wearing now, and she'd wondered if they belonged to Laura. On her own, Jayne had rinsed her hair in strong coffee. She was still blond, but the Arbuckle's had taken off the shine.

They had also decided to use her middle name, Elizabeth, which Ethan had shortened to Lizzie because it sounded more familiar. "Lizzie," he'd said out loud. "Lizzie Trent."

He'd tried to smile at her, but his mouth had twisted into a grimace and she'd felt the ache of the day all over again. Ethan had lost so much, but the sadness was for herself, for the things she was starting to want and couldn't have. Laura Trent had been a fortunate woman, indeed, and Jayne was an impostor with dyed hair, ill-fitting spectacles and a husband who did not love her.

Steeling herself against that truth, she focused on LeFarge and the danger at hand. She had to warn Ethan without raising the outlaw's suspicion. "My husband is working just over that rise. I'll get him, if you'd like."

"Actually, I came to see you."

"I'll tell you what I can." She motioned at the washtub. "I'll be done in just a minute. You can water your horse by the barn."

LeFarge hunched forward in the squeaky saddle and stared straight at her. "What did the widow look like?"

To hide her shaking hands, she reached into the washtub, raised the last of Ethan's shirts and wrung the life out of it. "She was blond. I didn't notice her eyes, just that she was crying."

Streams of water puddled at her feet as the outlaw shifted his gaze from her face to Hank's grave, and then to the narrow path leading to the meadow where Ethan was working. She wanted to shout for help, but her ruse called for calm and good manners.

"It's a nice day, isn't it?" she said.

LeFarge scratched his chin. "A bit too warm, I think. I better see to my horse." He tipped his hat and nudged the bay in the direction of the trough just as Ethan came over the rise. He was ambling down the path from the corral, carrying a shovel and a saw. He didn't know that LeFarge was just thirty feet away, hidden by the laundry.

Waving cheerfully, she called to him. "Hello, sweetheart! We have company."

His jaw hardened at the hint of danger and she saw him clutch the tools, no doubt wishing he was holding his Winchester instead of a shovel. As he passed the laundry line, LeFarge came into his view. The man was standing by the trough where his horse was taking a drink. Jayne saw him peering from beneath the brim of his hat, studying them both with his dead eyes.

"Hello, Detective." Ethan set the tools by the barn door. "What brings you this way?"

"I'm not so sure the widow's dead."

Jayne's stomach churned as she stepped to Ethan's side. Like wolves in the wild, the men locked eyes. LeFarge was armed. The situation called for cunning, not a physical challenge. Terrified that Ethan would start a fight he couldn't win, she prayed that he'd be wise and they would both stay safe. When Ethan scratched his head, Jayne knew that he'd sized up the situation the same way she had.

"I don't understand," he said, sounding slightly stupid. "I buried her a few miles from here."

"I live by hard evidence, Mr. Trent. A man's word means nothing to me. I want to see a body."

Ethan shrugged. "Sure, but it's late. How about tomorrow?"

"Tomorrow's fine, but it's a long ride from Midas. Perhaps I could impose upon you for the night?"

"It's not an imposition at all," said Jayne. "We'd *love* to have company, wouldn't we, dear?"

"Absolutely," he replied.

"That's very kind," said LeFarge. "The three of us can get to know each other. I'd like to ask Mrs. Trent a few questions, as well."

Ethan put his arm around her shoulders. "Ask away, but Lizzie doesn't know any more than I do."

Squinting through the glasses, she said, "We can talk later. I need to start supper."

Ethan gave her hand a hard squeeze. "Go ahead, sweetheart. I'll give Mr. LeFarge a hand with his horse. I can talk cattle all day long, and all night, too. How about you, Detective? Got any interest in ranching?"

"Not much."

The outlaw hadn't taken his gaze off her face, except to ogle her chest. His expression was crude, but she had to put up with it, at least for now. "Supper's in half an hour," she said. "You can clean up at the well."

"We'll be there." Ethan maneuvered the outlaw into the barn. "So what do you think of New Mexico? Lots of good grass, sky as blue as heaven. I can't think of a prettier place on earth…"

Ethan's rambling faded from Jayne's ears as she hurried to the cabin, closed the door and saw the bedroll on the floor. She kicked the evidence of their false marriage under the bed, lit both lanterns and started a fire in the hearth. Shaking inside, she surveyed the contents of the kitchen shelves, hoping to find something decent for supper.

The front door swung wide. She whirled around just as Ethan closed it with a thud. He came across the room and clasped her upper arms. "Are you all right?"

"I'm so sorry." Her voice cracked. "I didn't want to involve you. Where is he?"

"In the privy. We need to think quick."

Hysteria welled in her throat. "Maybe he'll fall in."

"I like the way you think," he said with a tongue-in-cheek smile. "How about we tip it over? Door side down?"

His presence alone bolstered her courage. She wanted to shout and laugh and cry, but then their eyes locked and the humor died like a wisp of smoke.

He tightened his grip on her arms. "I won't let him hurt you."

"I know you'll do your best, but—"

"There are no buts. If he lays a finger on you, he's dead. Do you have anything that might throw him off your trail?"

"There was an advertisement in Hank's coat." Easing out of Ethan's grasp, she opened the trunk and took out the paper. "Here it is."

"Tell him you found it wedged behind the drawers."

She touched his ragged sleeve. "Please, don't take chances for me."

His eyes narrowed as he shook his head. "That's not your choice. I protect what's mine, and right now, that includes you."

They both heard the slap of the privy door and the shuffle of boots coming down the dirt path.

"Just focus on supper," Ethan said. "I'll keep talking, and the night will be over before we know it."

As he strode out of the cabin, Jayne took the biggest pot off a shelf, started a stew with canned goods and whipped up a huge batch of biscuits. She didn't have butter or fresh milk, or a dozen other things a woman would keep on hand. When Ethan led Le-Farge through the door, she felt like a bird without feathers.

"Something sure smells good," said Ethan.

How many times had he said those words to Laura? Their charade seemed doubly cruel as she dished up his meal. "It's just a stew, but there's plenty. I hope you're hungry, Mr. LeFarge."

"Call me Tim."

She forced a smile. "Then I'm Lizzie."

Ethan sat closest to the door, forcing LeFarge to sit in the opposite chair. The outlaw craned his neck and peered at her face as she took the biscuits from the oven.

"Where are you from, Mrs. Trent? You look familiar."

She nearly dropped the pan.

"We're from Missouri," Ethan replied. "A man

needs land, don't you think, Detective? And what better place than New Mexico? Except maybe Colorado. That's pretty country. Have you ever been there?''

"Yes, I have," LeFarge replied. "And you, Lizzie, do you like New Mexico as much as your husband?''

"I love it," she said, taking her place at the table. It was the first honest thing she had said, and telling the truth calmed her. As soon as her backside hit the chair, Ethan began to say grace.

"Our...dear...Heavenly...Father...We come to you...with thanks...and gratitude...for this fine... delicious meal...prepared...with loving hands...''

Jayne bit back a smile. At this rate, LeFarge would die of old age before the prayer ended. Every minute counted. Every word bought her a second of safety. Ethan ran out of steam after the fourth Heavenly Father and gave a loud amen.

LeFarge reached for a biscuit. "So, Lizzie, tell me—''

"Sweetheart?" said Ethan. "Would you pour me another cup of coffee?''

"Sure.''

By the time she sat down, he was rambling about longhorns and Herefords. LeFarge grunted now and then, but when he tried to get personal, Ethan steered him back to talk of the weather or the train trip from Missouri. It was all very boring and normal, at least that's what she hoped LeFarge would see.

She couldn't help but notice the man's table manners, or the lack of them. He chewed with his mouth open, hunched over his plate and shoveled the stew as if he were slopping a hog. She nearly lost the small amount of supper she'd eaten when he pushed back from the table and let out a wet belch.

Ethan looked like he wanted to hold his nose as he pushed up from his chair. "Let's sit by the fire, Tim."

The men pulled their chairs to the hearth and set them at casual angles. Jayne watched as the outlaw curled into the seat with the ease of an alley cat, extracted a cigarette from his coat pocket and struck a match on the sole of his boot. Ethan cupped one hand around the pipe and lit the tobacco with a twig. "So, Tim, do you know any jokes?"

"Not a one."

"I've got a few. Have you heard the one about the three-legged pig?"

Ethan was scraping the bottom of the barrel, but she forced herself to smile as he told one shaggy-dog story after another while she rinsed the dishes. When the last plate had been put away, she dried her hands on a towel from the trunk, picked up a book of poetry and sat next to her husband.

The outlaw looked down the length of his cigarette. "Where were you born, Lizzie? I hear a hint of the South in your voice."

Ethan didn't jump in. She had to hold up her end of the lie, so she bent the truth. "I was born in Virginia."

"Tobacco country. The fellow pretending to be Dawson spent some time there, too."

Had he? She didn't know. It was easy to shrug. "It's lovely country. Almost as pretty as here."

Ethan slapped his thigh. "Speaking of Dawson, I should have thought of this sooner. Sweetheart, do you have the advertisement you found in the trunk?"

"I think so."

She rose, lifted the paper off the nightstand, handed it to LeFarge and sat back in the rocker.

The outlaw unfolded the paper and read. "I'm surprised I missed this."

Fighting the urge to glance at Ethan, she said, "It was wedged behind a drawer."

LeFarge sucked on his cigarette as he scanned the ad. "They were headed to California, all right. There's a name of a bank written here. Looks like Fowler's writing, too. May I keep this?"

"It's yours," Ethan answered.

Jayne opened Laura's book of poetry and looked for the longest passage she could find. "Would you gentlemen like to hear Thoreau?"

Ethan nodded. "Why, sure—"

LeFarge cleared his throat. "Tell me more about the widow."

The book pressed against her thighs like a stone threatening to drag her down into a lake of lies. Closing it, she forced herself to look at LeFarge. "There isn't much to tell."

"Did she say anything to you about family, or where she planned to go?"

"Not a word."

"I'm surprised she didn't have more to say to you. Women talk."

"It wasn't a social call. Some things are private, and a woman's grief is one of them." The line between saying too little and too much was like a fraying rope. The more she said, the more weight it would have to bear. Yet she had to hang enough lies to convince this man that Jayne Dawson was dead. "I wish I could help you, especially if she did something wrong, but I barely said a word to her, and she said even less to me."

"She was about your size, wasn't she?"

"Yes. You can tell from the dresses that we were about the same height."

LeFarge rolled the cigarette between his thumb and forefinger. "That was a fortunate coincidence."

"Life goes on," Jayne replied. "Ranching is hard work, and we can't afford to waste anything. Her clothes fit me fairly well, but we need other things as you can see. I'm using the red skirt for curtains, and I'll braid the scraps into rugs."

"You must be skilled with a needle and thread."

Jayne's blood turned to ice. "I am."

Ethan leaned forward in the chair with his forearms resting on his thighs. As cordial as a minister making a Sunday visit, he said, "It seems to me there isn't much else to say."

LeFarge stubbed his cigarette out on the hearth. "So it seems."

Timonius pulled a second cigarette from his pocket and lit it. He disliked Ethan Trent with an intensity he usually saved for lawmen and preachers. Tonight's picture didn't fit with the ragged man he had met yesterday, but some men were just plain lazy about personal hygiene.

The woman was clutching the poetry book in her lap, but that didn't mean much, either. He'd upset her on purpose. She'd stood the test well, though, answering his questions with facts and very little emotion. She seemed at home in the cabin and the dress from the trunk didn't fit her shape. Jayne Dawson had been a seamstress, and Timonius figured that her clothing would fit well.

Eager to take a few nips from the whiskey flask in his saddlebag, he took a long drag on the cigarette, tossed the butt into the fire and rose from the chair. "I'll bed down in the barn."

Trent stood, and the woman rose with him. "I'm sorry we don't have an extra room for you," she said.

"Don't trouble yourself." Turning to the rancher, Timonius let his coat fall open to reveal his gun. "I'd like to get an early start for the Dawson woman's grave, if you don't mind."

"I'd prefer that myself." Trent picked up the lantern, smiled at his wife and patted her arm.

Timonius wasn't familiar with the ways of husbands and wives, but the caress seemed natural. Mrs. Trent clearly had eyes for her husband, and Tim's suspicions slid to the back of his mind like pebbles falling in a pond. His fishing trip was over, at least for tonight.

As soon as the door slapped shut, Jayne took off the eyeglasses she'd been wearing and collapsed in the chair the outlaw had used. His body heat was still radiating from the wood and she jumped up as if she'd sat on a pine cone. Tobacco smoke had thickened the air, but she didn't open the window. As long as LeFarge was out of sight in the barn, she and Ethan would be safe. There would be no reason to carry on their charade by sleeping as man and wife, and she was sure he'd be relieved. LeFarge was the biggest threat by far, but their forced marriage had to cut straight to his heart.

She pulled the blankets from under the bed just as Ethan paced through the door. He scowled at the tangle of wool in her arms. "You can put those away. We're both sleeping in that bed tonight."

"It isn't necessary."

"Like hell it isn't." He lifted the blankets out of her arms and kicked them under the bed. Pivoting, he took his shotgun off the wall and snapped it open to check for cartridges. She stared with wide eyes as he raised the stock to his shoulder, aimed at the door and squinted down the barrel. Satisfied with the range, he lowered the weapon and faced her.

"Believe me, Jayne. LeFarge is no fool. He'll be watching us, and that makes sharing a bed *very* necessary."

After he leaned the gun against the wall, he stripped off his shirt, sat down on the mattress and yanked off his boots. They clattered to the floor like tumbling rocks, and she saw holes in his too thin socks.

Her heart skittered against her ribs. The moment was brimming with need, his and hers, the need to protect and the need to comfort. Her throat swelled with misery. She didn't want to hurt this man, to remind him of Laura in any way. Nor did she want to need the security he offered.

Clinging to her dignity, she said, "We have to deal with LeFarge, but it's not a good idea for us to sleep so close." Her voice drained to a whisper.

"I can stand it," he replied evenly.

But she wasn't sure *she* could. With her life in danger and the baby doing funny things to her breasts, she felt like dry wood ready to go up in flames. She wanted to shout at the moon and shake her fist at the stars. She wanted to be bold and brave, but she also wanted to surrender to tears, to escape the tension and the fear, to take comfort in Ethan's arms.

But that wasn't smart. She had to stay alert to protect herself and the baby from harm. Clutching the ends of her shawl, she said, "I'd like to wait for you to go to sleep before I put on my nightgown."

He leaned to the side and blew out the lamp. "That's all the privacy you get. There's not much chance I'm going to sleep at all."

She knew exactly how he felt. "Maybe not, but I'd rather sit for a while."

Obscured by darkness, he rose to his feet, stepped in front of her and rested his warm palms on her shoulders. His face glowed orange in the roaring light of the fire. "Come to bed. You and the baby need rest, and we have to come up with a plan."

"We can talk here."

His lips grazed her ear. "Not with LeFarge watching us. You can trust that I won't take advantage."

"Of course not," she said in a rush. "In your heart you're still married to Laura."

His eyes drilled hers for one tense moment, then he let go of her shoulders and strode across the room. Keeping his back to her, he said, "Get your nightgown."

He was standing by the heart-shaped mirror, with his feet planted wide and his arms crossed over his chest. Glancing over her shoulder, she unbuttoned the front of her dress, stepped out of it and put on her white night rail. Once she was covered, she said, "I'm decent."

Slowly, like a man not sure of what he'd see, Ethan turned and looked straight at her. Only then did she realize she was standing in front of a blazing fire in a thin cotton gown. She heard him suck in a breath, saw the twitch of a smile on his lips and heard the rustle of the sheets as he lifted the blanket from the bed.

"Go on now," he said. "Get in. It's not like I haven't seen you half-dressed before."

But it hadn't been like this. She'd been ill with fever and he'd been half dead with grief. Two healthy bodies presented a whole new set of problems. Politely, she said, "I'd rather sleep on the edge than by the wall, if you don't mind."

"I do mind. I want a clear shot at the door."

He was guarding her with his life, and it gave her some ease as she slid across the mattress. Rolling to her side, she faced the wall as he stripped off his shirt and climbed in next to her, still wearing his trousers.

As the bed dipped with his weight, gravity went to work. Her hips slid back as he rolled to his side. Their thighs met and then parted, staying close but not quite touching.

With Ethan lying next to her, she squeezed her eyelids shut and focused on the baby and staying safe. She imagined sleeping in her bedroom in Lexington, but with thoughts of home came memories of her mother.

You're strong, Jayne. Stand tall. Be brave.

Her throat squeezed to a pinhole. She *would not* cry. Except her chest was aching and she could feel Ethan's warmth spreading through the bed. If she moved an inch, she'd be pressed against him from her neck to her knees. She'd be safe in his arms, at least for now, and sheltered by his body, at least for tonight.

Tears pressed behind her eyes. She knew the value of a good cry. It healed the soul like rain ending a drought, but these tears were different. They had been born of weakness and want, and that wasn't acceptable.

Sucking in air for courage, she rolled onto her back. His face was inches away, giving her a clear view of the rage in his eyes. Having to deal with LeFarge was terrible, but being with her in the bed he'd shared with Laura had to be like slicing open an old wound. Guilt overwhelmed her, but she couldn't change the facts. She needed his help.

"I don't know what to do," she said, tugging the comforter up to her chin.

Ethan reached across his body, covered her hand and squeezed. "We should keep doing what we're doing. LeFarge wants to see a grave, so I'll take him out tomorrow. It's a big mountain and my memory's not so good, especially since the stream's running hard after that blizzard. I'll tell him the body must have been washed downstream. I'll ride with him all day if I have to. Though I've got to admit, I'm running out of things to say."

In spite of the tension, she chuckled. "You're trying to bore him to death, aren't you?"

"That's the plan, though I'd rather skin him alive."

"Aren't you worried he'll try something? I'm scared, Ethan. For both of us."

"I'll be back. I promise."

"Hank said the same thing."

Her voice trembled and the next thing she knew she was sobbing with her face pressed against the long johns hugging Ethan's chest. He smelled like new cotton, her favorite smell in the world, and she clutched a fistful of the fabric for reassurance.

"I'm not Hank Dawson," he said, pulling her close. "I'm older, smarter and a lot meaner when it comes to people I care about. I know these mountains better than LeFarge, and so far the ruse is working. I think he's about ready to hop a train for Los Angeles."

"Dear God, I hope so."

''After he's gone, we'll ride for Raton. It'll be safer than dealing with Handley.''

Jayne weighed the facts. If she left her trunk, she could roll her clothing and tie it to the saddle. The ten dollars was still in the hem of her skirt. If she left now, she could find work and be in Lexington by August.

''I'll pack my things,'' she said quietly. ''I don't need the trunk.''

''What are you talking about?''

''I can find a job in Raton.''

''It's not safe.'' His gaze held hers, a mix of amber and brown that melted into dark gold, then he touched her cheek with his thumb. ''We took vows, Jayne. This may be a marriage in name only, but I intend to protect you until LeFarge is dead or in jail. You'll be safer here than anywhere else.''

Danger had heightened her senses, making her aware of the taut cords in Ethan's neck and the heat of his skin. She'd lost so much—her home, her business, her dream of loving a good man. Tears welled and spilled from her eyes.

Ethan brushed them aside with his knuckles. ''It'll be all right. I promise.''

But she couldn't stop the throbbing in her chest. More tears spilled, thicker than the first ones, until Ethan tipped his head downward and kissed them away, trailing his lips from her temple to her cheek.

Did he feel it, too, this yearning for comfort? She couldn't be Laura for him, not ever. But just for tonight, she could meet a need, both his and hers. She turned her head an inch so that their mouths were almost touching. Neither of them moved. The question had frozen on her lips, silent and dry, until his mouth melted into hers.

Together they explored the ragged edges of that kiss, the mix of desire and healing, hope and desperation. She took pleasure in the scratchy texture of his face against hers, the tug of his hands in her hair, then the slow, lingering trail of his lips against her cheek, her jaw, her throat. The heat of his breath penetrated her cotton gown and warmed her skin until he stopped at the heart-shaped line between her breasts.

"I'm sorry," he said quietly. "I didn't mean for that to happen."

Bowing his head, he rested his brow on the hard bone of her chest, seeking an absolution she didn't want to give. Couldn't he feel this pull of life? An affirmation of a future bright with hope? Jayne did. It was pulsing low in her belly where the baby was a reminder that life was meant to be honored.

She took Ethan's hand and placed it on her breast. "It's okay. It's a gift. Just for tonight."

As she inhaled, the soft mound filled his palm. He jerked back his hand as if he'd touched the cold flesh of a ghost. "I can't."

"You mean, you don't want to," she whispered.

But he wasn't listening. His eyes were riveted to the door where a knife-edge of light was glowing through a crack. Hoofbeats thundered past the cabin and a wisp of smoke reached her nose.

In a single beat of her heart, a glimpse of heaven turned into a fiery hell.

Chapter Nine

"The barn's on fire!"

Ethan yanked on his boots and raced out of the cabin just in time to see Timonius LeFarge galloping across the meadow. Through the barn door, he saw flames slithering up the back wall like spidery vines. The screams of the horses split the air, and he grabbed a damp shirt off the clothesline and raced across the yard.

As soon as he reached the barn, he knew what had happened. LeFarge had tipped over the lantern and a bale of hay had caught fire. Either it had been arson, or the man had gotten too drunk to be trusted with matches.

Praying for time and the mercy to rescue the horses, Ethan ran the length of the barn to the stall holding the roan. The smoke was thicker here and embers shot off the back wall as he opened the gate. The panicked horse was close to rearing. While its spirit was admirable, this wasn't the time to fight.

"Easy there," Ethan crooned. As he moved closer, the roan backed into the corner of the stall, splayed its legs and snorted. Ethan grabbed the halter, wrapped the shirt around the animal's head and tugged. The horse wouldn't budge. The flames were higher now, close to the roof and spreading to the sides of the barn. The dry wood crackled and popped, thickening the air with smoke. He had to hurry if he was going to save the gelding, too, but the roan was pulling in the wrong direction. "Come on, fella," he urged.

Just as he gave the halter a second tug, a bale of hay exploded with a whoosh. The roan bolted from the stall, half dragging Ethan to the door. The shirt slid from the horse's face and Ethan lost his grip. At the smell of fresh air, the horse coiled and ran into the night.

Ethan scoured the yard for Jayne. The clothesline had fallen on the ground and a puddle of water from the washtub was glistening in the moonlight, but she was nowhere in sight. Terror ripped through his chest.

"Jayne!"

"I'm right here."

He whirled sideways and nearly lost his mind. She was inside the barn, silhouetted against the flaming wall with a wet skirt covering her back like a shield. Dragging a saddle with both hands, Jayne was as foolish and brave as any woman he'd ever known.

Flames were crackling just ten feet away. "Get the hell out of here!" he shouted.

"There's still time. Get the gelding."

She mattered a hell of a lot more than a horse, so

he grabbed the saddle and tossed it out the door. Much to his relief, Jayne raced after it.

A current of air whooshed upward, drawing his gaze to the roof where an orange halo of flame rimmed a black hole of starry sky. He had a minute at the most, maybe two. With smoke burning his eyes and the heat blistering his skin, Ethan ran to the back of the barn where the gelding was screaming and kicking at the stall.

He prayed to God the horse would calm down. But either God wasn't listening or the horse had a mind of its own. Because just as he opened the stall, the animal rose up and pawed the air, striking Ethan in the chest.

The blow sent him sprawling. His head smashed into the rim of a bucket and his back slammed against the floor, knocking the wind out of him. He couldn't breathe. Even as embers blistered his back, he couldn't make a sound.

A calm settled over him like a soft blanket. Was this what it had been like for Laura and the children? Had she told them to be brave? Had they struggled in the dark or had death come quickly from smoke and heat? This close to the ground, the air was almost cool, but he couldn't suck it in. A few more breathless seconds, a few moments of pain, the peace of unconsciousness and then…heaven, with Laura and the kids.

Was it his choice to make? Deep down, he didn't think so.

"Ethan! Oh, God. *Ethan!*"

At the cry of his name from Jayne's lips, he struggled to pull in a hint of air. His lungs throbbed with the effort, but he managed to draw in a small breath. No matter how much it hurt, he couldn't lie here and die. Jayne needed him.

At last able to pant, Ethan pushed to his feet. The rafters creaked and embers swirled like autumn leaves in a storm. The gelding was cowering against the wall. With hot air searing his throat, Ethan grabbed the animal's halter, covered its head with the shirt and gave a firm tug.

"Come on, Buck," he gasped. "You've got five seconds. Then I'm leaving without you."

The animal took a single step.

"Let's go, buddy."

The horse snorted once, took two more steps and then a third. The door was in sight.

Ethan looked up and saw Jayne staring at the roof in horror with her hands pressed against her cheeks. Buck whinnied in terror, drawing her gaze to the blazing interior of the barn. She ran in his direction, but a wall of heat pushed her back. Focusing on her eyes, Ethan staggered into a starry oasis of open sky. Behind him, the roof collapsed in a roar of flame and groaning timbers. Letting go of the horse, he fell to his knees and inhaled the fresh air.

Jayne crouched down beside him. She had filled a bucket with cold water and was dipping her hands to make a cup for him. Water ran down her elbows as she raised her hands to his mouth. "Drink a little," she said.

A little? He wanted to dump the whole damn bucket over his head, but instead he cupped her hands with his, as dirty as they were, and sucked down a mouthful of water. He'd never tasted anything so sweet.

"Heaven on earth," he gasped, wiping his mouth on his sleeve.

Tears welled in her eyes, then she stood tall and put her hands on her hips. Dressed in that fluttering white nightgown and unbuttoned boots, with her feet planted in the dirt and her hair in a tangle, she looked mad enough to scratch and bite.

"You scared the daylights out of me!" she cried.

He managed a wry smile. "It was close, all right. Buck had one more second to make up his mind."

Shivering in spite of the heat rising from the charred wood, she glared at the ruins. "This is all my fault. I brought LeFarge here. If not for me, you'd still have your barn."

If not for her, he would have chosen to die.

"The barn means nothing," he said. It was a bad memory, the place he had left her to grieve alone, where he had endured endless hours of his own despair. Rising from his knees, he raked his hand through his hair. "I'm glad it's gone. Sometimes it's better to start fresh."

When she looked at him with a stark curiosity, he realized they had to talk about the other sparks flying between them—the ones that came from a man and woman rubbing up against each other like two sticks—but this wasn't the time. The timbers were still burning and his lungs were aching with smoke.

Jayne raised her face to his with a question in her eyes. "Did LeFarge make it out?"

"I saw him gallop off right after the fire started."

"Do you think he set it on purpose?"

Ethan shook his head. "That wouldn't have been to his advantage, but I think he was sly enough to saddle his horse before he went spying on us."

She clamped her lips into a tight line and then blew out a worried breath. "I have to go to the authorities, but someone other than Handley."

Ethan had hoped to never see Raton again, but Jayne was right. LeFarge had to be stopped, and Handley was a fool. Even with the Reverend's help, Midas wasn't safe for her. There weren't any guarantees that the outlaw would leave for California. Even now, he could be watching from the ridge. Ethan coughed hard, got rid of a mouthful of black spit and wiped his forehead with his sleeve. "We'll leave for Raton tomorrow. Are you up for a ride?"

"I have to be. How far is it?"

"Three days, maybe four."

She pressed her lips into a grim line. "I'd walk if I had to."

He believed her, but walking wouldn't be necessary. The gelding was grazing in the meadow and the roan would most likely be back for breakfast. Jayne had managed to save both saddles and a hodgepodge of halters and bridles. Still, it was going to be a long ride through country that was open and dangerous. If LeFarge decided to follow them, he'd have an easy time picking up their trail.

On the other hand, they were sitting ducks on the ranch. Ethan looked at the smoldering barn. One by one, the orange embers were dying, like the poppies that bloomed at dawn and wilted by dusk. Smoke rose in ghostly pillars. His lungs hurt and the burns on his back were coming to life with a vengeance.

"The fire's just about out," he said. "Let's go inside."

He put his arm around her shoulders and cringed when she touched one of the burns. Stepping to the side, she looked at his singed long johns. "My God, what happened?"

"I took a tumble. It's nothing."

Her eyes filled with worry. "I have a jar of aloe in my trunk."

Walking side by side, they crossed the yard and entered the cabin where she told him to slide his arms out of his sleeves. He turned a chair backward against the table, straddled it and rested his head on his forearms. In the darkness, he heard the swish of her nightgown, the creak of the trunk and then fabric being torn.

Looking up, he saw her shredding one of her petticoats. "Don't waste your pretty things on me. Use some of that cotton I bought."

She shook her head. "This is softer."

When she finished tearing the cotton into strips, she filled a basin with warm water and set it on the table. Ethan put his head down, hiding his face as she positioned herself behind him. "These are deep," she said. "I'm sorry, but it's going to hurt."

"I expect it will."

She cleaned the wounds and then applied the aloe, smoothing it in small circles. He'd forgotten how good it felt to be touched by gentle hands. It calmed him, until her loose hair grazed his shoulder and he remembered being in bed with her. His shoulders tensed and he let out a miserable groan.

"Did I hurt you?" she asked.

No, but he'd almost hurt her. He had wanted her badly enough to take the gift she'd offered without thinking about the consequences. He had to apologize, but he didn't have the strength. "I'm all right."

She dabbed the aloe even more gently until every blister had been soothed. "There, I'm finished," she said. "You should lie down."

Ethan pushed out of the chair and faced her. She was drying her hands on a towel, looking at them as if they belonged to someone else. "We're both worn out," he said. "You take the bed."

Her cheeks flushed pink "No, you're hurt. I can't sleep anyway."

Ethan knew what pregnancy did to a woman's body. She needed her rest. "Even so, you should lie down. Especially if we're going to ride to Raton tomorrow."

"I'm so sorry," she said. "Of all the places to have to go…"

Raton was the last place on earth he wanted to be, but Las Vegas was seven days to the south over harsher terrain. A lump rose in his throat. "I don't like it, either," he said. "But it has to be done."

When she didn't reply, he nodded toward the bed and its tangled sheets. "Get some rest," he said. "I'm going to make sure the fire's out."

He snatched his favorite blue shirt off the hook by the bed, shrugged into it and glanced at the mattress.

He was sorely tempted to collapse on top of it, and even more tempted to ask Jayne to lie with him, just to sleep close. He wouldn't, though. A man could only put out so many fires at a time, and right now he had to tend to the one outside. Grateful for the distraction, he walked out the door and closed it tight.

Ethan had intended to leave the next day, but the roan had shown up at the cabin with a stone in his shoe and a bruised hoof. Taking off on a cross-country ride with a gimpy horse was just plain stupid, so he'd made his peace with the circumstances by sticking close to the cabin and carrying his Winchester everywhere he went.

It was at his side now, propped against a bucket while he surveyed the wreckage of the burned-out barn. He'd used the gelding to haul away the heaviest timbers and then hacked at the mess with an ax until he could manage the rubble with the garden shovel and a rake.

He had piled up a small mountain of charred wood and twisted metal on the edge of the meadow. Thanks to yesterday's rain, it reeked of mold and rot. As Ethan scraped at the debris, particles rose in a cloud and clung to his skin. He decided to wash off in the creek before supper, his third bath of the week.

"A penny for your thoughts?"

He looked over his shoulder and saw Jayne walking toward him with a wadded-up napkin in her hand. Her eyes were still blurry from her afternoon nap and she was sucking on a lemon drop.

"How're you feeling?" he asked.

"Better than this morning. I'm sure tired of tossing up my breakfast."

"I bet you are, but it'll get easier," he said. "In another few weeks you'll feel better than ever. At least, that's how it was with Laura."

"I hope so." Jayne shook her head. "I can't imagine doing this more than once."

Ethan managed a smile. "Just wait until the end. Laura used to say she felt as big as a house. I told her it wasn't true, that she looked more like Daisy, our milk cow."

"That's shameful!" she cried. "You should have told her that she was the most beautiful woman on earth."

"Actually, I did better than that. I painted the kitchen and—" He choked on dust as he remembered making love to his very pregnant wife and feeling the baby kick at them both. "You'll be fine, Jayne. Trust me."

"I do," she replied. "But I'm still annoyed with you."

Ethan knew why. She had wanted him to sleep in the bed so that he could lie on his belly while the burns aired, but he had flat-out refused. To settle the argument, he had dug out the two-headed coin he'd given to William on April Fools' Day. When he had bested Jayne by calling heads, he felt as if he'd shared a joke with his son.

Lowering his head, Ethan went back to raking the debris. "The floor's fine for me."

"It's not, but I'm tired of arguing." She held out the napkin. "I baked cookies. Do you want some?"

Laura used to bake cookies on Saturdays, and she'd scold them all for sneaking them off the tins. Ethan had been the worst offender. As the aroma of sugar and vanilla spread from Jayne's outstretched hand to his nose, the memories of Laura faded and his mouth started to water. He felt a twinge of guilt, but he couldn't help himself. He wanted a damn cookie. So what?

Grunting his thanks, he lifted one to his mouth and polished it off in three bites.

"Take some more," she said. "There's a whole batch in the house."

As he helped himself to seconds, she looked out to the meadow where the roan was grazing. "How's Rocky?"

She had named the horse when it showed up lame after the fire. "He's ready for the trip."

"Then so am I."

The taste of sugar turned to acid on Ethan's tongue. He couldn't bear the thought of coming within a mile of Laura's grave and the one next to it holding his sons. Seeing Katie's name on the marker would just about kill him. Raton couldn't be avoided, but hell would freeze before he'd set foot in that churchyard. Nonetheless, the trip had to be made. "We'll leave tomorrow."

He glanced at Jayne who was shaking crumbs from the napkin. The sun reflected off the crown of her head, turning the loose strands into gold filament. She had washed her hair at least five times since the fire. The honeysuckle soap had rinsed out the smoke and the dullness left by the coffee she'd used to change the color.

She was a lovely woman—tender and generous, kind and strong at the same time. His eyes drifted from her face to her throat and then lower still to her breasts. With a power of its own, the memory of lying in bed and touching her there came alive. He could almost feel her nipple against his palm and the soft mound filling his hand. He'd come within an inch of pushing aside the cotton gown and suckling her breast like a needy babe.

If a man loved a woman and wanted to make her his, nature was a powerful ally. If he didn't, it was a fearsome enemy. With Old Faithful threatening to make a fool of him, Ethan knew he had a problem as old as time. He wanted sex. He just didn't want to have it with Jayne, or anyone other than Laura.

He had tried it once. A few months after the Raton fire, he'd gone to Santa Fe, gotten stinking drunk and found a whore with big brown eyes. He had been both grateful and embarrassed when Old Faithful had hung there like an old rope.

That wasn't a problem today. Old Faithful was pointing due north, straight to Raton. Ethan took it as a sign that it was time to prepare for Jayne's inevitable departure.

"It's been a week since the fire," he said. "Maybe you should pack your things. LeFarge could already be in jail. If that's the case, we can get an annulment and you can be in Kentucky in a couple of weeks."

The smile faded from her eyes as she folded the

napkin and put it in her pocket. "I'll need to find work. I don't have enough money for train fare."

"I'll pay it," Ethan said. "It's a gift."

She shook her head. "It has to be a loan. I want to pay my own way. What about my trunk?"

"We'll carry everything we can manage and I'll ship the rest of your things when you're settled."

Ethan watched as she hooked that wayward strand of hair behind her ear and gazed past the cabin and out to the meadow stretching east. A breeze stirred and the grass shimmered in the afternoon sun. The scent of lemon drops reached his nose. Someday she'd make another man a fine wife.

After taking a deep breath, she put her hands in her deep pockets and faced him. "I appreciate all you've done for me," she said. "I know this has been hard for you."

Ethan grunted. "So is breathing."

Lowering his chin, he went back to sweeping up the soot.

Chapter Ten

Jayne dried the frying pan and hung it over the stove in the exact place she'd first seen it. Wiping her hands on the linen towel she was leaving, she looked around the cabin to make sure she wasn't forgetting anything.

Hank's letter, her mother's scissors and the silver dollars were tucked in the saddlebags she had saved from the fire. She had rolled her clothing last night, and Ethan had lashed the bundles to their saddles, along with supplies and his Winchester. At the thud of his boots on the front porch, Jayne looked through the open door.

Ethan stopped at the threshold and placed one hand on the frame. "Are you ready?"

"I think so."

She forced a smile, but a small lump rose in her throat. Under different circumstances, she could have been happy in New Mexico. The open spaces stirred her blood in a way that Kentucky never had. Bluegrass and white fences had a gentle charm, but the West had passion and grit. So did Ethan. He was a good man—far better than Hank—but his heart would always belong to Laura. That was a fact.

With a prayer for him on her lips, she closed the door and put on the old Stetson he'd given to her, telling her to keep it as a memento. Her farewell gift to him was just as practical. She had darned his socks, mended every tear in his shirts and replaced all the missing buttons.

He was standing in the yard, holding Buck steady for her. His wedding band caught a ray of sunshine and glimmered even brighter than the day. He had been particularly grim this morning, fussing about the weather and checking their gear at least three times. The trip to Raton would be miserable if he couldn't manage an occasional smile.

Jayne raised her face to the sky and took a deep breath. "It's a beautiful day," she said.

He gave her a dour look. "It's going to rain later. I want to get to shelter before dusk. Do you need a leg up?"

"I'm from Kentucky. What do you think?" Before he could answer, she swung into the saddle and took the reins. "You better hurry if you want to keep up with me."

"And you better take it easy. It's a long ride."

"Good," she replied. "I feel wonderful this morning."

Still scowling, he put his foot in the stirrup and mounted Rocky. His denim-clad thigh flexed as he assumed a relaxed posture that put the horse at ease without relinquishing a bit of authority. She couldn't help but notice the way Ethan took to the saddle. He rode a horse the way he kissed—with a gentle command.

Heat flared up her throat. She had to banish such thoughts. It wouldn't do any good to remember the way his mouth fit with hers, or the muscular flex of his shoulders as he held her. She had places to go and things to do, a job to find and a baby to raise.

With that plan in mind, she rode out of the yard, trying her best not to look back. She couldn't help it, though. When they reached the edge of the forest, she glanced down at the empty homestead where she imagined children playing in the yard, clucking chickens and a whitewashed barn.

Maybe someday Ethan would be able to love again. She hoped so, but only a foolish woman would settle for a man who didn't love her with his whole heart.

Louisa McKinney had made that mistake and paid dearly. Jayne had been fourteen years old when Arthur Huntington charmed her mother into marrying him. It had been a perfect match, or so it seemed until her mother caught him in bed with a woman who resembled his first wife.

On an ordinary Saturday morning, Jayne had gone downstairs for breakfast and found her mother dressed in her best suit. "Pack your things," she had said coldly. "We're moving back to the shop."

The whispers in town soon made Jayne wish that Mr. Huntington had never set foot in their lives.

Can you imagine! I heard it was Bettina Woolsey. Think of the humiliation.

Of course, you've got to wonder why. Men don't just stray, you know.

As she followed Ethan through the dappled shade of the forest, Jayne recalled her mother's firm voice. *Face the facts, and be ready to pay your own way.*

That's exactly what Jayne intended to do as soon as they reached Raton, but until then she wanted to enjoy every minute of this beautiful day. The morning sun reminded her of apricot jam, and the cloudless sky was flame-blue. Indian paintbrush glowed in patches along the trail and stalks of lupine were pointing straight to heaven.

Hope welled in her chest and a natural energy surged from her head to her toes. Needing to express it, to find release, she gave Buck full rein and left Ethan in the dust. "See you later," she called.

"Damn fool woman," he muttered.

Galloping off like that wasn't smart. He'd intended to keep their pace to a walk the whole way to Raton, stopping often in case she needed to rest. "Wait up!" he shouted, giving Rocky a kick.

The roan liked the idea of running just fine, and Ethan raced up behind her. The effort earned him a clear view of her stretched thighs and the teardrop curves of her bottom. The sight was unavoidable, and so was the urge it inspired. Old Faithful wanted to take a hard ride of a different kind, but so what? The woman looked good in a saddle. Ethan conceded that point gladly, but he sure as hell wasn't going to let her beat him in a horse race.

He rode close behind her until they reached a gentle slope. The main trail circled around a meadow, but he knew a shortcut. As Jayne raced by the drop-off, he turned the roan and sped down the hill.

The horse took flight and Ethan sailed with him, feeling like the kid who had dreamed of raising quarter horses. He wanted to ride like this forever—to go far and fast without a thought in his head. To relish the wind in his face and the rumble of hoofbeats. To be free to laugh, and maybe even love again.

But that couldn't be. Just like his life, the meadow ended at a granite rockslide caused by an unforeseen disaster. Slowing the roan, he turned west to the main trail where he saw Jayne riding at a full gallop, her face knotted in concentration.

Buck didn't have a prayer of catching up with Rocky, but she was giving it her best shot. The horse loved her for it, too. He seemed proud of himself, arching his neck as she rode up next to Ethan.

"You cheated!" she cried.

"You had a head start," he countered. "I just evened things up with the shortcut."

Her eyes flashed. "I want a rematch."

Lord Almighty, she looked pretty today. With her hair mussed and her cheeks glowing from the sun, she made him think of picnic baskets, bare skin and lovers hidden by tall grass. Ethan clenched his jaw until it hurt. He had no business thinking of her in that way. He had to keep his mind on other things, like cattle.

"We're near the spot where the herd usually grazes," he said. "Want to see some Herefords?"

"Sure," she said, smiling. "You ride well, by the way."

"You, too." Grunting at the memory of her cute little behind, he turned Rocky up the trail. "Riding like that isn't good for the baby."

"I'll give it up when my clothes get tight," she replied. "But not until then."

Ethan didn't like it, but the plan sounded reasonable and he didn't want to fight with her, in part because bickering made Old Faithful even more cantankerous. Hoping a little friendly camaraderie would ease that misery, he glanced at her from beneath the brim of his hat.

"Are you still hoping for a girl?" he asked.

"I am," she replied. "I want to name her after my mother. I just wish I knew more about babies."

"Mothering will come easy to you," he said. "Tucking a child into bed at night is the best feeling in the world."

A river of need tugged at his soul. He didn't like to think about his kids. It hurt too much, but he wanted Jayne to know that she had good things ahead of her. Keeping his eyes focused on the trail, he said, "My two boys were as different as night and day. And Katie—she was all girl with ruffles and bows."

Jayne rode up next to him, pulling so close that the tips of their boots brushed. "Tell me about them," she said. "That is, if you want to."

"I could fill a book," Ethan said wistfully. "Those two rascals fought all the time."

"How did you get them to stop?"

An honest chuckle rumbled in his chest. "They

were just being boys. Laura tried to lay down the law, but they were pretty wild. That is, with everyone except Katie. She had us all wrapped around her little finger.''

His eyes drifted over the meadow where stalks of lupine were bright in the sun. His throat tightened, but it felt almost good to remember. He glanced at Jayne and thought of the joys she had ahead of her. Then he flashed to the other side of the coin—colic, stinky diapers and spit-up. Throaty laughter spilled out of him.

''What's so funny?'' she asked.

''I was remembering the time Josh puked all over me right before a friend's wedding. Lord, what a mess. It was my best suit, too.''

''I have so much to learn,'' Jayne said. ''I barely know how to change a diaper.''

''That's not hard at all. Dealing with broken hearts and snakes in the house—that's hard.''

''Oh, no,'' she muttered. ''I *hate* snakes.''

Ethan pretended to be shocked to his bones. ''They're not any worse than mice, unless you find one in your bed.''

''Did that happen to you?''

''It sure did. William thought the snake was dead so he took it up to his room. The darn thing perked up in the warm house. Laura found it curled up on our bed and let out a scream that raised the roof.''

Jayne shuddered. ''I am definitely hoping for a girl.''

An ache took hold deep in his chest. She had so much ahead of her, good times and bad. He couldn't imagine raising a child alone, without the benefit of grandparents, aunts and uncles, or even friends. The loneliness of her circumstances struck him like a blow. He wanted to help her, and so for the next hour he told her everything he knew about raising children, and boys in particular.

He talked about Josh wanting to be a doctor, and how he'd rescued wounded animals like other boys collected toy soldiers. He did his chores like clockwork and tried too hard to make everyone happy. William had been the exact opposite. He couldn't pass a girl's ponytail without pulling it. Telling him that the stove was hot wasn't enough of a warning. He had to touch it for himself.

The stories rolled from Ethan's lips until the sun peaked in the noon sky. ''They were good boys,'' he finally said.

His eyes burned as the sadness descended over him like a black veil. The sun turned from warm to scorching, and he had to squint against the blinding light. Sometimes it hurt so *goddamn* bad…sometimes he couldn't even think—couldn't even breathe. This was one of those times.

He nodded in the direction of a distant bluff. ''We'll stop there.'' Before Jayne could say a word, he nudged the roan into a trot and rode off alone.

She hurt for him, low in her belly and deep in her chest. As he had talked about his sons, she felt his fleeting happiness as if it were her own. And when he spoke of his daughter, she had wanted to cradle his hand between both of hers.

She wanted to gallop after him, to wrap her arms around him and offer solace. It wasn't the same, but she had lost her mother suddenly to apoplexy. For a full year the pain had been sharp and unrelenting. Time had turned that wound into a scar, but she missed her mother every single day.

Jayne swallowed hard at the sight of Ethan riding up the rocky trail. His shoulders stayed straight and his back didn't bend. She yearned to take him in her arms and comfort him. To hold him to her breast until the pain eased. To wipe away those rare male tears he needed to shed. She wanted to give him so much more than his privacy, but this simple silence and her prayers were all he would accept.

"Oh, God, no," she murmured.

She'd fallen in love with him. Completely. Irrevocably. She had lost her heart to a man who cherished his first wife more than life itself. A man who liked home cooking but had no interest in sharing his dreams or his bed. He'd kissed her twice, and both times he'd been quick to regret it.

Staring helplessly, she watched as he rode to the crest of the ridge. A smattering of grass reminded her of the hill where they had taken wedding vows. The Reverend's words came back to her in a whisper.

Hope is a rope. Tie a knot and hang on.

Could Ethan ever love her the way he cared for Laura?

Her hands felt stiff and empty, and her throat ached. Every instinct told her to let go of the Reverend's rope and escape with her pride intact, but she couldn't leave Ethan to shoulder his grief alone.

Never mind that he slammed the door in her face every time circumstances pried it open. Whether he liked it or not, he needed her—like flowers needed the sun and grass needed rain.

Her heart made a daring leap. If she scattered seeds of love, maybe something wonderful would grow on its own. A field of primroses or a garden teeming with vegetables. Maybe a forest as lush as the one surrounding his empty homestead.

She had to be gentle, though. Too much heat would make Ethan push her away, and too much rain would keep him mired in despair. She had to find a middle ground, a safe place where the seeds could grow at their own pace.

Jayne knew that her mother wouldn't have approved of her plan, but she loved Ethan enough to fight for him, to hang on to that rope until her hands bled. The trick was patience, and knowing when to prod him with a sassy remark and when to lure him with a little sugar.

A half smile curved her lips. Earlier he'd offered to show her his cattle. It wasn't exactly a bouquet of summer roses, but it was a step in the right direction.

Knowing he needed a moment alone, she held Buck to a slow walk. By the time she reached the crest of the hill, he had spread a blanket beneath a pinyon pine and was taking jerky out of his saddlebag. His eyes stayed riveted to the worn leather as she approached.

''I'm starved,'' she said cheerfully.

When he didn't reply, she dismounted and walked to the edge of a bluff that overlooked a pasture where a dozen head of cattle were lazing in the sun. She laced her fingers behind her back. "In Kentucky I'd be looking at white fences and thoroughbreds. This is prettier."

Ethan shrugged as he handed her a strip of jerky. "It's a living. That's about it."

"So is sewing, but I still love it," she replied. "How much of this land is yours?"

He gave her some acreage figures, then talked about water and open range. "It's a good spot," he finally said.

"It sounds like you could run ten times as many cattle, or even better—why not raise quarter horses like you'd planned?"

He tossed the stub of his jerky on the ground. "That dream died in Raton."

"I understand," she said, reaching for his hand. "Nothing will ever be the same for you, but you still love horses. This is beautiful country, Ethan. You can use it for good things."

He blew out a hard breath and clutched her fingers. "I miss them so damn much," he said. "The land, the dream—it was all for them."

Knowing that words couldn't touch his pain, she let go of his hand and put her palm flat on his back. They turned to each other at the same time, coming face to face in complete understanding. He needed comfort, nothing more, and that's what she offered as he pulled her into his arms and simply held her.

Jayne put her whole heart into that hug. She held him tight and smoothed his shirt, patted his shoulders and breathed with him in perfect time. For that single moment they were knit together in perfect under-standing. Then his throat twitched against her fore-head and he let her go.

Taking a step back, she peered into his eyes where she saw the humblest of human needs—the need to be fed—milk for the body and kindness for the soul.

He gripped her hand. "What about your dreams, Jayne? Is going back to Lexington enough?"

Her heart rose into her throat. Maybe he felt the same stirrings that she did. "What are you asking?"

"You should think big. Sew all you want, but don't lose sight of the things that matter most in this life. Find a good man and raise a houseful of chil-dren."

"Maybe I will." Her voice faded to a twinge. He was pushing her away again. Wanting to lighten his mood, she managed a winsome smile. "The problem is finding a good man. Any ideas about where I should look?"

"I sure do," he replied. "Hardware stores."

Laughing softly, she pulled her hands out of his grasp. "I'll have to keep that in mind."

"I'm serious. Go to the counter and ask for picture hooks. Every young buck in earshot will whip out his hammer and follow you home."

She crossed her arms over her chest and looked directly into his earth-brown eyes. "And what if I'm not interested in 'every young buck'?"

A strand of hair caught on her lips. As she hooked it behind her ear, she saw Ethan's gaze firm on her mouth. The memory of kissing him burned through her and the glimmer in his eyes said he was remembering, too. "Ethan, I—"

"Don't say it, Jayne. We'll both be sorry."

"How do you know what I was going to say?"

When her eyes twinkled, Ethan realized that he'd just tripped over Old Faithful. Hugging her had made him feel whole, and all sorts of yearnings had sprung to life. He'd pulled back before he'd embarrassed himself, but he'd been staring at her mouth and drooling like a hound dog. Lust did that to a man. He'd have to be more careful.

"Never mind," he said, waving his hand in the empty air. "I interrupted you. Go on."

"I was just going to say that hardware stores don't really interest me. I'd probably have better luck at a church social."

That was a fine idea, except Ethan didn't like it nearly as much as he wanted to. "Just watch out for wolves in sheep's clothing," he warned.

She crossed to the saddlebag where he'd stowed biscuits with the jerky. She lifted one out of the stash and took a bite. "Is the Reverend married?" she asked.

Hellfire and matches! "What do *you* care?"

"He's nice."

John Leaf wasn't the least bit *nice*. He was a man with eyes in his head and natural appetites. Ethan knew for a fact that the parsonage got lonely at night, and he sure as hell didn't want to think about Jayne staying in Midas and getting cozy with the Reverend. Scowling, he said, "Hand me a biscuit."

When she put the bread in his hand, he grasped her wrist. "Don't go thinking about the Reverend, Jayne. He's not right for you."

She huffed at him. "Since when is that for you to decide?"

Ethan said the first thing that popped into his head. "We took vows. I pledged to take care of you."

"I pledged the same thing," she said evenly. "So why doesn't this advice about 'thinking big' apply to you?"

"It's not the same." He raised his eyes to the meadow, spotted a calf suckling its mother and loosened his grip on her wrist. "I've already had my day in the sun. Yours is yet to come."

"You don't know that," she said. "Maybe Hank was the love of my life."

"Dawson was a drip-ass fool and we both know it. If he'd been a real husband to you, he would *never* have lied and left you to pay for it." Ethan felt a full-blown lecture coming on, but he couldn't stop himself. He'd been churned up for days now.

"There's more," he declared. "Did he make the world stop when he kissed you? When you saw him first thing in the morning, when he was scruffy and scratching himself, did you feel an ache down low and deep in your chest?"

"No," she whispered.

A smart man would have stopped running his mouth, but Ethan wasn't feeling particularly brilliant today. He wanted to hold Jayne in his arms. At the same time he wanted to hit himself upside the head with a fence post. He wanted to do a lot more than talk to her about the awkward pleasures of love, but that could never be. In his heart, he would always be married—to Laura.

Except he also had an obligation to this sweet, young woman who had held him close while he was hurting. She was far too innocent to face the world as a young widow. Men would make assumptions and take advantage. He was her husband in name only, but those vows gave him the right to dish out advice.

He put his hands on his hips. "We have to talk."

"About what?"

"The birds and the bees."

Chapter Eleven

A light chuckle spilled from her lips as she arched an eyebrow and patted her tummy. "It's a little late for that, don't you think?"

"I'm not talking about the how-to," Ethan rumbled. "I'm talking about the what-for."

At the sight of her palm on her still-flat belly, he wished to God he'd kept his mouth shut. He couldn't help but imagine her in a few months' time, round and lush. If she took his advice and married again, more babies would come. She'd be baking cookies for some damn fool who'd have no idea how fortunate he was to have her.

Ethan looked up from her tummy just as she stifled a yawn. "I'm sleepy," she said. "Do you mind if I rest while you talk?"

He nodded at the blanket. "That's for you. I won't be insulted if you doze off."

She ambled to the wool square and curled on her side, using her arm for a pillow. It would have been easy to stretch out next to her and offer his shoulder for her head, but he had to keep his mind on the task at hand. He just wasn't sure where to start.

Scratching his head, he said, "Love is...good. It's the best thing in the world. Lust is...second best."

She burst out laughing. "Is that so?"

This wasn't going well at all. To make matters worse, his feet hurt and he wanted to sit down on the blanket. Well, why the hell shouldn't he? Keeping his boots on the grass, he planted his backside behind the soles of her feet and rested his forearms on his bent knees.

The feel of the earth and the smell of new grass gave him purpose. "I'm making a mess of this, Jayne, but I'm sincere. Love is amazing. At first it's a mountain stream, all fresh and new. Sometimes the excitement trickles to nothing, but other times the stream grows big and strong and it turns into a river. Rivers feed farms and families. They're the blood of the land."

"I know about rivers," she replied. "They carry away the rain."

Her voice was barely a whisper, faint with coming sleep, so he said nothing. Instead he listened to the hum of the earth, the stirring of a breeze and the sleep-induced rhythm of her breath blending into the day. He didn't bother to stifle a yawn of his own. Instead he laid himself next to her and curled on his side, being careful to keep a good twelve inches between them.

He was staring at a tiny mole on the nape of her neck when she scooted back and nestled her hips against his. He should have pulled away, but instead he slid his shoulder beneath her head. Earlier today, she'd offered him comfort with a simple hug. He was just returning the favor.

Soaking in the rays of the sun, Ethan closed his eyes and fell sound asleep.

Jayne woke up from her nap with Ethan's knee pinning her legs to the ground and his hand resting on her tummy. His quiet snores filled her ear, and puffs of his breath were tickling her neck and making her shiver. She wanted the moment to last all afternoon, so she held still and let him sleep.

As his snoring changed to deep inhalations, he slid his hand up her torso and cupped her breast. A rush of heat pulsed from her chest to toes, and she had to force herself to lie still. Ethan would be horrified if he woke up now and, to tell the truth, she was enthralled with the sensations coming from his touch. His fingers were doing wicked things to the tender tip of her breast, and he didn't seem at all inclined to stop. To keep from moaning, she bit her lip and clutched a fistful of the blanket. Ethan pressed tighter, cupping her bottom with his hips, fully aroused and searching.

Struggling to breathe evenly, she thought about his mountain stream. Maybe this was their start. Maybe he was dreaming about her and not remembering his wife. Maybe they had a chance. She was about to test that hope with a touch of her own when his hand stopped moving in mid-caress. His breath caught and he jerked away from her.

''Holy hell,'' he muttered, pushing to his feet.

Jayne pretended to be asleep, but she stole a peek at him as he walked to the roan. After adjusting his pants, he unhooked the canteen, gulped water and then scrubbed his face with his hand. Without looking at her, he said, "Wake up. We have to go."

He'd helped himself to a little sugar. Now it was time for a little sass. Jayne sat up, stretched her arms over her head and yawned. "I fell asleep. What were you saying about the birds and the bees?"

He glowered at her. "Nothing I'm going to repeat."

"Are you sure? I liked what I heard before I dozed."

Ethan jammed the plug in the canteen so hard that the water sloshed, then he looked straight at her. "I'm a damn fool. Don't listen to a word I say. Ever."

That was fine with Jayne. Actions spoke louder than words, and he'd just been holding her close. Raton was miles away and they'd be alone on the trail, sharing meals and a blanket of stars. A smart woman could do a lot of persuading in that time, and that's what she planned to do.

Two days later, Ethan decided that he had lost his mind. What else could explain these strange mood shifts? One minute he'd be telling Jayne a funny story about growing up in Missouri and the next he'd feel so bitter he could taste his own bile. It was all so damn unfair. For no good reason, he'd lost his family to a pointless fire. His wife was dead, and he wasn't.

Mother Nature had driven *that* point home in spades when he'd woken up with his hand on Jayne's breast and Old Faithful rubbing up against her bottom. He'd been dreaming in vivid color and full sensation. It had been the kind of dream he'd once cherished because it brought Laura to life. He could see her again, smell her skin, touch her hair—but it wasn't Laura who had been in his thoughts at that moment.

It was the damnably cheerful woman riding about twenty paces in front of him. The ride to Raton had turned to pure hell, and it was all her fault.

Ethan, did you see those wildflowers? They're gorgeous... Look at that cloud. It's shaped like a cottontail rabbit... Ethan, breathe deep. You can smell spring...

Like a fool, he'd inhaled through his nose. Sure enough, he smelled warm grass, but he wasn't about to admit it. Instead he'd huffed. "It smells like cow dung to me."

And as for the damn cloud, it hadn't looked a thing like a cottontail. It looked like what it was—a cloud—and that's what he had told her. He'd been trying to make her mad enough to shut up, but instead she had pointed to the sky, told him to squint and darn near convinced him that the cloud had two ears and a puffy tail.

She had a way of sliding into his thoughts, but he'd managed to keep his distance in a physical sense. He had made it a rule to stay at least five feet away from her at all times and especially at night. The downside of the plan was having a clear view of her in the firelight. Her hair shimmered when she brushed it, and her breasts filled her shirt in a way that left little to his imagination.

"Ethan, look!"

At the sight of her peering over the trail's edge, he swallowed a curse. He knew what she'd discovered. Rainbow Falls was a piece of heaven on earth, and he had intended to ride by it without stopping.

Scowling, he rode up next to her and peered into the canyon. Just as he recalled, a rushing creek spilled over an old rockslide, curved along copper-colored boulders and formed a deep pool. The still water mirrored the sky and the trees, and patches of primrose were in full bloom.

It was too damn pretty to be tolerated. "We have some daylight left. Let's keep going."

Jayne smiled up at him like an elf. "Remember what you said about boys learning to fish?"

"Yeah, I remember."

"You can teach me." She gave a deliberate yawn. "Plus I'm plain worn out. I'd really like to stop."

Ethan didn't stand a chance against the fatigue in her wide eyes. He had a string and a hook in his pocket, but under no circumstances would he break his five-foot rule. "I'll make you a deal," he said. "I'll catch and clean, and you cook. How does that sound?"

"We have a deal." When she offered him her hand, he took it before he could think. Fire shot through him. Why did she have to be so damn pretty and so god-awful optimistic? Why did she have to turn clouds into bunny rabbits and trout into a feast?

With a quick grin, she turned Buck and rode down the narrow canyon trail. Ethan wanted to ride in the opposite direction, but he couldn't. He'd just have to be careful to keep his distance. Five feet wasn't far enough, but surely ten would be plenty.

After they tethered the horses and set up camp, Ethan went fishing. He had a knack, and soon they were eating trout and canned peaches. Just as he planned, Jayne was on one side of the fire and he was on the other. She had to shout to be heard over the rushing water, and that was just fine by Ethan.

After she'd taken the last bite of her meal, she set the plate down and flopped on her back with her fingers laced behind her neck. Peering into the pinyon branches, she said, "We have company."

Ethan looked up and saw a pair of squirrels chasing each other. Every now and then, the male stopped and shook his tail at the female. It was mating behavior in all its earthly splendor.

"It's looks like Sammy Squirrel is in love," said Jayne.

Ethan harrumphed at her. Sammy Squirrel was a lust-filled rodent. He wanted one thing from the female, and Ethan knew for a fact that it wasn't love. "He's just being a squirrel," he said.

A pinecone thudded to the ground as the female leaped to a lower branch with Sammy in hot pursuit. When a high-pitched twittering crescendoed, there wasn't a doubt in Ethan's mind that Sammy was having his way with the female.

He glanced at Jayne. Her cheeks had blushed a

pretty pink and she looked both wide-eyed and shy. Overhead, the pine needles were still shivering. A twig landed smack in Ethan's coffee cup.

"Damn rodents," he muttered as he fished it out with his finger. "I hate squirrels."

Jayne's lips pulled into an odd smile. "Why?"

He wasn't about to engage in a debate about the worth of horny rodents, not when he had been having similar thoughts all day. Old Sammy had it easy. He'd eat his supper, have a go at the female and fall asleep. That's exactly what Ethan wanted to do, but he had a conscience that wouldn't let him use Jayne in that way, even if she'd let him. He had promised to protect her, and that meant from himself as well as LeFarge.

Heaving a sigh, he stared up into a tree where the two squirrels were perched on a branch, eating nuts and no doubt resting up for round two. Ethan was giving serious consideration to fetching his rifle and making squirrel stew when the critters scampered away.

"Ethan?"

"What?" he growled.

"Are you upset? You've been cross all day."

Hell yes, he was cross, but it was none of her business. "I'm all right."

Jayne nodded and then looked up. He followed her gaze to a scrub jay that had perched on a low branch just above his head.

"The birds in Kentucky are bright colors," she shouted over the rumble of the stream. "Do you have cardinals here?"

When Ethan turned his head to shout his answer, the jay took off. A glop of something vile landed smack on his shoulder. "Holy hell!"

The damn bird had crapped on him. It wasn't just a little splat, either. The damn thing had left a blessing the size of a pancake.

"Oh, my God!" Jayne jumped to her feet, hurried to him and dropped to her knees between his sprawled legs. Before he could wrap his tongue around something other than a curse, she had opened the top two buttons of his shirt. "I've never seen that happen before."

Ethan could only sputter.

"Take your shirt off," she ordered. "I'll wash it in the creek."

He shook his head, not knowing whether he wanted to howl with laughter, cry with the need he felt with Jayne between his legs, or shake his fist at God who'd taken his wife and left him alone to suffer the wants of being a man. He ended up doing all three, with the hard laughter making his eyes water.

Chuckling with him, Jayne finished undoing the buttons while wrinkling her nose at the glop on his shoulder. "This is disgusting. Now I know why cowboys wear hats."

Ethan laughed even harder, but wearing a hat had nothing to do with birds. He wore a hat to keep the sun off his face. With Jayne so close, he was taking the full force of her special heat and light. She smelled like the mesquite smoke from the campfire, and her eyes had a glow that tore his heart in two.

Feelings—good ones and hard ones alike—welled

like a spring flood, and his heart thumped like a rock being dragged along the bottom of a streambed.

Being careful to keep the bird mess from his skin, she was sliding the shirt off his shoulder. He crooked his elbow to free his arm and sat still as she maneuvered the cotton around his back.

He turned his head to help and accidentally pressed his cheek against the side of her breast. When she didn't pull away, Ethan knew that she'd say yes if he asked her to sleep with him tonight. The humor of the moment dissolved into a haze of miserable desire. His heart would always belong to Laura, and he intended to honor his wife's memory until the day he died. He *had* to keep that promise. It was all that kept him from loving Jayne, and loving again meant risking a heartache he couldn't endure.

After she freed his other arm from the sleeve, Jayne crouched between his knees and looked into his eyes, asking questions he didn't want to answer. All he could do was stare at her, stony and silent, until she pushed to her feet with his dirty shirt crumpled in her hand.

Ethan stood and reached for the cotton. "You stay here. I'll wash the damn shirt."

She stuffed it into his hand and pulled her face into a frown. "Go right ahead. I'll be upstream. Don't come looking for me."

Not sure what to say, he watched as she trudged past a boulder, then he glanced down at the spot where he'd been sitting. The bird had shed a pretty feather. It reminded him of Josh and everything he had lost, so he put it in his pocket and then walked to the pond.

Crouching behind a thicket of willows, he swished the shirt in the clear water and splashed his upper body. It wasn't enough to clear his thoughts, so he stripped down to bare skin and waded into the waist-deep pool. His whole body tingled with the shock, but he still dunked below the surface. Holding his breath, he felt a pressure building in his lungs as Laura's gentle presence came to him. He could see her eyes, her hair up in a loose knot, the tilt of her chin. It would have been a fine moment, but he had the distinct feeling she was annoyed with him.

Now, Ethan, be nice.

How often had she nudged him to hold his tongue? Almost every day, it had seemed. His chest burned with the old memory and a new shame. Jayne had done nothing but offer kindness and respect, and he'd been as sour as vinegar. She deserved better.

As he broke through the surface, he sucked in a lungful of air. The five-foot rule had to stay in place, but tonight he'd manage a bit of conversation. It was the least he could do for the woman who made him see bunny rabbits in the clouds.

Chapter Twelve

Needing to get away from Ethan, Jayne fled upstream to the base of the rockslide where water was rushing in a roar that matched her thoughts. She found a flat boulder and sat, drawing her knees to her chest. The sun had dipped below the horizon and she felt the weight of dusk on her shoulders.

Tonight would be awful. They would sleep on opposite sides of the fire. She'd listen to Ethan's breathing, or else he wouldn't sleep at all. She'd ache to go to him, but she wouldn't. He'd just made his feelings clear, and last night he had hurt her even worse. Jarred awake by a howling coyote, she had seen him standing with his hands on his hips, staring at the stars.

"What do you see?" she had asked.

"I see heaven."

She had understood that he was remembering his family. Wanting to share that need, she had started to stand.

He had waved her off with a scowl. "Go back to sleep."

She'd been hurt to the core. She had nothing but respect for his memories. Laura was as much a part of him as the schoolhouse where he had learned to read or the farm where he had grown up. Jayne understood that fact. She didn't begrudge him a past love. What mattered to her was the here and now. She wanted to share his feelings, good and bad, but he'd cut her off as if she were a stranger.

Her rope of hope was beginning to fray. She'd had plenty of time to reflect on Ethan caressing her during that afternoon nap. She'd been the woman in his arms, but Laura most likely had been the woman in his dreams.

Aching inside, Jayne slid off the rock, stripped to her underthings and splashed water on her exposed skin. She was still worried about LeFarge, but her heart was in danger, too. The longer she stayed with Ethan, the harder it would be to leave him. She had her sewing tools and most of her clothes. If she stayed in Raton, she could find work and save.

She also had a new name. Tears pressed behind her eyes. Ethan had marked her as his wife in a legal sense, but he didn't love her and he never would. It was time to face facts and move on with her life.

As she stepped out of the creek, a roll of thunder filled the canyon. Her heart hammered against her ribs. She had once weathered a tornado in a cellar, and she hadn't forgotten the raw terror that had gripped her in the dark. To this day, thunder scared her half to death.

Jayne yanked on her clothes and hurried down the path to the camp where Ethan had already gathered their things and moved the horses. He had put on a fresh shirt and was dousing the campfire when he saw her.

"Mother Nature's going to put on a show," he said. "There's a place to shelter in those rocks. We'll have a view you won't believe."

Jayne glanced at the sky. "I hate storms."

To her utter shock, Ethan broke into a smile. "That has to change. Storms are meant to be enjoyed, and that's what we're going to do."

A clap of thunder rumbled through the air. "We better hurry," he said, nodding at two leaning boulders that formed a huge vee. "I've already set up camp."

The thunder clapped again and Jayne took off faster than a rabbit. A drop of rain smacked her cheek and the wind howled through the trees as she ran. She dived for cover in the vee just as the sky let loose with a deluge.

"We made it." Breathing deep, she sat on the blanket Ethan had spread, drew her knees to her chest and covered herself with a second blanket.

"Are you cold?" he asked. "I can build a fire."

She gave a tight shake of her head. "I'm fine. The blanket's enough."

He dropped down about five feet away from her. When the sky flashed white, he started to count. "One one-thousand, two one-thousand—"

At an earsplitting kaboom, Jayne buried her face against her knees. She felt like a child cowering at a storybook monster, but she couldn't stop herself from trembling. Some feelings ran bone-deep and her fear of storms was one of them. When the reverberations passed, she dared to peer up at Ethan who was grinning like a fiend.

"You're enjoying this, aren't you?" she said.

"I like storms." In the purplish light she saw him staring across the landscape, lost in thought until he turned to her. "I didn't start really watching them until I moved to the ranch. The thunder made me feel less alone, as if God really did understand the misery. As for the lightning, those flashes of brightness gave me hope."

It was the most personal thing he'd said in two days and she wondered if perhaps her rope had a few strands left. To encourage him, she managed a rueful smile. "Storms scare me to death. I was ten years old and visiting a friend when a tornado struck. The cellar was so small I thought I'd be sucked through the door."

"It sounds terrifying," he said quietly.

"It was. My friend had her mother to hold, but I was all alone."

When a sudden flash lit up their shelter, Ethan slid across the rock floor and grabbed her hand. Before she could brace for the coming thunder, he was next to her, pressing her face into the hard muscle of his chest even before the blast roared through the canyon. Being held felt wonderful, but she knew it didn't mean anything. He was comforting the little girl in the storm cellar. When the thunder stopped, she looked up. "Thank you, but I'm—"

A crackling sizzle made her hair stand on end. *Kaboom!* Thunder nearly split the rock in two. She

screamed and pulled herself into a ball. With the reverberations pulsing through the cave, Ethan
wrapped his arms around her and pulled her close.
He felt like a wall of muscle and bone, strong and
tender at the same time. When the thunder passed,
he slid behind her so that her back was resting
against his chest and his arms were around her middle and upper chest.

"I'll keep you safe," he said. "Now look up and
watch the pond."

A bolt of lightning strobed through the canyon,
illuminating the darkness with jagged white fingers
that vanished as quickly as they appeared. When the
thunder cracked, she listened to the changes in pitch
and tempo. Ethan was right about storms. The thunder matched the longing in her body and the lightning gave her hope. She put her hands on top of his
and pressed his forearms tight against her. "I have
to ask you something."

"Go ahead," he replied.

"Do you think God wants you to be alone for the
rest of your life?"

She felt the sharp intake of his breath against her
neck, then he pressed his temple against hers. "No,"
he finally answered. "The choice is mine, but I'll
never love again. It hurts too much. Do you understand?"

"I do," she said. He had locked the door to his
heart because he was afraid, just as that little girl had
been afraid in the storm cellar. But Jayne remembered the aftermath. The storm had passed and dawn
had come with a brilliant splendor. She wanted to

give Ethan that gift—the joy of a new day—so she turned in his arms and clasped her hands around his neck. Knowing she was taking a chance, that he was wounded and might turn away, she kissed his lips, warm and openmouthed.

Though stiff-necked and reluctant, he kissed her back, taking small nips as he murmured, "Oh, God."

Jayne didn't know if it was a plea for the mercy to surrender to love or for strength to resist the desire, but it didn't matter. She'd been tapping on the door to his heart for two days. Tonight she intended to pound on it with both fists and even kick it down, if that's what it took to remind him that love was… good.

A storm as savage as the thundering sky erupted in Ethan's soul. The five-foot rule had been burned to a crisp with that first burst of lightning. He'd seen honest terror in Jayne's eyes, and protecting her had been as natural as breathing. One instinctive touch had led to another and now he was hungry for more.

He had to fight the urge to simply not think. All it would take was silence and he'd be inside her tonight. He wanted that to happen, but only if she understood what he was offering—comfort and friendship, nothing more. He couldn't love her. Not ever.

He whispered into her ear. "I have to be sure you understand."

"I do," she replied.

Ethan wasn't sure he believed her, but the urgency in her tone spoke for itself. She had heard his talk on love and lust. She was his wife in name. Why not in body? It was his heart he couldn't share. Honor demanded that they talk a bit more, but before he could find the right words, the clouds parted and a full moon illuminated her face.

She had opened her eyes wide and was biting her bottom lip, tense with a case of nerves that went beyond anticipation. "I have to tell you something," she said.

Relief filled Ethan's chest. If she had doubts, he would take the honorable road and back away. "You can tell me anything," he said.

"With Hank, it was just one time, and it wasn't very nice." Her voice dropped to a hush. "I'm afraid you'll be disappointed."

Holy hell. Ethan was mad enough to do serious battle for this woman's honor and show her the full range of her charms, but he understood the power of sex. A smart man would run from that innocence. He'd tell her to save herself for a man who could love her right.

But Ethan wasn't smart. He was a complete idiot. He wanted Jayne to feel wild, beautiful and as aroused as all hell. As for his heart, he'd draw a line and stay behind it. He'd give her pleasure, but for himself, he'd take only what was required for nature's release.

Peering into her eyes, he made his voice firm. "If Hank Dawson made you feel bad on your wedding night, he was a disgrace to every man in America. It's *my* job to satisfy *you,* not the other way around."

When her eyes flared wide, he nuzzled her ear.

"All you have to do is breathe for me. Can you do that?"

She whispered yes and Ethan took on the serious business of kissing her breathless. It had been a long time since he'd given pleasure to a woman, but he hadn't forgotten how. Whispers, touches, and demands—he'd use each one as needed, or asked for.

Focusing on Jayne's rapid breath, he trailed his lips from her mouth to the base of her throat where he kissed the soft hollow above hard bone. When she bent her neck to give him better access, he smiled. "You like that, don't you?"

"Yes, I do," she whispered.

Enjoying the taste of her, he worked his way down her chest. One by one, he undid the buttons on her shirt, then using both hands, he spread the cotton to reveal a lacy white camisole. Thankful for the full moon, he studied her breasts. Soon he'd see them bare. They'd be round and firm, he guessed, tipped with pebbled flesh and far more sensitive than she'd expect.

"You're beautiful," he said.

Holding her gaze, he slid her shirt off her shoulders and wadded it into a pillow of sorts. Mindful of the hard rock, he gently put her on her back, cushioned her head with the cotton and stretched next to her.

Stroking her bare shoulders, he dipped a finger beneath the camisole and traced the sweetheart line of her breasts. She tried to kiss him, but he wouldn't let her. Instead he made a game of it, avoiding her lips while caressing her in places she didn't expect.

Her elbow, her wrist, her palm—whenever she came close to his mouth, he dipped away, until he distracted her completely by untying the ribbons on the camisole and baring her breasts to moonlight and the cool air.

As she became aware of his gaze, her nipples hardened even more. He ached to suckle her, but first he wanted to touch the tips. At last kissing her mouth, he caressed her nipples with his fingers, focusing on her breath, her thighs seeking his, the small whimpers in her throat.

When she clutched his head and thrust her breast to his face, he kissed the white flesh in a leisurely circle. "How's that feel?" he asked huskily.

She could only moan.

More pleased than he had a right to be, he finally took the tip between his lips and drew hard. Over and over, he teased and pulled, until she was tense enough to shatter with a touch. Showing no mercy, he broke the suction and switched sides. In the tender cries spilling from her throat, he heard a plea for release, but he wasn't quite ready to grant her wish. "So you like this, too," he said.

Trembling with need, she shocked him with a low chuckle. "All I can say is 'holy hell.'"

Feeling more eager than he wanted to be, Ethan slid her trousers down her thighs, taking her drawers and socks with them so that she was naked from head to toe. Keeping his eyes on her face, he slid out of his clothes, laid next to her and stroked her belly, her thighs and everything in between, until she was oblivious to everything but her own body.

He'd succeeded in tonight's quest. He'd made her feel glorious and wild, and his own heart was still untouched. Sure, it was beating like a hammer, but he still had his wits about him. Positioning himself above her, he was about to finish her pleasure and take his, when she raised her hand and curled her fingers around the part of him that no one but Laura had ever touched.

He wanted to tell her to stop, that it hurt too much to be held in that way, but he couldn't say the words. Instead he looked down at her fingers, unschooled yet generous as she caressed him, and he let her do it.

The moment stretched with each stroke until the night blurred in a mist of need and desire, moonlight and a woman's power to turn a man into a hungry child. Lost to himself and unable to endure the wanting, he filled her with a searching fierceness. He wanted to go home. He wanted warmth for his flesh and light for his soul. He wanted to feel…good.

He couldn't get close enough to her, couldn't feel enough of her skin. Naked, blind and needy, he rocked in the cradle of her hips and fed on her mouth until he saw a blinding light, stars bursting behind his eyes and the joyous glimmer of creation. As the first tremors rocked him, a sheen of sweat broke out on his forehead. He was filled to the brim with heat and light and…love.

No, dammit! He couldn't love her. He wouldn't.

A horrible moisture filled his eyes. He had to focus on the pain of losing his family, on Laura looking down from heaven. Except Jayne was feeding him and he wanted to stay inside of her forever. She was clutching at his back, drawing him deeper as she clenched at his need, whimpering and teary-eyed as she shattered in his arms.

As he spilled his seed, Ethan felt sick with regret. He didn't know which woman he'd betrayed—the wife he had loved first or the one he wanted to love now but couldn't.

As the sensations faded to an awareness of the rock floor and the empty night, he buried his face in the crook of her neck and prayed that she'd fall asleep. He needed to be alone to figure out how to make things right, but she was rubbing his back with both hands, firm and gentle at the same time, stirring up more hunger and making him weak.

When she nuzzled his neck, he felt how much she cared and silently rebuked himself for using her for sex. He was about to pull out of her and tell her he was sorry, when she put her hands on his temples and raised his face so that their eyes were just inches apart, while their bodies were still joined.

"I love you," she said.

Anguish roared through him. He couldn't stand the hope in her voice, the generosity and the warmth. Old Faithful shriveled like a worm. Pushing up on his arms, Ethan rocked back to his knees and reached for his pants. "Don't say that."

"But I do." She grabbed his hand and squeezed. "It was so good, Ethan. So right. Can't you feel it?"

He pushed to his feet and hiked his trousers up to his waist. "Of course I can feel it. It's called lust. I used you. I—"

"You did no such thing," she said. "I gave myself to you, and you can't stop me from speaking the truth."

"Jayne—don't."

"Why not? Because you're afraid?" Sitting upright, she picked up her shirt and put it on with that matter-of-fact air that made him crazy. "I know you've suffered terribly, but we all live with dread and uncertainty. Those feelings are part of life, but so is happiness—if we're brave enough to fight for it."

Looking down at her face, Ethan took in the stubborn tilt of her chin and the tangle of her blond hair shimmering in the moonlight and defying the dark. She'd finished buttoning her shirt and was hoisting her hips to skim into her pants. If he walked away, she'd follow him. She'd find a way to get close, and they'd be rolling in the grass and he'd die all over again.

He had to stop her from saying another word, so he snatched up his shirt and stepped to the mouth of the cave with the intention of leaving her alone. "Nature's calling," he said. "I need to take a walk."

"I'll go with you."

Whirling to face her, he shouted, "Dammit! Don't you see? I'll *never* love you! I can't. I don't want to."

She pushed to her feet and crossed her arms over her chest. "Then how do you explain what just happened?"

He told himself to walk away before he said something hateful, but he was spoiling for a fight. If he'd been at the ranch he could have punched another hole in the barn, but right now that wasn't possible. Instead he hocked up a mouthful of spit and sent it flying out of the cave.

"You are so goddamn naive," he said with disgust. "We didn't 'make love.' We had sex like a couple of horny squirrels, and that's the whole story."

She turned as brittle as dry pine. "I see."

"I told you how I felt before any of this happened," he said, sounding superior. "I thought you understood."

He clutched at his shirt and decided to hike down to the stream. If he stayed within twenty feet of her, he'd be weeping at her feet and begging for her to forgive him for his meanness. He had to go now, before he hurt her again. It was best for both of them.

As soon as he rammed his arms into his sleeves, he jerked on his boots and looked up to say he'd be down by the stream. She spun out of his view, but not before he saw smudges of moisture on her cheeks.

All hell broke loose in Ethan's soul. He wanted to run from her tears, but he was deeply ashamed of himself for causing them. She had just given him her most precious gift—her love—and he was treating her like a glob of manure stuck to his boot.

Tired of his own stinking self, he forced himself to survey the damage he'd done. What he saw made him flinch. Her face was as blank as slate, empty of all joy. He'd sworn to protect her, but instead he had stomped all over her heart.

Slouching against the rock wall, he pinched the bridge of his nose and bent his neck in remorse. "Jayne, I'm sorry," he said. "I should be shot for acting this way."

She shook her head. "I pushed you, but I have to know. Was it me? Did I disappoint you? I thought you were—"

"Oh, God." Every instinct told him to show her again just how pleased he'd been, but he didn't have the guts to do it. Instead he reached for her hand. When she took it, he covered her fingers with his left palm and squeezed.

"Don't you dare doubt yourself," he said. "Tonight was beautiful. I won't ever forget it."

She looked down at their entwined hands. "Then why—" Her voice caught.

Ethan followed her gaze and cringed at the sight of Laura's ring on his finger. His stomach turned bitter. He'd just made love to one woman while honoring the other with that circle of gold. He felt disloyal to both women, and to himself. He had taken pride in being a faithful husband.

Jayne slid her hand from his grasp. "It's because of Laura, isn't it?"

"I guess so," he replied, but in his heart he knew he'd lied. The problem wasn't that he couldn't love Jayne. The danger was in loving her too much. Silently praying that it wasn't already too late to prevent her from more pain, Ethan touched her arm. "None of this is your fault. Get some rest. We'll leave early and make Raton late in the day."

Before she could say a word, Ethan turned his

back and walked alone to the edge of the swollen stream. With the rush of water filling his ears, he searched the heavens for understanding, but instead of bringing him peace, the stars glared down with pity.

Laura wasn't too happy with him right now. With an uncanny certainty, he understood she was waiting for him in Raton. He had to visit her grave, and he wasn't going to like what she had to say.

Jayne watched Ethan vanish into the shadows, then she dropped to her knees and sobbed. She loved him enough to fight for him, but how could she compete with Laura's memory? It was hopeless. Her mother would have understood. She would have told her to stay strong, made her a pot of tea and focused on the future. Louisa McKinney had walked a similar road.

Don't ever settle for second best.

Jayne curled on her side and hugged her knees. Ethan had made his feelings clear. What they'd shared tonight had been lust, second best to his love for Laura, and he profoundly regretted their coupling.

Chewing on her bottom lip, Jayne knew that she had to stay in Raton even if LeFarge was still on the loose. The outlaw was a lesser danger than Ethan. She supposed the marriage had been consummated, but an annulment was still fitting. They weren't really married, and she was sure Ethan wouldn't object.

Focusing on the baby, she closed her eyes and tried to sleep. Leaving Ethan was going to hurt like a toothache, and she'd need all the strength she could muster to yank him out of her life.

Chapter Thirteen

They arrived in Raton late the next afternoon and checked into a boardinghouse. Jayne spent the evening pressing her dresses and quizzing the cook about local seamstresses who might be hiring. Ethan disappeared after supper and spent the evening alone in his room.

During the ride, they had decided to visit the police chief together. If LeFarge was still a threat, she would keep Ethan's name. If not, they would obtain an annulment and she'd be Jayne McKinney again. When she told Ethan she intended to stay in Raton regardless of the outlaw, he had argued with her, but she wouldn't change her mind. Laura's ring was snug on his finger, and that was the only sign Jayne needed.

After spending a fitful night alone, she had put up her hair and donned her best dress. With Ethan stoic at her side, they walked to the police station where she told the entire story to Chief Benjamin Roberts and presented Hank's letter.

The chief listened carefully, but his expression

turned grim. "I believe your story, Mrs. Trent, but it's for the district marshal to decide if you're telling the truth. As it stands, you're an accessory to a crime. In fact, I should take you into custody right now."

"But I brought you proof!" Jayne cried.

Chief Roberts shook his head. "That letter could be forged, for all I know. You were seen with this Dawson-Fowler character in St. Louis, and I have a Wanted poster with your picture on it."

Squinting in irritation, Ethan leaned forward. "Are you calling this woman a liar?"

"No," replied the chief. "I respect her for coming forward. If you're willing to post a bond, I'm willing to let her wait at your ranch for the district marshal. Otherwise, she can stay here in Raton and check in twice a day."

"I'll stay here," Jayne said. "I need to find work."

Glowering, Ethan stood and pulled his billfold out of his pocket. "How much is the bond?"

"Fifty dollars," the chief replied.

Jayne opened her mouth to protest, but Ethan had already slapped the greenbacks on the chief's desk and was headed for the door. "Let's go," he said.

Jayne stood and addressed Chief Roberts. "My husband and I have some differences to settle. I'll check in tomorrow at nine. Is that acceptable?"

"If I'm not here, you can leave word at the front desk."

After shaking the chief's hand, Jayne ran to catch up with Ethan. Under the circumstances, she had no intention of going home with him. "You should have saved the fifty dollars,'' she said as she came up next to him. "I'm staying here."

He stopped dead in his tracks and gripped her shoulders. "I don't give a damn about the money. I'd put up my last nickel to keep you and the baby safe."

Hope spread in her chest as she gripped her reticule. "What are you saying?"

The planes of Ethan's face hardened into stone as he released her shoulders and stepped back. "I'm not saying anything. The bond is to show the authorities that you're telling the truth, and to give you options if LeFarge shows up and you can't reach Roberts. I don't expect you to come home with me."

She wished he had said something else, but she had learned her lesson about wishful thinking. "All right," she said. "In that case, thank you."

As he blew out a breath, he glanced across the street, looking everywhere except at her face. "I guess we'll be saying goodbye. You can write to me when it's time for the annulment. I'll handle the papers."

She didn't know what to say, so she said nothing. Finally he heaved a sigh and looked at her. "I'm sorry, Jayne, for everything."

She had held him while he was hurting. She had cooked his meals and nursed his burns. She had made love to him, and he was *sorry?* She had a good mind to hit him over the head with her reticule. Instead she made her voice sharp. "After all we've shared, that's insulting."

"You know what I mean."

She raised her chin and gave him her hardest stare. "What I know is this—I'd do it all again. I'd marry you and mean every word. I'd make love under the stars. I'd cook for you and hold you while you grieved. I'm not the least bit sorry for me, Ethan, but I'm very sorry for *you*."

She waited for two beats of her heart, praying he'd rise up and fight, but instead he looked down at his boot. When he finally raised his gaze, his eyes were as lifeless as stones in a pond. "Parting ways is best for both of us," he said.

He was dead wrong. A fence post had more sense than he did right now. Realizing that arguing would only make him dig a deeper hole, she decided to face the facts. "When are you leaving?" she asked.

"This afternoon, right after I take care of some business. I thought we'd have lunch and then say goodbye."

The thought of sitting with him in a restaurant as if they were a couple made her furious. She shook her head. "I have to find a job."

Nodding, he pulled out his billfold. "I want to give you some money. I said I'd pay you for housework."

At the sight of his wallet, she exploded. "Do you have any idea how belittling that is? At the very least, we were friends, and now you're treating me like a ranch hand you'll forget in a week."

"It's not that way. I want to help you." He pinched a stack of greenbacks, pulled them from the leather and held them out to her.

She pushed his hand away. "I don't want your money, or your help."

What she wanted was to kick him in the shins. A man in pain could be comforted. A man wallowing in self-pity needed a talking-to. She wanted to give it to him, but he was trapped in a hole so deep that he couldn't hear her.

He shoved the billfold into his pocket. "So I guess this is goodbye."

"Yes, it is." The business between them was over, so she held out her hand. "Good luck, Ethan. I'll contact you about the annulment as soon as LeFarge is caught."

A haunted shadow filled his eyes as he grasped her fingers. She would remember this moment as long as she lived—the emptiness, the lost hope, the powerlessness of loving a man who loved someone else. When he released her hand, they both stepped back. With nothing left to say, she hurried down the street in a fog of unshed tears.

Ethan hated the thought of Jayne wandering around Raton by herself, but he had to let her go. Last night had been awful. Sleeping in a bed for the first time in weeks, he'd dreamed about making love to her. He'd woken up on his belly with Old Faithful hard and hungry, and his wedding ring as tight as a band on a barrel of water.

Nothing felt right, and that wouldn't change until he faced Laura. Pivoting, Ethan walked to the churchyard where his family was buried. The sun was high and the air stirred with a warm breeze. It was a beautiful day, but he felt like a kid who'd been called to the woodshed.

In that way of men who'd been married awhile, he knew Laura was mad at him. They hadn't argued often, but an occasional shouting match had kept them both honest. Things always blew over quickly. What they couldn't settle with words, they had settled in bed. He had liked that part of marriage—the tussle that was a kind of fight—the mutual need that brought forgiveness.

Jayne would have liked it, too. Ethan gritted his teeth. He had to stop thinking about her.

For the next three blocks he focused on the tap of his boots on the boardwalk and the puffs of dust as he walked down the dirt path to the church. Wishing he could stop his heart from pounding, he opened the squeaky gate to the garden and stepped into the cemetery.

His gaze landed on the bushes lining the white picket fence. He walked to the hedge and pinched off two roses—a pink bud for Katie and a full-blown white one for Laura. As he approached the graves, he dug in his pocket for treasures for his sons. His fingers curled around William's two-headed coin. The blue jay feather was for Josh.

With the familiar stab of tears behind his eyes, Ethan set the trinkets at the base of the marker and stepped back. With his arms laced across his chest, he let himself remember every detail that made his sons distinct—Josh's curious eyes, William's stubby fingers, their skinny arms and their muddy shoes. When he closed his eyes he could even hear their laughter, bits of conversation, the scrape of their forks at the dinner table.

Standing still, Ethan remembered everything, and it felt…good.

Wiping his eyes but oddly happy, he stepped to the grave holding Laura and Katie. Dropping to a crouch, he placed the roses at the base of the marker, with the stems crossed and the white and pink petals touching. The flowers made a heart of sorts, and he started to talk to Laura in his head. He told her that he had cheated on her, and that he was sorry.

No words came in reply, but he had a sudden vision of her in their Missouri kitchen. She was wearing a dove-gray dress and a white apron with huge pockets. As if he'd just barged in with mud on his boots, she crossed her arms over her chest and gave him her most irritated frown.

Ethan, you fool! I'd like to tan your hide!

He had it coming. He'd betrayed her memory. He could almost smell her hair, almost touch her skin. Instead he caressed the rose, but in his mind's eye, Laura turned away. She snatched up a broom and started to sweep the floor. Out of the blue, she turned so that she was looking straight at him.

That girl is just plain sweet. And what did you do? You hurt her, and then you hid behind my skirts. You're a better man than that.

His fingers stilled on the rose. But—but—

Laura shook her head. *There are no buts about it, dearest. I know you too well. You get angry when you're scared, and you get mean when you're sad.*

In his mind's eye Laura leaned the broom against

the wall and poured two cups of coffee. He could smell it—truly, he could. She sat down, took a sip and hummed with pleasure. She had made that sound over coffee every morning of their marriage. They would sit together and talk about the kids, the weather, anything at all. It had been the best part of the day.

As Ethan straightened the white rose, Laura lowered her china cup to the saucer and gazed at him thoughtfully. *Do you remember the morning we left Missouri?*

Of course he did. The morning had been bright with hope, but she'd been in tears as she said goodbye to her mother and sisters. Still, she'd clung to his hand and forced a smile. She'd said that the change would be good, and she was happy to start a new life.

She smiled at him. *I meant every word.*

A cloud passed over the sun and her picture faded. To bring her close again, he shut his eyes. This time he saw her sitting next to him on the train. Katie was in her lap and the boys were in the seat in front of them, poking at each other and bouncing with excitement. Laura shushed them with a mother's firm word, and then she turned to him.

It's your turn, dearest. It's time to leave what you've loved the most and start over. I did it for you, now you do it for me.

He whispered that he was afraid, that he didn't have the courage, but Laura shook her head and smiled.

Oh, yes you do! That young woman is a gift,

Ethan. I asked God to send her to you. It's a new day. Grab it and live. Don't you dare stay here with me.

But—but—

I love you with my whole heart, but it's time to say goodbye.

Shortly after leaving Ethan, Jayne walked out of Madame Marchand's dress shop with a job that paid almost as much as she could have earned in Lexington. The old French seamstress had recognized Louisa McKinney's name and pulled Jayne into a warm hug.

"Your mother was a talent," she had said in accented English. "I am so happy to know you, *mademoiselle.*"

At the thought of her mother, tears welled in Jayne's eyes. What would Louisa McKinney have said to her daughter? *Stay strong and trust God.* She would have told her to focus on the baby and the future, and that's what Jayne intended to do.

Since Raton would be her home for the next few months, she decided to take a walk to learn the streets. She passed a bakery, a telegraph office and several other shops before she saw a tin steeple poking above the line of wooden roofs. She liked the idea of sitting in a quiet spot, so she walked toward it.

When she reached the walkway leading to the church, a cloud drifted past the sun. The fleeting shadow drew her gaze to the fenced yard where she saw a man kneeling in front of a grave. At the sight of Ethan's broad shoulders, she gasped.

She had no desire to intrude on his grief, but neither could she leave him to suffer alone. Standing at the open gate, she laced her fingers together and said a prayer.

"Some things never change," Ethan said to the headstone. "You're still as smart as a whip and just as pretty as I remember."

He knew what he had to do. Still on his knees, he gripped Laura's ring between his thumb and forefinger and slid it over his knuckle. The air felt cool against the circle of white skin and he flexed his hand to stir his blood. He considered putting the ring in his pocket, but it belonged with Laura, in a place apart from his life now but where he could always find it.

Using his fingers, he scratched a hole below the marker, set the gold band in the center and covered it with sod grass and the white rose. Taking a deep breath, he pushed to his feet.

"Am I intruding?"

At the low pitch of Jayne's voice, he turned his head and stared, speechless because he was so happy to see her.

"I know this is private," she said. "I can leave—"

"No, don't go." He wanted to pull her close, but his fingernails were full of dirt and he didn't want to soil her dress. Instead he called to her heart with his eyes and spoke the truth for the first time.

"I lied to you at Rainbow Falls," he said. "For that, I'm sorry. But I'm not the least bit sorry you came into my life."

Her blue eyes brightened. "Neither am I."

"I'll always love Laura and the kids. I wouldn't be much of a man if I could forget them, but she's not the reason I pushed you away that night. You made me feel good again, and I got scared."

Raising her chin, she took his hand in spite of the dirt. "I can understand why. You're a good man and that night was hard for you, for all sorts of reasons."

A flood of gratitude washed over him like rain after a drought. What had he done to deserve such love twice in one life? Laura had been right. Jayne was a gift and he'd almost lost her. With the sun shining and the grass thick beneath his feet, he vowed to earn her love and make her his wife in every sense of the word.

It had been awhile since he'd courted a woman, but he knew where to start. Giving her hand a squeeze, he put a meaningful glint in his eye. "I want to take you to supper tonight, but be warned. I'm going to talk you into coming home with me."

"That's a possibility," she replied, "but I have two requirements of my own."

"I expect you do."

"First, I want to go to Frau Hester's Kitchen for supper. I'm craving sauerkraut."

Ethan chuckled. "I can't stand cabbage, but sauerkraut it is. What else?"

She looked him straight in the eye. "What happened at Rainbow Falls won't be repeated until I can trust your feelings. You hurt me, Ethan. I forgave you the minute it happened, but I don't want to go through that misery again.''

''I don't, either,'' he said solemnly. ''We're starting from scratch.''

To make his point he stepped to the hedge of roses, picked all the red ones and wrapped the bouquet in a bandanna to protect her fingers from the thorns. ''These are for you,'' he said, putting them in her hands.

When she took a whiff and smiled, he felt ten feet tall and hungry enough to eat anything—even sauerkraut—as long as Jayne was at his side.

When a four-year-old boy stomped on his foot, Timonius decided he hated children almost as much as he hated Jesse Fowler and his sneaky wife. The train was crowded with families, salesmen and single men in new dungarees, all headed to California. The company and discomfort made him feel old and sour. His cough had kicked up, too, and he was hocking up green phlegm.

Pulling his hat low, he slept through Arizona and most of the Mojave Desert. When he finally arrived in Los Angeles, he walked out of the train station and headed for the First Bank of Los Angeles. Glancing at his pocket watch, he saw it was noon, the perfect time to find a clerk in charge while his boss was having his midday meal.

No one saw Tim enter the First Bank of Los Angeles and no one heard the door click shut behind him as he introduced himself. ''Good afternoon,'' he said to the young clerk. "I'm Detective Samuel Goode with Pinkerton's. Is your manager in?"

"He's gone for the day, sir."

Timonius gave the young man a sincere smile. "I'm sure you can help me. I'm investigating a robbery that took place in Wyoming. Does the name 'Dawson' mean anything to you?"

"No, sir. You'll have to ask Mr. Higgins, but he won't be back today."

"This can't wait." Timonius slid a gold piece across the counter.

The kid eyed the money. "I guess I could check for an account."

The clerk fingered through a file drawer and paused at a single card. His face flushed crimson. "You'll have to come back tomorrow and see Mr. Higgins."

"I don't have time for games. I want to see the card."

"There's no account. It's the truth!"

Timonius barged through the gate to the working half of the bank, elbowed the kid out of the way and inspected the file for himself. The boy had been telling the truth about the card, but he'd neglected to mention a note that advised bank personnel to contact local law enforcement concerning any inquiries on this account. Then he saw the written description of Jesse and a woman who could only be Ethan Trent's so-called wife. Below those words, he saw a second note describing a man in his fifties with red hair, an outlaw wanted for murder.

Timonius aimed his cut-off Colt at the kid's chest. "Find a bag and fill it up."

Not surprisingly, the kid obeyed. In less than two minutes, Timonius had a sackful of greenbacks. He also had to dispose of a witness. As cool as winter, he said, "Now, turn around and put your hands behind your back."

Expecting to be tied up, the clerk complied. It was the last thing he did before he died. Whether the kid was destined for heaven or for hell, Timonius didn't know or care. He had only one purpose now, and that was to find Jayne Dawson. Jesse might have turned over a new leaf, but he was savvy enough to keep a good portion of the money on hand. The widow had to be lying, and Timonius intended to make her pay—right after he left Los Angeles, found a first-rate hotel and slept until his damn cough went away.

Chapter Fourteen

If John Leaf hadn't been wearing the black coat that marked him as a preacher, Ethan might have shot first and asked questions later. Keeping an eye out for LeFarge had made him edgy, but the real source of his tension ran deeper. He was happy again, but not an hour passed that he didn't feel like a man perched on the edge of a crumbling cliff. Jayne could be snatched away tomorrow, and he couldn't imagine going back to living alone.

Since coming home from Raton, they had talked for hours. On warm nights they took a blanket to the knoll where they could lie close and look at the stars. Talk had led to touching, and lots of it, but Ethan wasn't in a rush to take her to bed. He felt like a kid again, and he wanted Jayne to have the pleasure of being courted. Plus he had to be sure that he had earned her trust. He had hurt her once and he didn't want it to happen again.

As good as he felt, he also suffered moments of stark terror. Whenever she left the cabin, he broke into a sweat. The hour she had spent bathing at the creek had made him edgy enough to check on her three times. The view had made him crazy with love, but the thought of losing her turned him livid with fear.

Maybe that's why his first reaction to the Reverend sitting at the table eating cookies wasn't kind. "What the hell are you doing here?"

The preacher lowered his coffee cup and chuckled. "Well, hello to you, too, Ethan. I came to pay a call, and your wife kindly offered me refreshments. Want a cookie?"

"I'm not hungry." Ethan dropped into his chair and glowered at their guest as Jayne filled their coffee cups.

"The Reverend invited us to church on Sunday," she said. "The women are planning an ice-cream social. Doesn't that sound nice?"

"Hell no! It's not safe," declared Ethan.

John leaned back in his chair and arched his eyebrows. "Are you sure about that?"

"I'm dead sure. People will gossip. If LeFarge comes back, he'll head straight this way."

Jayne sat between the two men and turned to Ethan. "It's been three weeks since we left Raton. Maybe LeFarge is in jail and we don't have to be afraid."

Ethan grimaced. "Or maybe he's sitting in the Midas saloon and asking nosy questions."

The Reverend pushed back from the table. "I should be going. Ethan, why don't you walk out with me?"

He wanted to ask John to wire Chief Roberts, so

he stood as the preacher put on his hat and nodded his thanks to Jayne. "I hope to see you on Sunday."

"I hope so, too," she replied. Her words were for John, but her eyes stayed firm on Ethan's face. He turned away and followed the Reverend out the door.

As they walked to John's mare, he glanced at Ethan. "Do you mind if I switch from visiting to meddling for a minute?"

"You'll do it anyway, so go ahead."

"Stay on your toes, but don't be too cautious. It's not courage that gets people killed, it's fear."

Ethan's gaze drifted to the pile of black rubble from the fire. No one had to tell him about fear. He lived with it every day in a way few men could understand. "I appreciate the advice, but I intend to take precautions. LeFarge is a real threat."

"Maybe so," John replied. "But it's time to clean up the mess he left, including that pile of rotten wood. Your wife doesn't enjoy looking at it."

"How do you know?"

"She told me. You need to get busy on a new barn, too." A trace of a smile curled the Reverend's lips as he climbed into the saddle. "Think about Sunday. You can sit in the back row and I'll watch the door from the pulpit."

"It's just not safe."

"Sure it is." John pulled back his coat to reveal a Colt Peacemaker with a custom hammer. With a cocksure dip of his chin, he said, "I like a good fight now and then."

Ethan didn't doubt John's sincerity. He'd been known to use his gun *and* his fists. Rumor had it that he'd knocked Zachary Biddle all the way to next week when he'd caught him abusing his wife and baby daughter.

As he took the reins, John studied Ethan's face. "Can you stand one more piece of advice?"

"I doubt it, but go ahead."

"Take your pretty wife to bed and forget this crap for a while. Something tells me you two haven't figured out how to be married yet."

Ethan's mouth gaped wide enough to catch a fly and then he chuckled. "Are you always this direct?"

"Hell yes," the preacher replied. "If you have a lick of sense, you'll finish what God and nature started, and you'll do it soon. You're both tense enough to snap."

When Ethan didn't deny it, John turned serious. "Do you love her?"

"I do."

"Then why don't you tell her?"

Ethan shook his head. "I don't think I could survive losing her."

"So you're wasting today because you're afraid of tomorrow." The Reverend's stare was hot enough to start a fire. "Don't be stupid, Ethan. Grab the joy God has for you and don't let go."

Without another word, he clicked to the mare and rode into the meadow. Ethan's gaze stayed on the man's back. He couldn't tell John to go to hell because he'd already been there and had decided to leave. Grateful for a friend who understood him, Ethan raised his chin and shouted, "Hey, John. We'll see you Sunday."

The preacher acknowledged with a wave, and Ethan walked into the cabin. Jayne was standing at the counter with a dishcloth, rubbing a tin plate hard enough to give it a shine. At the sight of him, she squared her shoulders.

"I'm going to church and you can't stop me," she declared. "I'll walk if I have to."

She looked mad enough to beat him at arm wrestling, not that it was necessary. She had already won the argument, but Ethan was in the mood for a bit of a tussle. Besides, manly pride demanded at least a grumble about going to church, if not a full-fledged whine.

He settled for a huff. "I can put up with gossipy old biddies if you can, but that out-of-tune piano is too much. We'll go, but we're sitting in the back pew."

Two beats of silence told him that he'd surprised her. He liked having the upper hand, but it didn't last long. She crossed her arms over her chest. "All right," she said. "But we're staying for ice cream."

"Agreed." If they were going to be a couple in public, he wanted to be one in private first. He made his voice husky. "Saturday night comes first. Wear something pretty, just for me."

When her mouth gaped, he walked out the door before he changed his mind about waiting until Saturday to make her his wife in all the ways that mattered.

As soon as the door closed behind Ethan, Jayne hugged herself and bounced on her toes. The circle of white flesh on his ring finger was nearly as brown as the rest of him now. With all the talking they had done, she felt as if Laura were a pen pal, someone she hadn't met, but whom she knew and liked just the same. Best of all, not once had Ethan turned away from her to hide his feelings.

With thoughts of Saturday night making her blush, she decided to fix a special dinner, including a cake to celebrate. In her trunk she had the perfect dress to wear. She had intended to sell the stylish evening gown in California, but wearing the royal-blue silk for Ethan had far more appeal. With its off-the-shoulder bodice and lace trim, the dress was both alluring and bridelike.

The only thing missing was a gift for Ethan, but if she hurried, she could make him a Sunday-best shirt. She had worn her beige skirt just once, and the fabric was ideal for what she had in mind. After glancing out the window to make sure he'd gone to the corral, Jayne lifted his most ragged shirt off the nail by the bed. It fit him perfectly. She knew it was his favorite because he'd worn it every day until he had made that first trip to town and bought something new.

The garment was beyond repair, but it would make a perfect pattern. Pleased with her plan, she opened her trunk and took out her mother's scissors. Imagining a look of pleasure on Ethan's face, she cut the shirt into pieces.

For the next few days Ethan kept busy by working on the corral and putting the glass panes into the cabin windows. Jayne had chased him away every afternoon by saying she wanted to nap, but he had managed to finish the project by late Saturday afternoon.

With the sun low on the horizon, he set his tools on the porch and walked to the well. Stripping off his shirt, he splashed water on his chest and arms and raked back his hair. This morning she'd given him a trim and he'd enjoyed every minute of it. She had been cooking all day, too, and a tantalizing aroma tickled his nose. Unless he missed his guess, she had baked something special for dessert.

With his stomach rumbling, he shrugged back into his work shirt and walked through the door. His gaze went straight to Jayne who was inspecting her face in the mirror and pinching her lips to give them color they didn't need.

No woman had ever looked more beautiful. The bright blue silk matched her eyes, and the front of the dress was cut low enough to give a man something to look at. "You're lovely," he said.

"Thank you."

He dragged his eyes away from her just long enough to hang up his hat. "Supper smells good."

She gave him a shameless smile. "I baked a cake for dessert."

Ethan nearly blurted what was in his heart. *I love you. I want you to be my wife, my soul mate, my best friend and lover.* He wanted to take her to bed right now, but he also wanted to give her candlelight and shadows, the pleasure of a man's anticipation and the memory of a proper marriage proposal. So instead of scooping her into his arms, he walked to the wall where a clean shirt was hanging on a nail. "I need a minute to change," he said.

She usually made a point of turning her back when he undressed, but tonight she watched as he lifted a fresh shirt off a hook just above her scrap basket. He had seen that basket before, but tonight it caught his eye and wouldn't let go. His old blue shirt, the last one Laura had made for him, was in tatters.

She had given him that shirt for his birthday, and he had worn it nearly every day for two years. On cold nights he had slept in it. On warm ones he had held it against his bare chest and remembered his wife. It had been like a second skin to him. At times it had been *her* skin. Air hissed through his lips and his fingers went numb. The soft glow of the lantern brought back pictures of Laura loving him, of her fingers unbuttoning that shirt. Heat rushed up his neck and he was back in Raton, standing helplessly at the fire.

He didn't want these memories *now*. He wanted Jayne. He wanted to tell her he loved her, but he couldn't turn around, and he was painfully aware of her gaze on his back.

"Is something the matter?" she asked.

Why the hell couldn't he talk? He shook his head.

"Oh, God." She clasped her hands to her cheeks. "It's the shirt. Laura made it for you, didn't she?"

His throat had closed to a pinhole. He tried to tell her that the shirt didn't matter, but his voice came out in a strangled grunt.

"I'm so sorry," Jayne cried. "I made a present for you, and I used that shirt for a pattern."

He wanted to tell her that these feelings were just a reaction, like stubbing his toe and yelping with pain. Seeing the shirt had hurt like hell, but it would pass in a minute or two. Except he didn't have a minute. Jayne was starting to sob.

"I—I should have known it was special," she said. "I used it because it f-fit you so well. It was too worn-out to mend, and I thought—"

"It's not as simple as you think." His voice was none too steady, but it was a start. Swallowing hard, he looked at her. "That shirt doesn't matter."

"Yes, it does." More tears welled. "I thought we had a chance, but I was wrong. Laura will always be first in your heart. I'm just here."

"That is *not* true!" Ethan hurried to her side and gripped her arms. "We had plans for tonight. Don't let a knee-jerk reaction ruin it."

She pulled away from him and walked to the stove where she began to dish up their supper. "It's too late, or too soon. Or maybe it's just not meant to be. I can't stand feeling second-best. Oh, God, Ethan. I saw your face. I feel so bad."

He came up behind her and clasped her shoulders with both hands. "Listen to me. What you *saw* was a man get bit by a snake."

Ignoring him, she picked up their plates and set them on the table with a clatter. Then she sat down and straightened a linen napkin in her lap. "We might as well eat."

Ethan dropped into his chair and willed her to look

at him. When she finally glanced across the table, he started to talk.

"Have you ever seen a snake?" he asked. "I got bit when I was about thirteen. You don't see it coming. One minute you're walking through the woods and the next thing you know you have fang marks on your boot. That's what it's like to live with memories. They sneak up and bite you. Everything hurts again, but just for a while."

She gave him a look full of pity. "I know you, Ethan. I can almost read your thoughts. You can't hide the truth."

"I don't intend to." He put iron in his voice. "You need to understand that I felt all sorts of things when I saw that shirt. I'll always love Laura and the children. There isn't anything wrong with that, and I'm not going to apologize. But that was then and this is now."

Ethan waited until she swallowed a bite of food and then looked up. "I love you, Jayne. I want you to share my bed, my future, everything."

When she sucked in a breath, he felt a glimmer of hope until she picked up her knife and buttered a slice of bread. "Eat before it gets cold," she said.

A smart man ate what a woman cooked, so Ethan raised a bite to his lips, giving her time to think. Silence hung between them like too much salt on a good meal. Their cups clanked on the table. Knives scraped against the plates. As soon as he polished off the last bite, she snatched away the tin and carried it to the scrub bucket.

In one smooth motion she picked up the cake and

set it on the table. The scent of vanilla was more than he could stand. "You didn't answer my question. I want this marriage to be complete."

"If you need an answer tonight, it's no. If you're willing to wait, the answer is maybe."

Ethan pushed back from the table, scraping the chair legs against the floor as he rose to his feet. "Dammit, Jayne. You're stubborn beyond words."

"I'm being sensible," she said. "I know what it's like to live in someone's shadow. My mother did it with Arthur Huntington, until she caught him cheating on her."

Ethan saw six shades of red. Propping his hands on his hips, he said, "Do you think I'd *cheat* on you? That's an insult to who I am."

"You wouldn't hurt me on purpose, but you'll always think about Laura. I realized something tonight. I don't want to feel like a hand-me-down that's been made over and doesn't quite fit."

"What do hand-me-downs have to do with anything?" Ethan scratched his head in confusion. "I love you. I want to spend my life with you."

After giving him a look that said he had missed the point, she walked to the hook where she hung her clothes, reached behind a dress and lifted out a shirt. "Maybe this will explain it. I made it just for you. It won't replace Laura's, but maybe you can get some wear out of it."

He imagined Jayne's fingers measuring the seams and working the needle. He didn't know a thing about stitchery, but he could see that the garment would be a perfect fit. "It's the nicest shirt I've ever owned," he said. "Thank you. I'll wear it to church tomorrow."

"I'm glad you like it." Her chest rose as she took a deep breath. "I'll be staying in Midas after the service. I can pay for a night in the hotel, then I'll take the train to Raton. With a little luck, Madame Marchand will still need a seamstress."

How the hell had they switched from talking about shirts to going their separate ways? Baffled and furious at the same time, he raked his hand through his hair. "You can't leave."

She looked him straight in the eye. "I need time to think. It's true that I love you, but you keep trampling all over my feelings. I know it's not on purpose, but it still hurts."

"I understand that. We can talk it out."

After shaking her head, she walked back to the table where the cake was sitting untouched. "I'll be in Raton. You can visit me in a few weeks."

The thought of *visiting* her made him mad enough to spit. Crossing his arms over his chest, he rocked back on one hip. "I don't particularly like being told what to do."

She looked ready to hurl the cake at him. "I'm trying to find a compromise! You're the one being stubborn."

"Oh, no, I'm not." His voice picked up volume. "You're my wife, dammit. You're carrying a baby I consider mine, and you're acting as crazy as a loon!"

As soon as the words left his mouth Ethan realized that he'd stepped in a giant cow pie. He'd been through three pregnancies with Laura. Rule Number

One was never tell a pregnant woman she looked fat. Rule Number Two was never call her a loon. He needed to back up, and fast. "I'm sorry, sweetheart. It's just that—"

Jayne's cheeks flushed red. "Don't you dare 'sweetheart' me!"

"You're just a little emotional," he said, holding up his hands to calm her. "I can understand that. We can wait awhile before we make this a real marriage. We can do whatever you want."

"What I want is to leave!" She spun on her heel, opened her trunk and started to fold the clothes hanging by the bed. "How dare you call me a loon! I'm being perfectly logical about the whole mess. You're the one who's confused."

"Like hell! I know *exactly* what I want. I want you." *Right now. Under my roof. At my table. In my arms.*

She shook her head. "You want someone to cook for you and warm your bed. Any woman would do. As soon as I get to Raton, I'll ask Chief Roberts to wire the bond money to you."

"I don't *want* the goddamned bond money!"

"And I don't want to live with ghosts or, for that matter, a man who'd call me crazy just because I have concerns."

Ethan rubbed the back of his neck. "I'm sorry about the wisecrack, but you're not being fair. After all we've been through, I can't believe you're letting one little incident get in the way of our future."

"This isn't 'a little incident,' at least not to me." She crouched down and pulled her everyday shoes out from under the bed. Pushing to her feet, she said, "Would you please excuse me? I want to change clothes."

Ethan had a good mind to stand his ground, but he was getting angrier by the minute. He'd already apologized about his insensitive remark and declared his intentions. What more could a man say? If she so much as blinked, he'd be taking her to bed, but it was up to Jayne to decide.

Mindful of her cold glare, he hoisted a chair with one hand, opened the front door and looked over his shoulder. "I'll be right outside. Let me know if you change your mind about sleeping alone."

"I won't."

"Maybe not," he replied. "But you're going to think about us tonight. You're going to wonder what our children would look like, and you're going to imagine making love to me in that bed. You're going to think about waking up together, all tangled up and ready for more. All night long, you're going to dream about us."

When she looked down at her feet, Ethan felt a surge of hope. He lowered his voice to a gravelly drawl. "I can make those dreams come true. All you have to do is ask."

Neither of them slept well. Jayne spent the night alone in bed doing exactly what Ethan had predicted. From the occasional thumps of his chair against the door, she knew that he hadn't budged from the porch. True to his word, he was waiting for her to ask him inside.

The empty hours had given her time to think. The logical part of her mind was convinced she belonged in Lexington where she could support herself and the baby. She'd step into her old shoes, the ones like her mother had worn, kid boots with pointy toes and hard soles.

Her heart ached at the thought of leaving Ethan. Maybe he was ready for a new life and the upset over the shirt had been nothing.

Or maybe not. Maybe she'd rue the day they met, just as her mother had regretted her second marriage. At least she'd had her shop to fall back on. After the divorce, her mother had thanked her lucky stars that she'd kept her business.

With dawn pushing through the new glass windows, Jayne climbed out of bed and opened her trunk. Her green traveling suit was on top, neatly folded and ready to wear. She put on fresh unmentionables, stockings and the white shirtwaist she'd been wearing the day she arrived. It was snug across the bust, but it would have to do. After putting on the skirt and jacket, she twisted her hair into a knot and stepped into her city shoes.

They pinched. So did the waistband of the skirt.

As the morning sun chased away the gloom, she made coffee and opened a can of peaches for her breakfast. She had just taken the last bite when Ethan walked through the door and headed for the coffee-pot. His face was red from scrubbing, and she guessed that he'd shaved outside with cold water. He was also wearing the shirt she had made.

At the memory of last night's fiasco, she directed

her gaze to Ethan, curious to see what he'd say. If he apologized, she would, too. They had both been upset.

But instead of softening, he gave her a hard stare, poured coffee for himself and downed it in six gulps. He set the cup on the counter with a thud. "Chores are done. We can leave whenever you're ready."

"I'm ready now," she replied. *Unless you have something to say.*

He gave her a stiff nod and walked to the bed. Kneeling, he reached under the oak frame and took out a leather satchel.

She pushed to her feet. "What are you doing?"

"Packing."

"What for?"

"I'm staying in town."

She watched as he gathered long johns, socks and an extra shirt. Not bothering to fold anything, he stuffed the garments into the satchel, worked the buckle and hoisted the bag off the bed.

Jayne glared at him. "I don't want you to wait with me."

"You don't have a say in the matter. I want to order wood for the barn and hire men to help build it. I can't do that until Monday. And then there's the matter of buying a new wagon."

"Suit yourself," she said. Ethan's presence in Midas didn't change a thing. She'd be on the train to Raton in the morning.

He carried his satchel to the buckboard, leaving her with the trunk. It was too heavy for her to lift, so she waited for him to come back for it. A full minute passed. What in the world was he doing out there? Heaving a sigh, she stepped onto the porch and saw Rocky tied to the back of the wagon. Ethan was lazing against the side with one boot draped over the other.

"Would you please get my trunk?" she said.

He curled his fingers into his palms and flicked at a cuticle. "Since you're so determined to take care of yourself, this seems like a good time to start. You get it. I'll wait here."

His snide tone reminded her of old Mrs. Teeter back in Lexington. The woman had been a thorn, but a wealthy one who bought a new wardrobe every spring. Jayne had learned that common sense trumped rudeness any day of the week.

Shrugging, she said, "Never mind. I can manage."

She walked back into the cabin, grabbed one handle of the trunk and dragged it across the floor. Who cared if it scratched the planking she'd waxed just yesterday? She tugged the heavy case through the door, barking her knuckles on the doorjamb and nearly tripping on her hem as she backed down the porch steps.

She could push and pull the heavy trunk, but she didn't have a prayer of lifting it into the buckboard as long as it was packed. After untwisting the wire holding the broken latch, she opened the lid.

Ethan's shadow touched her feet. "What are you doing?"

"I'll be able to lift it when it's empty." Her voice had risen a notch, betraying her nerves.

"Jayne, don't." His touch burned through her sleeve. If only she could forget his wife…if only he would kiss her until she couldn't think…

Instead he blew out a hard breath. "I was trying to make a point, but never mind. I'll get the trunk."

He dropped to one knee, grasped the handles and hoisted it into the wagon as Jayne walked around to the seat. She was gripping the frame with the intention of pulling herself up when she felt his hand on her elbow.

"Watch your step," he said.

The old wood creaked as she sat and then creaked again as he climbed up next to her. He loosened the reins and the gelding plodded down the trail.

The ride to Midas was bumpy and silent. When she finally saw mining shanties and the steaming kettles of a laundry, she breathed a sigh of relief. A few minutes later Ethan steered the horse down a street lined with storefronts and adobe buildings. The sun was bright and the boardwalk was dotted with people headed to church.

As fragments of conversation drifted to her ears, she wondered if she would ever feel at home again. Folding her hands in her lap, she sat ramrod-straight as Ethan shifted one boot against the floorboard. The church was a block away and they had decisions to make.

"I'd like to check the train schedule," she said. Her stomach quivered at the thought of bidding him farewell, but she had to be sensible.

"We'll check in at the hotel first," he replied. "After the service, I'll walk with you to the depot."

When they arrived at the hotel, Ethan paid for adjoining rooms and put her trunk in one and his satchel in the other. Next, they visited the livery stable where he boarded the horses and wagon and posted a For Hire notice.

The church was situated apart from the local businesses. As they stepped off the boardwalk and onto a dusty path, Ethan raised his hand to the small of her back. She smelled the sweetness of spring grass as families dressed in their Sunday best climbed out of wagons and walked into the wooden building.

Blinking in the sun, she couldn't help but wonder where she'd be in five years. Maybe she'd be strolling to church in Lexington, holding her daughter's hand, or perhaps she'd have a boy, like the one doing jumping jacks in front of the church. When the boy's father hollered at him to be still for a change, Jayne felt a lump rise in her throat.

With one last look at the brilliant sky, she let Ethan guide her into the church, where Reverend Leaf was glowering from the pulpit.

Chapter Fifteen

"Anyone here ever kill a man?"

From her seat in the last pew, Jayne saw forty people shake their heads as John Leaf paced across the front of the church. Dressed in a black frock coat and staring into the congregation with piercing eyes, he reminded her of a hawk on a hunt. He barely resembled the friendly man who had munched cookies at Ethan's kitchen table.

The Reverend peered ruthlessly into the crowd. "Anyone here every lied or cheated at cards?"

The room grew even quieter.

"How about stealing?"

Silence.

"Okay, how about you men? Has anyone here ever bedded another man's wife?"

The air thickened like fog on the Ohio River, the kind that formed when cold air hit warmer water. The woman seated in front of Jayne leaned close to her husband and whispered, "Well, I never!"

Reverend Leaf must have caught a hint of the talk because he stared at the woman as if he were getting ready for a gunfight. Then he tapped one boot, pivoted and paced some more. When no one else stirred, he squared himself in front of the congregation, crossed his arms over his chest and smiled. "All right, since you folks are all so perfect, you can go on home and I'll eat the ice cream myself."

The crowd teetered with laughter until an old man said, "Like hell, Reverend. I'll join you."

"Count me in."

"Me, too, John."

Several women nodded, but the young woman sitting next to Jayne had tears in her eyes. She was also wearing a cherry-red dress that was too garish for church but perfect for a woman trying to attract a sporting man's attention. The girl had stitched lace across the neckline to hide her bosom, but her feeble effort didn't mask who and what she was. Or used to be. The dress was old and worn.

Jayne saw the Reverend's eyes focus on the back pew as if he were willing the girl to look up at him. She sniffed once and then raised her chin. Her cheeks were as red as winter apples and they grew even redder when John Leaf gave her a smile.

His gaze traveled to Jayne, whom he greeted with a friendly nod, and then to Ethan. Rocking back on his heels, he hooked his thumbs in his pockets and pulled back his coat just enough to reveal a glimmer of blue metal. It looked like a pistol, but Jayne couldn't be sure.

When Ethan nodded, the Reverend lowered his arms so that the flaps of his coat closed. Then he scanned the room one more time.

"This is your last chance, folks. Anyone who's never made a mess can leave right now, because what I've got to say today isn't for those of you who have always been saints. It's for those of us who have had to clean our boots a few times.

"You see, ladies and gentlemen, I've done all those things I mentioned, and some more than once. I'll carry those marks until my dying day, but God forgives, and we've got a duty—" he zeroed in on Ethan "—to forgive ourselves."

Then he looked at Jayne. "And the people we love."

This wasn't the church service she had been expecting. Her pastor in Lexington had been stout and pink-cheeked with a fringe of white hair around his bald head. John Leaf didn't fit that image, but it was obvious the people in Midas loved him.

An old lady in the front row let out a hoot. "Now, John, we all know you've got a past. Speculating keeps us widows entertained, but what *you* need is a *wife*. She'll fix your wagon!"

The Reverend laughed out loud. "Well, Mabel, my wagon needs fixing, but that's not going to happen today, or tomorrow, either. Frankly, there's not a woman in the world who could put up with me."

Female laughter rippled through the room.

"I get cranky when I'm tired. I cuss now and then. I toss back a shot of whiskey on occasion, but I think about it all the time. I'm weak-minded when it comes to looking at pretty women but strong-willed about everything else. I guarantee you. There's not a lady here who'd want to wash my smelly socks."

He shook his head. "I'm greedy, selfish and lazy as sin. Ask Mrs. Cunningham. She's the parish housekeeper."

A middle-aged woman gave an exaggerated sigh. "It's true, ladies. Our good Reverend is the messiest man ever born, and I've outlived three husbands. He's worse than my five sons all put together."

Laughter filled the church. Even Ethan was smiling.

Reverend Leaf managed to look both sheepish and incorrigible. "It would take a saint to put up with me." He cocked a grin. "Or a crazy woman. I'm pretty irredeemable, but I do have one or two good qualities. Anyone want to know what they are?"

"Oh, we know, Reverend." The remark came from a butterball woman in the middle of the church. "You'd die for any one of us. You made the sheriff lock up Herbert Jones when he beat up Sally, and whenever there's trouble, you're the first one to show up."

"And?" He arched one eyebrow and gave the old lady a wicked smile.

She huffed at him. "You're nice-lookin' to boot."

"That's right, and I'm modest, too."

As John Leaf told tales and spun stories that wove together parables and proverbs, Jayne became enthralled. He preached about life in all its heartache and glory. About failed hopes, promises still to be kept and about loving imperfect men. And imperfect women.

Long before he reached the final amen, she decided to talk to him after the service. She loved Ethan and wanted to believe he loved her, but her heart was still bruised from last night. She didn't think she could bear that pain again.

After a final hymn, the congregation rose to its feet and Reverend Leaf closed the service with a prayer and a sincere "Amen." Smiling men and women streamed from the front pews.

Ethan sought her gaze. "Are you ready?"

"Not quite. Would you mind waiting for me outside? I'd like to talk to Reverend Leaf in private."

He hesitated, then lifted his hat off the bench. "All right. I'll be out front."

As the last few people approached the door, Jayne joined the greeting line. Out of the corner of her eye, she saw the girl in red lurking by the cloakroom. Realizing that they both wanted a private moment with the Reverend, and that the girl had been fighting tears all morning, Jayne took her place in line.

Shaking John Leaf's hand, she said, "I'd like a word with you in private, but I think someone else needs you more right now."

He'd already seen the girl. "Come back in fifteen minutes or so."

"All right."

She didn't want to see Ethan yet, so she slipped out the side door and ambled through the church garden where someone had planted roses. With her hands laced behind her back, she bent forward, closed her eyes and sniffed.

The sweet fragrance brought to mind the bouquet Ethan had given her at Laura's grave. Her heart swelled with longing, but her stomach was in a knot.

She understood that last night's argument had been the kind of tiff couples had all the time, but how did she stop feeling the shadow of Laura's presence? She was wondering what the Reverend would say when a man's rough hands grabbed her wrists and spun her around.

"Sheriff Handley!" she cried.

"Jayne Dawson, you're under arrest. Or should I call you Jayne McKinney?"

"I'm Jayne Trent now. Please, I have to find Ethan."

Smirking, the sheriff let go of her hands but stepped closer, trapping her against the thorny bush. Crossing his arms over his chest, he looked peeved to say the least. "I'm taking you to jail, miss."

"This is a mistake," Jayne cried. "We posted a bond in Raton. If you speak with Chief Roberts, you'll see—"

"What I see is your face on a Wanted poster in my office. Let's go." He planted his hand on her back and shoved her into the middle of the garden.

"No, please," she begged. "Ethan will be panicked. I can't do that to him."

"No way, lady. I let you out of my sight once and I'm not about to do it again."

Ethan was getting tired of tapping his toe in front of the church. A good half hour had passed since the Reverend's last amen, and neither Jayne nor John Leaf had moseyed over to the picnic table where men were cranking the ice-cream freezers.

Annoyed with both of them, he marched up the

church steps just as the girl in red pushed through the door. For some fool reason, she smiled at Ethan and wished him a good day as he walked past her. He entered the sanctuary just in time to see the Reverend slip out a side door. Before it could swing shut, Ethan strode into the garden.

"Where the hell's my wife?" he demanded.

The flash of surprise on the Reverend's face put Ethan's heart into a spin. "She's not with you?"

"Hell no! She was waiting for you."

"She was supposed to come back inside. I figured she would join the crowd until I finished up."

Ethan grabbed at shreds of hope. Maybe she had walked to the train depot or the hotel, but it wasn't likely. Even if she was still mad at him, she would have told him where she was going. Staring down the path leading to town, he said, "It's bad, John. I can feel it in my bones."

"I can, too."

The Reverend was known for an uncanny ability to see trouble coming, and having him agree brought Ethan no comfort. "I hate to go to Handley, but I don't think we have a choice."

The two men headed straight to the sheriff's office where Ethan pushed through the door first. His gaze ricocheted from Handley lazing at his desk with a newspaper to a cell where he saw Jayne locked up next to Horace Little, the town drunk and a lecherous piece of scum. Mercifully, Horace was passed out and snoring.

Ethan strode to Handley's desk and pounded it

once with his fist. "What the *hell* is my wife doing in your jail?"

After taking his sweet time to lower the newspaper, Handley rocked back in his squeaky chair and smirked. "You better be civil, Trent, or I'll toss you in jail, too. You've been harboring a wanted woman."

Provoking Handley wouldn't help Jayne, so Ethan lowered his voice. "She's a witness, Sheriff, that's all. We have proof."

The sheriff pointed to a Wanted poster on the wall. "That's all the proof I need. I've got plenty of cause to lock Miss McKinney up for a few days."

"She's *not* Miss McKinney," Ethan said forcefully. "She's my wife, and I want her out of that cell."

All three men looked toward Jayne, who was grasping the bars. "Sheriff, you *know* this is a mistake."

"What I know is that you've got a little payback coming for ditching me on the trail. You disobeyed the law, young lady."

Ethan's temper flared. "This is just plain wrong. I could—jeez!" As pain shot from his foot to his head, he realized that the good Reverend had stomped on his foot.

"Now, Tom," John said, sounding as wise as Solomon. "Let's think this through. I married these two awhile ago, so Ethan has a right to be concerned. We both know you can't leave a woman locked up next to Horace. It isn't seemly. Plus she's innocent, and you know it."

"I don't know any such thing. I don't make judgments. I just enforce the law."

As Jayne sighed with frustration, Ethan balled his hands into fists. With his throbbing foot reminding him to stay civil, he faced Handley. "Okay, Sheriff. What will it take to get her out of here? Another bond?"

"Nope. She'll rabbit off somewhere."

Jayne interrupted. "I won't. You have my word."

Handley harrumphed. "That means nothing to me, young lady."

The sheriff's loud grunt must have disturbed Horace's slumber because he rolled to his side and thumped his head on the bed frame. At the sight of Jayne, he bolted upright. His bloodshot eyes popped wide and his fat lips curled into a leering grin. Wobbling to his feet, he curled his greasy fingers around the bars and let out a catcall. "Whooo-hoooo, I got me a *skirt* to look at."

John raised an eyebrow at Handley. "Do you intend to spend the night here, Sheriff? If not, I'm going to have to let the ladies of this town know that you subjected a young woman to Horace's bad habits."

Horace chose that moment to grab his crotch and squeal like a pig.

"Ah, hell," the Sheriff muttered. "Get her outta here, but don't leave town. I want to see you both here at twelve sharp every day until this is settled."

As soon as Handley opened the cell door, Jayne bolted for the front door. Nauseous from the stench of Horace's body odor, she collapsed on a bench and pressed her hands to her cheeks to steady herself. Ethan and John followed in her steps and planted themselves in front of the bench.

Ethan reached down and touched her shoulder. "Are you all right?"

"The fresh air is helping." She smoothed a wrinkle out of her skirt, wishing all of her problems could be solved so easily. John Leaf was standing like a silent black wall with his hands on his hips, while Ethan was rubbing her shoulder, as if to convince himself that she was safe. Not knowing if she was giving comfort or seeking it for herself, she put her hand on top of his.

Looking into his worried eyes, she said, "I'm so sorry to scare you. Handley wouldn't let me tell you what happened. He just locked me up and started talking about bank robberies and murder charges."

John shifted his weight. "Handley's just plain mean, and stupid to boot. You both seem calmer. Do you want to go back to the church?"

Jayne shook her head. "I'm not up for conversation."

"Neither am I," Ethan added.

"I can understand," said John. "I've been in jail a few times. Whether it's five minutes or five years, the feeling's the same and it's awful. Supper and sleep will help you both. I don't think Handley will bother you at the hotel."

As soon as the Reverend departed, Ethan dropped down on the bench, put his arms around her and pressed her head against his shoulder. The solidness of his body took her back to the storm at Rainbow Falls, and what had happened afterward.

I love you...

She heard the cry in her heart, but her mouth refused to work. If she became Ethan's wife in the truest sense, there would be no going back to Lexington or starting over in a new town. She'd be sharing him with Laura for the rest of her life, no matter how much it hurt. Her mother's voice haunted her thoughts.

Be careful, Jayne. Don't risk your heart.

Side by side, she and Ethan sat in silence until he loosened his grip on her shoulders and nodded toward the café across the street. "I wonder if that place serves sauerkraut," he said, making his voice light.

In spite of herself, she smiled. "I don't think I could eat a bite."

"Maybe a cup of tea then. Besides, it'll give us a place to talk. We have a few things to settle."

Chapter Sixteen

Pushing to his feet, Ethan took Jayne's hand and led her across the street to the café. Her fingers felt like ice in his, and her cheeks were still as white as a new petticoat. Last night's argument had to be addressed, but right now she needed a friend more than she needed a man's stubbornness. Ethan intended to be strong for her, today and always, but with Handley's threats ringing in their ears, "today" took precedence.

After they entered the café, Ethan guided her to a table against a wall where they would have some privacy. He ordered tea and toast for her and a plate of tamales for himself. As soon as the waitress left, she spread her napkin in her lap and looked at him with stark confusion.

A lot had happened to her in twenty-four hours. Together they'd tumbled from the mountaintop of a wedding night to a valley full of shadows and danger. He couldn't change the facts, but he could put her at ease about their personal differences. He made his voice gentle. "We have some unfinished business."

"Yes, we do," she replied. "I wanted to talk to the Reverend about what he said today, but then Handley nabbed me. I feel like I'm still in jail, like decisions are being made for me."

"I know how that feels." He'd been made helpless by circumstances when his family died. "You want to have choices."

"Exactly."

"I want you to have a choice, too, that's why I'll wait as long as it takes for you to feel right about being my wife. I love you, Jayne, and that's why we aren't going to share a bed until you say so."

To his horror, she started to cry. "You're being so kind to me. Maybe I *am* as crazy as a loon."

"No, you're not," he said. "You're smart and beautiful and brave. Do you know when I first realized I could love you?"

She shook her head.

"At Dawson's grave when I saw you tramping through the snow. You risked everything for a man who didn't deserve to walk on this earth with you. That took courage, and I admired you for it."

She managed a smile. "But it probably wasn't smart."

"That's a matter of opinion," Ethan replied. "I think it's the smartest thing you've ever done. You saved me, Jayne. Do you know how it feels when your foot falls asleep? It's all numb and dead, and then the blood starts to flow and it hurts like hell. That's how I felt with you, like a dead man coming back to life."

"I'm glad I could help. You're a good man," she said sincerely.

"If I am, it's because of you. You gave me back the best parts of myself, and I can't thank you enough for all you've done—everything from giving me a haircut to that night at Rainbow Falls."

When she looked up with wide eyes, Ethan felt his blood heat to a near boil. She was on the verge of saying yes to him—he was sure of it—but the waitress interrupted with their food. His mouth started to water at the spicy aroma of the tamales, but he wouldn't take a bite until Jayne broke the silence.

She took a sip of tea, then lowered the cup. "I heard everything you said, but I still need to think. I have to be sure."

"I'd expect nothing less." Ethan cut into the corn husk wrapper and raised the bite to his lips. At least one of his natural appetites could be satisfied. As for their marriage, he'd have to be patient while nature took its course.

With their sleeping arrangements settled, he decided to address more practical concerns. "We need to wire Chief Roberts, then we'll go to the store. I need a few things."

"All right," she said, nibbling the toast.

After they finished the meal, they left the restaurant, sent a wire to Chief Roberts and walked to the Midas Emporium holding hands.

As soon as they entered the store, Ethan saw Mrs. Wingate arch her eyebrows. She was a talker, the kind of person LeFarge would find and use. Too late,

Ethan realized he wasn't prepared to answer questions about Jayne.

The clerk beamed a smile. "Hello, Mr. Trent."

"Good afternoon, ma'am."

Before she could probe, Ethan steered Jayne down the aisle holding personal items. He had forgotten his shaving tools, so he picked out a new razor, a mug and soap. Turning, he saw Jayne fingering the blue gingham he had wanted to buy for her the last time he'd been in town. Reaching around her waist, he picked up the bolt with one hand and tucked it under his arm.

She shook her head. "You shouldn't—"

"I want to." Nothing short of a bullet could have stopped him from buying the fabric for her. It matched her eyes, and pretty soon she'd need loose-fitting clothes to accommodate the baby. He wanted to buy her something else as well, something lasting, but what?

While Jayne looked at sewing notions, Ethan perused a display case of jewelry. He saw a silver band inlayed with turquoise, but he didn't want to give her a ring until he was sure that she'd wear it. He ruled out a gold locket etched with hearts. It was a courtship gift, and he'd done all the asking he intended to do.

Still, he wanted to send her a message. As he strolled the aisles, a shiny frying pan caught his eye. Under the circumstances, it seemed like the perfect way to mark his second marriage. In fact, his entire kitchen needed to be reoutfitted. With children in mind, he picked out the biggest skillet he could find, a pot for vegetables and a Dutch oven. He was about to add a set of enamel dishes when Jayne came up behind him.

Glancing at the cookware, she said, "You don't need those things."

"Who says?" If she intended to leave, she had no say in how he spent his money. If she decided to stay, then they would have something to talk about.

After surveying the pots and pans, she stood on her toes and scanned the higher shelves. "What you really need are biscuit tins." She reached above her head, lifted two round pans and inspected them. "These are nice."

He held in a smile. "Anything else?"

"Pot holders. I left you one of mine, but it won't last forever."

Together they picked out everything a new bride could want for her first kitchen. Ethan's heart swelled with hope as they carried the cookware to the counter where Mrs. Wingate looked ready to bust with curiosity.

"And who is this pretty young lady?" she asked.

Jayne smiled at the busybody. "I'm Mrs. Trent." The words made Ethan feel ten feet tall. *Let it be true…*

Mrs. Wingate clasped her hands at her breast. "I had no idea!"

"We were married a month ago," Jayne replied.

A rush of panic swept through Ethan. They had told LeFarge they'd been married in Missouri. If the outlaw pumped Mrs. Wingate for information, he would learn the truth. Rude or not, he had to stop the women from talking. Reaching for his billfold, he addressed the clerk. "How much do I owe you?"

Frowning, she named a price and made change.

Jayne glanced at him with annoyance and then turned back to Mrs. Wingate. "It's nice to meet you. Maybe we can chat some other time."

Ethan snatched the box to his chest and headed for the door. "Let's go, sweetheart."

As soon as they reached the street, Jayne gave him a sideways glance. "I'm not foolish. I said I was your wife because it fits with the story we told LeFarge."

"Not quite," he said in a firm tone. "He thinks we've been married for years."

The pots and pans rattled with each step as they paced to the hotel and then climbed the stairs to their rooms. Bracing the box against the wall, he fumbled in his pocket for the key. When it dropped to the carpet with a soft plunk, Jayne picked it up and opened the door. It struck Ethan as fitting. She held the key to his heart as well.

He followed her into the room and set the rattling box on the floor.

"I'd like to rest a bit," she said.

"Sure, it's been a hard day."

He opened the door to the adjoining room and stepped back, allowing her to pass through the entry. As soon as the last inch of her skirt brushed his boot, he closed the door with a soft click.

Frustrated, he rubbed his hand over his jaw. When a day's worth of whiskers scraped at his palm, he decided to shave and put on fresh clothes. The decision to share his bed was hers, but as sure as the sun would rise, he'd be ready to make love to her the minute she asked.

Jayne dropped down on the hotel bed in an exhausted heap. The soft mattress shaped itself to her back and hips, lulling her into a fitful slumber for the rest of the afternoon. Dreams came with the twilight. She saw herself riding hard and fast across a grassy plain with LeFarge in pursuit. She startled awake with her pulse pounding and her hands wrapped around her belly to protect the baby.

Still exhausted, she dozed again. This time she dreamed of Rainbow Falls and Ethan caressing her breasts and thighs. She drifted awake in a languid fog, but her pulse was racing even faster than it had before.

How could she long for his touch and, at the same time, fear the consequences? Loving Ethan meant admitting to needs she didn't want to have. For love. Companionship. A strong shoulder to lean on. It also meant trusting that he was truly over losing Laura.

His voice echoed in her ear. *I'll wait as long as it takes…*

Twilight filled the room with dusky shadows. Through the thin walls she heard the tap of Ethan's boots on the floor, then the trickle of water filling the washbowl. She shut her eyes to block out the picture of him stripping off his shirt, but the darkness only made the ivory of his skin more vivid. Her fingers ached to touch the hard muscles defining his back. She remembered the purpose in his voice when he promised to be patient, and it made her tremble.

Opening her eyes, she sat on the edge of the bed and peered through the window. The sky had deepened to a purplish blue, like a lake at midnight. Feeling like a moth trapped behind glass, she raised the sash a few inches. A man's voice drifted upward from the boardwalk and a woman chuckled at his joke. A dog barked and its mate howled in perfect harmony.

Battling a wave of loneliness, she lit the oil lamp on the dresser and slipped out of her dress and undergarments. The air prickled against her bare skin, making her nipples pucker with the sensation. Fighting the sudden tension, she lifted a white nightgown from her trunk and lowered it over her head. As she reached down to close the lid, her gaze landed on her mother's scissors.

She would have given a year of her life to talk to her mother just one more time. *Mama, Mama…what should I do?*

Stay strong. Be sensible.

Louisa McKinney's voice echoed in her daughter's mind, but tonight it brought no comfort.

But I love him, Mama. He says he loves me.

She could almost see her mother's skeptical gaze. Louisa McKinney had loved two men and been hurt by both. Except the circumstances weren't the same as the ones facing Jayne. Her father had died in an accident no one could have predicted, and Ethan was nothing like Arthur Huntington. He'd never hurt her on purpose. The problem was that he loved too well. His feelings for Laura were proof.

Sighing, Jayne slipped her fingers through the loops of the scissors and worked the blades, thinking of the blue gingham Ethan had bought for her. Someday she'd cut it into a familiar pattern—

Familiar patterns.

Shimmering silk or lush velvet—she loved them equally. Poplin or linen—they both made up into nice day dresses. Fabrics changed with the season. Styles changed with the times in a woman's life.

With a sudden clarity Jayne understood Ethan's love for her. She and Laura were like two beautiful dresses in the same closet, each one a perfect fit and right for an equally special occasion. He loved them both, truly and deeply.

She longed to open the door between their rooms and rush into his arms, but old habits and new doubts kept her feet glued to the floor. She was an incurable optimist. She saw things at their best, but Hank had shown her how wrong she could be. What if she had misread Ethan's feelings? What if they made love and he turned his back on her and wept for Laura?

Needing fresh air, Jayne opened the window as wide as it would go. At the same instant she heard a matching scrape from another sill. The hiss of a match drew her gaze to Ethan's room, where an orange glow flared in the darkness. She heard one long draw as he sucked on the pipe, then silence.

Vanilla smoke wafted into her room.

Needing to clear her head, she clutched at the high sash and tried to push it down. The wood refused to budge. Another curl of smoke drifted across her face and into her eyes. Standing on her toes, she pushed with all her might.

The sash broke loose and fell to the sill with a crash. Glass shattered in the air and fanned across the carpet in a sea of crystal splinters. There was nothing left of the window, nothing left to stand in the way of the cool night air, the stars, her destiny.

Ethan burst through the door. With a glance, he took in the broken window and her bare feet. "Don't move."

"I—I'm fine," she stammered. "The window just fell."

"The counterweight probably broke."

He walked to her side, pulverizing the biggest slivers beneath his boots. Without giving her a chance to argue, he scooped her into his arms and headed for his room, the only place on earth she wanted to be.

Wrapping her arms around his neck, she decided to enjoy the ride. When the hem of her nightgown slid down her thigh, she let if drift to her hips, feeling like a bride as he carried her over the threshold.

"You take my room," he said. "I'll check with the clerk about another one for me."

She trailed her fingers from his neck to the back of his head, forcing him to look down at her bare thigh. When he came to a dead stop, she decided he needed another hint.

"You can put the thought of separate beds out of your head right now," she replied. "I want us to be married, Ethan. Tonight and always."

His eyes lingered on her face, then burned as bright as embers turning into full flames. "I think that can be arranged, Mrs. Trent."

He carried her across the room, set her on his bed and sat down next to her. The scent of his pipe tobacco filled her nose as he smiled.

She had expected him to pounce on her, but instead he squeezed her hand. "We're not going to hurry anything," he said. "God knows I want to, but we only get one first time."

"Except this is the second," she said.

His expression turned somber as he cradled her hand in both of his. "Rainbow Falls was a beautiful night, but things got muddled at the end. Tonight, I want you to know how much I love you, right from the start."

"I do," she said. "I love you, too."

Her husband raised their entwined fingers, so that their hands made a shadow across her breasts.

"This time we're making promises," he said. "I'll never leave you nor forsake you. I'll never give you cause to doubt my love. I'll take care of you and our children—including the one you're carrying now—from this day on, until death us do part."

Putting her palm on top of his knuckles, she looked into his eyes. "I promise you, Ethan, that I'll give you comfort every day and every night. I'll feed you cookies and scratch your back. I'll give you babies, too, as many as you want. I believe in you. I trust you, and I couldn't be happier than I am right now."

With their gazes joined and void of secrets, he

curved his mouth into a smile. "It's time to kiss the bride."

Pulling her close, he matched his mouth to hers in an act of bold possession. Jayne flashed back to their first wedding kiss, the one on the knoll that had been sweet and sincere. A seed had been planted that day, and it was about to burst into full bloom—a red rose, a ripening garden, endless meadows of rippling grass.

Wrapping her arms around her husband's neck, she savored the fullness of his desire for her and her desire for him. She wanted the moment to last forever, but Ethan broke it off with a husky whisper. "I'm going to turn the lamp down a bit."

An aching heat pulsed through her veins as he walked to the dresser, dimmed the light and then faced her. His gaze lingered on her ankles, her knees, then upward to her thighs and breasts. As if a thread were pulling them together, he walked back to the bed, where he sat down and tugged off his boots. They hit the floor with two soft thuds, then he twisted on his hips, pinned her against the pillows and kissed her.

Tonight he wasn't asking for anything. He was telling her with his tongue exactly what he intended to take. He was staking his claim on her body, to mark this moment for all time, for all the world to know that they were a couple.

Filled with excitement, Jayne decided to do the exact same thing. Breaking the kiss, she put her hand on his chest and pushed him back. "Get undressed," she ordered.

Ethan gave a throaty chuckle. "I'll be damned. You're just as bossy in bed as you are everywhere else. I don't know why I'm surprised, but I am."

Jayne arched an eyebrow. "Are you going to argue with me?"

"Hell, no. This is one time I don't mind being told what to do."

After pushing off the bed, he squared himself in front of her, raised his hand to the opposite wrist, and oh-so-slowly unbuttoned the cuff. When he took even longer to undo the second sleeve, Jayne pushed to her knees and went to work on the buttons running down his torso.

"By the time you finish with that shirt, I'll have gray hair," she complained.

Ethan cupped her bottom and pulled her close, matching their hips. "Are you in a hurry?"

"Aren't you?"

"Nope. I intend to take my time."

Moving like a lazy river, he stepped back and rolled the shirt off his shoulders and hung it on the bedpost. His belt came next, then the dungarees and everything else.

She nearly lost her breath at the sight of him in all his glory. The muscles in his torso were tight and hard, his waist narrow, his thighs strong and close. He was flesh and bone, a man who could bleed and cry, but he also knew how to love and fight. Her husband would do anything to protect her. Anything to nurture and love their children.

His eyes locked on to hers with an intensity that pierced her soul. Still on her knees, she pulled her nightgown over her head and flung it on top of his shirt. Taking his hands in hers, she scooted forward on her knees so that her breasts grazed his flat chest and her smooth thighs were flush against his hairy ones.

"Are you still intending to take all night?" she asked, wiggling her hips to tell him what she wanted.

His male flesh stirred against her belly. "Maybe just half the night. Old Faithful is getting more ornery by the minute."

"Who?"

When Ethan gave a meaningful glance to his nether region, Jayne burst out laughing, then nuzzled his ear. "I think he's waited long enough. I know I have."

Before Ethan could reply, she trailed her lips down his chest, kissed the coppery discs of his flat nipples, and followed a line of hair down his belly, tasting his skin and breathing in his scent.

When she reached the triangle of brown hair between his legs, he sucked in a breath and groaned. If she had her way, they weren't going to endure this torment for half the night or even five more minutes. Sliding to her bottom, she took his heavy flesh in both hands, caressed and stroked him, and then looked up at his face.

He had closed his eyes, and his chest was shuddering with the effort to breathe evenly. A lump rose in her throat. She'd never felt so triumphant and aware of her power as a woman. Joyous and awed, she followed her instincts and explored the new territory of her husband's body—all of it—with deep kisses.

"Holy hell!" he cried. "I've never—"

Before she knew it, she was on her back and Ethan was suckling her breasts and driving her crazy with his hands. In an instant she went from being a woman in control to one who didn't want to be. Tangling their tongues and limbs, they braided their bodies into a single strand, forever erasing the line between giving love and receiving it.

In its own way, this odd dance made perfect sense, but Jayne was long past thinking about it. She and Ethan were creating a new world with its own language of touch—a place where asking was no longer necessary and telling wasn't the least bit selfish. She belonged to this man and he belonged to her.

With a soul-deep moan, he filled her body and made her his wife. With tears of happiness, she welcomed him home with pleasure pulsing through her body and joy brimming in her soul. Again and again, her husband journeyed into her, filling her with heat and hope and love, until he shattered in her arms, and it was…good.

Chapter Seventeen

Five days had passed since Ethan had first made love to his wife, and each morning he'd woken up with her warm feet tucked against his calves. Staying in town hadn't been all bad. He had been able to give Jayne a honeymoon, complete with suppers in the hotel restaurant and lazy days in bed.

With the morning sun streaming across his shoulders, he tucked his arms more securely around his wife. Smiling in her sleep, she rested her hand on his chest, displaying the silver-and-turquoise wedding band he'd given her last night. After supper he'd slipped it on her finger and given her the larger one to slip on his. Just as he'd expected, one thing had led to another and they'd skipped dessert…sort of.

Ethan grinned at the thought of last night's lovemaking. He had been blinded by the sun and lost in the stars all at once. At the telling moment when all conscious thought was lost to him, and only instinct and wanting were left, he had called her name, again and again, until his body exploded and the storm faded into gentle darkness. Spent and happy, he'd started to untangle himself, but she had stopped him.

"Thank you," she whispered.

"For what?"

"My name."

Considering her worries over Laura, it was natural that she'd have doubts. He had pushed up on one elbow and tipped her chin, putting them eye to eye. "Do you remember all those nights I slept on the floor?"

"Of course."

"I'm going to let you in on a secret," he had said. "I did a lot of imagining between dusk and dawn, and making love with you is everything I dreamed it would be and more. I've never felt this way in my life."

In no way was the confession a disservice to his first wife. Because he had loved Laura so well, his senses were keener, his expectations higher. Jayne had taken him back to some of the best times of his life and then to a place that belonged only to them.

Wanting to drive the point home, he'd put on his most bodacious smile. "I mean it, Jayne. You make me crazy."

She blushed. "Really?"

"Most definitely." He cocked a grin. "Now it's your turn to tell me I'm ten times the man Hank Dawson was. Only you don't have to, because I already know it."

"Try a thousand times the man…"

"Try a million."

"Two million."

With the last declaration still on his lips, she had pushed him onto his back and straddled his hips. For the fun of it, he had let her pin him to the bed, where he'd proved again how patient he could be.

Now, glancing down at her relaxed face, he considered kissing her awake, but he decided to wait. After all, she was with child and she needed her rest. Instead he thought about the changes he wanted to make to the ranch.

After he hired a crew and finished the barn, he'd draw up plans for a four-bedroom house. Someday he'd teach his sons how to ride and his daughters how to dance. He and Jayne would grow old together. They'd watch their grandchildren ride ponies and eat birthday cake, and he'd cherish every minute of every day.

It all seemed too good to be true. Ethan shivered in spite of the morning sun warming the sheets.

As usual, this afternoon they'd check with Handley to see if he had heard from Chief Roberts. Maybe LeFarge had been caught. The thought gave him hope, and he let his mind wander to the day ahead of them. His most pressing need was finding a cow and buying a dozen chickens. Soon there would be milk for his wife and child, eggs for breakfast and fried chicken for Sunday dinner.

Ethan closed his eyes and drifted from one pleasant dream to another. He hadn't been this happy in years.

Sheriff Handley slapped a telegram down on his desk. "Roberts says your story is true, Mrs. Trent, but *I* expect you to stay nearby."

Ethan squeezed his wife's hand to stop himself from mouthing off to Handley. "You know where we live, Sheriff."

"So does LeFarge." Handley rocked back in his squeaky chair. "There's news about him. A bank teller in Los Angeles was murdered about ten days ago. It might have been a simple robbery, but a ticket clerk at the train station saw a man fitting LeFarge's description. Unfortunately he couldn't remember where the man was headed. He could be anywhere by now. San Francisco, Mexico, even here."

Ethan's jaw tightened. "What else do you know?"

"Not much, just that the federal authorities are doing their best, but it's a big country with lots of places to hide." He stared at Jayne. "If I were you, ma'am, I'd be very careful. You're a sitting duck on that ranch."

The sheriff had a point. Situated in a valley bordered by mountains and pine forest, the cabin offered no protection. LeFarge could lurk for days, watching them from the hillside, and they would never know it. "We'll think about it," Ethan said.

Jayne shook her head. "There's nothing to think about. I won't let that awful man rule my life. If he robbed that bank, he could be in Alaska for all we know."

Handley rocked back in his chair. "I hope you're right, but don't say I didn't warn you. The bank clerk was shot in the back. He didn't know what hit him."

Fear gnawed at Ethan's ribs like a trapped animal. As he pushed to his feet, Jayne rose with him.

"We'll be in touch," he said, praying their next visit to town would bring word that LeFarge was locked up or dead—preferably dead.

Gripping Jayne's hand, he guided her out the door and down the boardwalk. When he had first laid eyes on her, he'd been afraid to touch her. Now he was afraid to let go of her hand. His eyes darted from one street corner to another, making note of strangers and narrow alleys.

LeFarge could be anywhere. Watching. Waiting. Planning his revenge. Ethan felt sicker by the minute. When they reached the store, he pushed through the door first and surveyed the aisles. Seeing no one, he hauled Jayne off the street and into the safety of the shop.

She stumbled against him. "Ethan! I'm not a mule!"

He grunted an apology, but he knew how her mind worked. That comment about LeFarge being in Alaska said it all. She had turned a wish into reality, and the determined tilt of her chin told him she was going to be stubborn about it.

He handed a list of things they needed to Mrs. Wingate and listened to the women chat while the clerk assembled their order. Still on guard, he walked to the front window and peered through the glass. A train had just arrived and the boardwalk was crowded with strangers. As he studied the unfamiliar faces, his wife's cheerful voice drifted to his ears.

"The baby's due in November," she said shyly. "Do you think this flannel will be warm enough?"

Ethan's shoulders rippled with tension. He didn't

want anyone to know she was expecting a baby, not until LeFarge was out of the picture. He glanced over his shoulder just as Mrs. Wingate unwrapped a length of yellow flannel.

"Three of my children were winter babies," she said cheerfully. "This will be perfect. Where are you from, dear?"

"Kentucky."

The information was too close to the truth for Ethan's comfort. Turning abruptly, he paced down the aisle. "Jayne—"

"Do you have family back home?" Mrs. Wingate asked.

"No. My mother passed away a year ago. I miss her every single day."

Ethan gave her hand a hard squeeze. "I almost forgot. I need to get to the lumber mill before it closes." It was a made-up excuse, but he had to shut her up.

"Couldn't we go tomorrow?"

Ignoring the question, he turned to Mrs. Wingate. "I'll pick up the order in the morning. How's that?"

The older woman scowled down her nose. "That's fine by me, Mr. Trent, but your wife might have questions only a woman can answer. I was about to ask her to stay for tea. She has special needs, you know."

Of course he knew that, but mostly she needed to stay safe. "That's very nice, but we can't stay," he replied pleasantly. "Maybe another time."

The clerk turned to Jayne. "If you have questions, dear, visit me alone and we'll talk."

Jayne thanked the older woman and followed him out the door. As soon as they reached the boardwalk, she grabbed his sleeve. "Ethan, what's the matter?"

"Everything," he growled.

"It's LeFarge, isn't it?"

"It's more than that." He couldn't bear the thought of losing her or seeing the baby come to harm. He had to make her understand that the outlaw wasn't in Alaska and that he posed a real threat. He went straight for her motherly instincts.

"You shouldn't tell anyone about the baby," he said.

"Why not?"

"The less people know about us, the better." His dry throat turned his voice into a buzz saw. "I want to keep this marriage as quiet as possible."

"I had no idea you felt that way."

"Well, I do."

"Then maybe I should stay in town," she said in a shaky voice.

He let out a relieved sigh. She finally understood the danger, and so he paused to weigh the option of staying in Midas a few more days. It wasn't a clear-cut choice. The town offered the protection of more people and access to Handley and a telegraph, but the ranch was their home and he had a family to support. "We can't stay in town," he finally answered.

"I didn't say *we*. I said me."

He stopped short in the middle of the boardwalk. "What does *that* mean?"

Tears filled her eyes and she pressed her lips into a tight line. A scene on the busiest street in Midas was the last thing they needed, so Ethan hooked his arm around her waist and guided her to the hotel. They hurried through the lobby and up to their room, where he closed the door and turned the lock.

As he faced his wife, he saw that she was struggling with something vast and personal. He didn't know what to say, so he waited as she squared her shoulders, gathering her dignity as if she were putting on a pair of fancy gloves.

Raising her chin, she said, "I don't understand. Did I say something to embarrass you?"

"You couldn't embarrass me if you tried." He was proud of her courage, the spunk that made her strong.

"Then why did you tell me not to talk about the baby? Is it because of Hank? Are you ashamed—"

"God, no! I don't give a hoot about Dawson. I love you more than I can say. I'd die for you."

"But you dragged me out of the store!"

His ribs nearly broke apart. Couldn't she feel the fear, the threat? Didn't she remember how much it hurt to lose someone you loved?

Bracing her elbows against her waist, she started to twist the wedding band off her finger. Understanding dawned on him. Not once in her life had a decent man given her shelter or love. While he saw secrecy as a way of keeping her safe, she saw it as a sign of disgrace because of that damn fool Dawson and her mother's cheat of a husband.

He wrapped his hand around her shaking fingers and pressed the ring back into place. "Don't take it off, Jayne. Not ever. This baby is mine, and I'm proud to claim you as my wife."

"Then why—"

"Mrs. Wingate means well, but she's a gossip. The whole town will talk. If LeFarge shows up and hears about the baby, God knows what he'll do. The man's hell-bent on revenge."

Air whooshed from her lungs. "I see."

As her shoulders sagged, he eased her into his arms. She pressed her face against his chest and he felt her blood rising to her cheeks. A tremor passed through her body and her breathing warmed his neck. A breeze stirred through the window, drawing their gazes in unison to the fluttering curtain. A cloud covered the sun, and gray shadows fell across the mountains between Midas and their home. Tomorrow they would be alone on the trail to the ranch.

Ethan pondered the hellish possibilities. An ambush. A sniping. LeFarge lying in wait at the cabin. Protecting Jayne and their child meant seeing evil everywhere. It was the coldest feeling he had ever known. Only the heat of his wife's body kept his hope alive. "I have to keep you safe," he said.

As she curled her hand against his chest, she raised her chin. "I want you to teach me how to shoot."

"I will, but that's not enough." He ran his hands up her arms and cupped her face between his palms. "I won't leave you alone for a minute. We can't risk it."

"Nothing is going to happen," she said fiercely. "I won't let it."

But she didn't have that power. People died. And he knew from experience that tears of regret tasted bitter, not sweet.

The clouds shifted in the late-afternoon sky, filling the window with orange light. The sudden glow threw shadows across the bed and against the wall. The glare reflected on Jayne's upturned face, making her both fiery and fragile. Heat surged through Ethan's veins. With a moan, he drew his wife into his arms and closed his mind to everything but her shape, her scent. Trembling, she clasped her hands around his neck. He kissed her then, with a mix of torment and faith, fear and affirmation.

They fell to the bed in a tangle of arms and legs. In seconds her dress was off, her underthings gone, his pants dangling from one ankle and his shirt open and loose. With a fire that matched the setting sun, he made love to her, losing himself in the melting heat of her body.

She climaxed quickly, but he held back. He wanted the moment to last and last. He wanted to love her like this forever, but when she wrapped her arms around his waist and kissed the center of his chest, he lost control.

As fast as their lovemaking had started, it was over, and he was afraid again.

Timonius LeFarge cursed himself for a fool.

His train ticket had been good through Santa Fe,

and that's where he was now, sitting in a saloon wishing he had never wagered his entire stake on a full house with nines high. He was also wondering how much of his money Jayne Dawson had kept for herself.

He had left Los Angeles three weeks ago. With the generous proceeds of his bank robbery, he could have opened that saloon in Denver, but instead he'd blown almost every dollar on women, whiskey and bad poker hands. Plus he was feeling as sick as a rabid dog. His head was full of snot, his lungs hurt and flashes of fever made him sweat through his clothes.

Dammit to hell. He needed another stake, and the Dawson woman had it. Plus he owed her a night of punishment for lying to him. Tipping back the dregs in his whiskey glass, Timonius decided to pay a visit to the Trents. He'd hold a gun to the woman's head, rape her a few times, and either she or the rancher would hand over the cash.

He left two bits on the bar and sauntered out the door in search of a cheap hotel. As he passed the sheriff's office, he saw five Wanted posters in the window, including a new one bearing his own likeness. The printing said he was wanted for bank robbery, murder and arson. The last crime made him scowl. He'd tipped over the lantern and burned down the barn out of sheer carelessness and it had cost him dearly.

Timonius hated the thought of bouncing in the saddle all the way to the Trent ranch, but the Wanted poster increased the risk that he'd be recognized. Instead of taking the train, he'd have to steal a horse, preferably one with a good saddle and a warm bedroll.

A thick cough rumbled in his chest. A few more days and he'd have money again. All he had to do was find Jayne Dawson and make her suffer enough to tell him what he wanted to hear.

Chapter Eighteen

"No, Ethan. I won't do it. I can't stand being inside all day. I know you're worried, but I want to hoe the garden myself."

They had just finished breakfast and were sitting at the table. Jayne was determined to spend the day outdoors, but her husband had other ideas. He was sitting across from her, squeezing his coffee cup. "It's too risky for you to just walk around," he answered. "That bastard could be watching us right now."

"Or he could be in Mexico."

Ethan shook his head. "We don't know where he is. I have to split wood for a second corral this morning. Promise me you'll stay inside."

They'd had the same conversation every day for a week.

I think I'll walk down to the stream.

No, Jayne. It's not safe...

It's a beautiful day. I'll do the wash.

Stay inside and rest. I'll help you tomorrow...

At first she had complied with his wishes, but three

full weeks had passed since they had received any news about LeFarge. The outlaw wasn't coming back. She was sure of it. Looking at her husband scowling across the table, she put iron in her voice. "Ethan, it's time to get back to normal. I know you're worried, but I can't stand being cooped up like this."

He shook his head. "Do it as a favor to me. Stay inside if I'm not in sight. We can't take chances. Not yet."

"Then when?"

"After LeFarge is in jail or swinging from a rope."

Jayne bit her tongue to keep from quarreling. Ethan had turned into her jailer, and yet how could she argue with him? He was a bundle of nerves. He didn't sleep more than an hour at a time, and some nights he didn't sleep at all. Even after making love, he stayed rigid and awake at her side. More than once, she had woken up alone and seen him standing guard at the window with his Winchester in hand.

Jayne heaved a sigh. "All right. I'll stay in the cabin. For today."

Ethan carried his half-eaten breakfast to the counter, retrieved a pistol from the nightstand and set it on the table. "Do you remember what to do?"

"Of course." He'd hammered the signal into her during their shooting lessons. "If I need you, I fire one shot."

"That's right."

She grimaced at the sight of the gun. She needed both hands to hold it steady, and even then she couldn't aim it properly.

"Don't hesitate," Ethan said for the hundredth time. "If you see anything suspicious, shoot and I'll come running."

She didn't doubt it for a minute. With the Winchester tight in his hand, he bent down, kissed her cheek and then pulled the door shut behind him.

Depressed by the sudden gloom, she rose from the chair and stepped to the window where dust mites swirled in a ray of sunshine. She hated feeling like a bug trapped in a jar. She had told Ethan she would stay inside, but the porch was as much a part of the cabin as the kitchen. What difference could a few feet make? Besides, she liked having the trail in sight. If trouble was headed her way, she wanted to see it coming.

Feeling better, Jayne positioned the rocking chair on the sunny side of the porch and fetched her sewing. Sitting with the basket at her feet, she took pleasure in threading the needle and sliding it through the yellow flannel she had cut into baby gowns. The familiar motion caused her shoulders to relax and she yawned in the pleasant warmth of the sun.

As the tension of the morning drained from her body, she fell sound asleep.

An irritated huff jarred her awake. Startled, she shot to her feet and came face to face with her furious husband. "I guess I dozed off," she said.

Ethan's eyes churned like a muddy flood. "You said you'd stay inside. I could have been LeFarge. It could have been too late."

The panic in his voice nearly broke her heart, but she'd had enough of his worry. The time had come to face facts. "Ethan," she said firmly, "I'm tired of being afraid. I've never hidden from trouble in my life, and I won't start now."

"But we don't have a choice, not until LeFarge is out of our lives."

"Of course there's a choice."

"Jayne, listen—"

"No! *You* listen!" Her voice rose to a shout. "If I want to go for a walk, I'm going to do it. If I want more water from the well, I'm going to pump it myself. I won't let that man ruin our happiness."

Ethan's brows pulled together in irritation. "You can't wish away the truth. He's a real threat."

"But I can't live like a prisoner!" She loathed herself for being near tears, but she was close to hating her husband for his high-handed ways.

His gaze clung to her face. "I can't risk losing you. If I have to stay awake every minute of every day to protect you and the baby, I'll do it."

A horse whinnied in the forest. Ethan jumped as if a gun had gone off.

"It's probably the Reverend," she said.

"You don't know that," he snapped. Shielding her with his body, he propelled her through the door. "Get inside and close the curtains."

She wanted to argue with him, but this wasn't the time. Instead she unhooked the red curtains she had made last week. They fluttered into place, changing the gray gloom into crimson shadows. Ethan peered

through the crack between the curtain and the glass
with the Winchester tight in his hand.

"Can you see anything?" she asked.

"Not yet."

She relaxed when she heard the rattle of a wagon
and the clop of hooves entering the yard. LeFarge
would have snuck up on horseback. When the rattling stopped, Ethan poked the rifle barrel out the
door. "Hold it right there!"

Jayne took his place at the window and peeked
outside. The driver was a lanky adolescent with a
bowl-shaped haircut and a pair of skinny arms that
he had raised over his head. "I'm just delivering the
lumber for the barn, sir."

When her husband continued to aim the rifle at the
youth, Jayne wondered if he had lost his mind.

"It's okay," she shouted to the boy. Coming up
behind Ethan, she pressed down on the gun barrel,
aiming it safely at the ground. He hung his head and
let out his breath.

The boy's face had turned as white as her cotton
drawers. As he lowered his arms, he glanced ner-
vously at Ethan and then spoke to her. "I'm not supposed to say anything, ma'am. It was going to be a
surprise, but maybe you should know that more folks
are coming."

"Who?" Ethan demanded.

"The Reverend and some families from church.
They're coming to build your barn."

Ethan nearly dropped to his knees with gratitude.
People were coming to help him. For a few hours

he could drop his guard, maybe even laugh and listen to a few jokes, perhaps doze for a bit after the noon meal. Even if LeFarge was watching, a crowd of men with ringing hammers would keep the outlaw at bay, at least for today.

God knew he needed some relief. He hadn't felt this bad since Laura and the children died. And just like then, he couldn't make the feelings go away. For Jayne's sake, he had tried to stuff down the fear, but he couldn't escape it. He would never forgive himself if LeFarge harmed her or their baby in any way.

The boy's voice cut through his thoughts. "Where do you want the lumber, sir?"

"Over by the meadow," Ethan answered. "You'll see the burn mark."

As the youth steered across the yard, Ethan looked down the trail. A second wagon crested the hill, and then another came along. Altogether he counted five wagons, each one carrying a mix of men, women and children. Three of the wagons were loaded with lumber. Another one held a makeshift chicken coop and a passel of clucking hens. Behind a buckboard, he spied a fat milk cow.

Lastly, he saw John Leaf on horseback, bringing up the rear. He was wearing work clothes, a worn hat and a smile that filled Ethan with pure relief. He owed the man more thanks than he could give. For the moment they were safe. Ethan slipped his arm around Jayne's shoulders and smiled at her. "It looks like we've got company."

She gave his waist a happy squeeze. "I better get to work. These people are going to be hungry."

He watched as she went inside and opened the curtains wide. As their eyes met through the sunlit glass, his wife smiled at him for the first time in a week.

The crowd unloaded the wagons in minutes. As the men set up the plank tables they had brought with them, the women marched into the kitchen with bowls and serving spoons in hand. Jayne scratched every family into her memory.

Andrew and Margaret Ripley had two little boys.

Elliot and Gertie Moorehead came with one set of twins and more kids than Jayne could count.

Frank and Susanna Hyatt had two daughters and a baby on the way.

Isaac Lindstrom, a widower, rode silently with his son, Howdy.

Priscilla and Luther Chandler were the parents of two young boys and an eighteen-year-old daughter. Amy was engaged to be married, and the family was from Kentucky.

Dishes clattered as the women set plates of food in the kitchen, and the pump handle squeaked endlessly as two young boys filled buckets for the thirsty men working on the barn. The older boys helped fetch tools and nails, while the older girls watched over the younger children.

With laughter rippling through the air, Gertie Moorehead smiled at Jayne while she unwrapped a plate of apple dumplings. "Mrs. Wingate tells me you're expecting," she said.

"Yes, I am," Jayne replied shyly.

"I'll never forget what carrying Ben was like," Gertie added. "I thought I was going to pop before he was born."

"That's not how it was with my Cindy," said Susanna Hyatt. "She came three weeks early and I've been trying to catch up with her ever since."

Gertie gave a friendly harrumph. "If you think Cindy's a handful, you should try chasing twins."

As the women worked, stories rolled from their lips. Jayne's questions about birth and babies received not one answer, but three or four. When her time came, she'd have plenty of help.

Wanting to share her happiness with Ethan, she excused herself from the kitchen and strolled to the barn. With her hands in her apron pockets, she watched as the men hoisted the fourth side of the frame and hammered it into place. Ethan climbed up the scaffolding and began hammering. Someone told a joke and her heart nearly burst with joy when her husband laughed and told one himself.

With hammers ringing in different rhythms, she watched as he reached into a bucket for a nail. When her white apron caught his eye, he smiled at her with a promise for the night to come. She wanted the moment to last forever, but one of the older girls broke the spell by banging on a frying pan with a spoon.

"Supper's ready," she called.

"Let's eat," shouted Reverend Leaf.

The men came down in a wave, washed up at the well, then bowed their heads for the quickest grace

Jayne had ever heard from a preacher. Amid jokes and laughter, they feasted on the meal. The children ate next, and then the women.

When there wasn't a speck of food left, the ladies washed the dishes, spread blankets in the sun and talked about their lives. From babies they moved on to older children and finally to Amy Chandler's wedding.

"She has her heart set on a wedding dress like mine," said Priscilla. "But the only dressmaker in Midas doesn't have time for us, and the wedding is in August."

"Maybe I can help," Jayne said eagerly. "I was a dressmaker in Lexington."

"That's where I grew up," said Priscilla. "Where was your shop?"

"On Beaumont Street. My mother—"

"Oh, my goodness! You're Louisa McKinney's daughter. I should have recognized you. You have your mother's hair and her fine features." The older woman's eyes widened with admiration. "She made my wedding dress almost twenty years ago. I still have it, but it doesn't fit Amy."

"I'm sure I could make one just like it."

"She'd be thrilled," Priscilla said. "She loves that dress, but as you can see, I'm not much bigger than a bug and she takes after her father."

Jayne had already noticed that Amy was six inches taller than her mother and as big-boned as her father. "I'm sure I can make something that she'd like. I just need to see the dress and take her measurements."

Priscilla sighed. "I don't know when we can come back. Luther's due to ride out, and I don't dare leave the boys alone all day. Is next week too late to start? Or maybe we should just bring the boys with us."

The Chandler boys were bona fide terrors. They had been bickering all day, and Jayne didn't think they'd do well at a dress-fitting. It sounded far easier for her to ride to the Chandler place. Besides, this was the excuse she needed to take a day away from the ranch.

"It will be easier if I come to you." Ethan might not like the idea, but he would have to understand. "I can ride out tomorrow if you'd like."

Priscilla smiled with excitement. "That would be wonderful!"

"No, Jayne. Absolutely not!"

"But this is important to me. I'm making friends, and I can help someone."

Still warm from their lovemaking, she had been curled against her husband's side when she told him about Priscilla Chandler's wedding dress. Mistakenly, she had thought that spending the day among men would put him in a better frame of mind.

"Do you know what you're asking?" he said.

"I know you'll be worried, but I want to go." She laid her cheek against his bare shoulder. "We both talked to John yesterday. Handley says no one has reported seeing LeFarge since he left Los Angeles, and even Chief Roberts thinks he went to Mexico."

Rigid with exasperation, Ethan swung his bare legs

over the side of the bed, yanked his pants over his hips and paced to the window.

Rising up on one elbow, she watched as he leaned against the wall and stared through the glass. In the dim moonlight she saw his shoulders tighten as he raised his hand to his face and tried to scrub away the tension. Finally he said, "Would you stay if I asked?"

Something hard and needy passed between them, and her pulse quickened with dread. "Are you asking?"

Turning slowly, he said, "Yes, I am."

His eyes glistened like obsidian, hard and black, and she wondered where this stranger had come from. Pushing to a sitting position, she untangled her nightgown from the sheets and pushed her arms through the sleeves. "If I don't go tomorrow, then when? Next week? Next year?"

Ethan shook his head. "LeFarge is still a threat."

"But we don't know that."

"*I* know it. If he thinks you have Dawson's money, he'll come back for it. He could hurt you, Jayne, and the baby, too."

Tremors shot down her spine. She raised her hand to protect her belly and yet it was the baby that spurred her on. "I'm sorry, Ethan. But I don't want this child growing up in a house where every sound makes her jump like a scared rabbit."

Sliding his gaze from her face, he turned to the window where the moon had dropped below the mountains and the sky absorbed the light like black velvet. She saw him grip the sill as if he could push back the night, but nothing moved. His fingers turned white. Then his shoulders sagged and he dropped his chin to his chest.

With a startling clarity Jayne saw the brutality of the choice she had asked him to make. He could follow his instincts and protect his wife, or he could go against that urge and trust her judgment. For a man who had blamed himself for his first wife's death, the choice was cruel.

But *his* plan was just as harsh. She had trusted one man's judgment and lost everything. Sometimes a woman had to stand on her own in spite of the cost. It was a matter of principle. Her heart thumped against her ribs as she stepped to his side and touched the tight muscles in his arm.

"I don't want to hurt you, Ethan, but I *have* to go tomorrow, just to prove that I can."

He shook his head. "One more month. If we don't hear anything by then, I'll forget the man ever breathed."

It was a reasonable request, but she had already made plans with the Chandlers. "I need time to do a good job. I want the dress to be special."

"All right," he said, heaving a sigh. "Then I'll go with you."

"No," she said firmly. More than the dress was at stake. Ethan had married a capable woman, and she hadn't changed just because he'd slipped a ring on her finger. She touched his arm. "That won't solve the problem."

"You're being stubborn."

"Call it whatever you want, but I'm going tomorrow and I'm going alone. You have to understand. I've got a mind of my own and I'm going to use it."

"I know," he said, shaking his head. "That stubbornness is one of the things I love most about you. I won't stand in your way, but I'm going to ask you to please be careful."

"I will. I'll be back long before sundown. I promise."

"If you're not, I'll be all over this mountain looking for you."

He had made his voice light and she loved him all the more as she slipped into his arms. As he pulled her close, she felt a stirring deep in her body. It was small and alive, a feather-like tickle, and she caught her breath. "I feel the baby!"

Belly to belly, they stood with their foreheads touching. Humming with contentment, she leaned against her husband.

As he tightened his grip around her waist, his breath grazed her ear. "Are you sure you have to go?" he said.

"Yes," she answered. "More than ever."

Ethan woke up with a pounding headache. Three cups of coffee didn't take it away, and neither did Jayne's promise to stay alert. As he walked across the yard to saddle her horse, he squinted up at the gray clouds and tried not to think about bad weather.

He had asked her to take the buckboard and follow the main road, but she had been adamant about riding over the ridge. It was the same trail they had taken to Raton, so she knew the way. It was also shorter, a fact that gave him some comfort.

After cinching the saddle and checking it twice, he led the gelding into the yard where Jayne was waiting on the porch. Dressed in a split skirt and a brimmed hat, she looked liked an ordinary ranch wife calling on a friend. This morning he'd watched her pack the red sewing bag dangling from her hand. It held a tape measure, a packet of pins, a sketch book and two pencils. For the hundredth time, he wondered if he had made the right decision.

"I could still go with you," he offered.

She shook her head. "I'll be just fine."

With an air of confidence he envied, she mounted the horse and settled into the saddle. He knew what it was like to be left with things unsaid and undone, and so he forced a smile as he handed her the reins. "It's a beautiful day for a ride," he said. "Enjoy yourself."

Smiling sweetly, she leaned down and kissed him on the lips. "I'll be back before you know it."

Ethan doubted it. He was in for the longest day of his life. "You have the gun in your pocket, right?"

She nodded. "Yes, but I'd rather leave it here."

He almost agreed with her. The woman couldn't shoot worth a damn. During their lessons, half the bullets had ended up in the dirt and the other half had flown over the stack of tin cans and into the trees.

"Keep it where you can reach it," he said firmly. "You might need it to scare away a coyote, or if you get lost, or if—'' If he didn't stop thinking, he'd never let her go. ''Just take it.''

When she glanced at her pocket as if it held a live snake, Ethan worried even more. Finally he said, ''Have a good day.''

''Thank you,'' she said. ''For everything.''

He forced a smile, but he didn't deserve her gratitude. He wanted to pull her down from the saddle and lock her in the cabin.

She was being foolish, and he hated it.

She was being courageous, and he admired her for it.

She was doing what a normal wife would do, and he envied her that confidence.

After nudging the horse into a fast walk, she turned in the saddle, waved goodbye with a smile and disappeared down the trail.

Timonius couldn't believe his good luck.

Sitting like a statue on the broken-down gray, he watched the Dawson woman ride off alone. He'd been spying on the couple for two days now. Yesterday, when she'd fallen asleep on the porch, he'd been about to strike when those do-gooders had shown up and ruined his plans.

Shaking with fever, he endured another fit of coughing. His lungs felt like wet sponges and his bones ached like he'd been in a fight. He belonged in bed, preferably a clean one, but the past few days had been well spent. He'd learned that the rancher was expecting him, and he kept the woman in the cabin as much as possible. He probably fancied himself to be in love with her, a notion that Timonius intended to use against him.

The woman wasn't nearly as cautious, and Timonius watched like a buzzard as she rode away from the ranch and took the right fork, probably to visit a neighbor. Wanting to put distance between himself and the rancher, he decided to shadow her for a while.

A good hour passed.

It was time…except he had a catch in his throat. He knew what was coming. To cover up his coughing, he buried his mouth in the crook of his elbow. When the spasm hit, his chest shook so hard that he nearly toppled from the saddle. His ribs felt close to cracking and he tasted blood from his torn-up throat. When the fit finally passed, he was so weak that a child could have knocked him flat.

Through the thinning trees, he saw the Dawson woman ride out of the forest. The path led to a ranch with a two-story house and a couple of boys playing mumblety-peg in the yard. Let her have her day, Timonius thought. He'd ambush her on the way back.

As soon as Jayne vanished over the hill, the air in Ethan's lungs turned sour. His head throbbed worse than ever, but he wasn't about to sit inside the cabin nursing a headache. He'd go crazy if he thought too much, so he looked around for something to do.

The problem was that he had finished every job that kept the cabin in sight. He didn't want to ride out and check the cattle, though he should have. Somehow the cabin connected him to his wife, and he couldn't bear the thought of being more alone than he already was. The barn was nearly done, too. The men had put on the first coat of white paint just before dusk, and he needed to buy more before he could finish the job.

Looking at the new building, Ethan felt a rush of gratitude. It rose from the landscape like a child's first tooth, and he thought of the one chore that still had to be done. The black mountain of debris hadn't been touched, and next to the white barn it looked like pure filth.

Yesterday, John had been blunt about it. "When are you going to get rid of that mess? It's an eyesore and it stinks to high heaven."

"I'll get to it," Ethan had replied. He'd turned away before the Reverend could see his eyes. The mountain of debris was a reminder to be careful, to hold tight to each day, and part of him didn't want to tear it down.

Now, standing in the yard with his hands on his hips, Ethan looked long and hard at the rotting wood. In his mind's eye, the misshapen heap took on the face of the devil himself, of LeFarge threatening Jayne, and even Ethan's own dark side—the part of him that would have broken his wife's spirit because of his own fear.

He didn't like what he saw. If Jayne could get on with her life, so could he. It was just a matter of doing what had to be done.

Striding into the barn, he snatched the pickax, marched up to the rubble and swung the blade high and hard. He flashed back to digging Dawson's grave and seeing Jayne for the first time. As the metal head bit into a rotting timber, a chunk of debris flew six feet in the air.

Ethan swung the ax again, even harder this time. He worked in a fury until sweat soaked his shirt and black dust clung to his face and hair. The stench of rot filled his nostrils, and he tasted particles of burned wood in the back of his throat.

Picturing the outlaw's gaunt face, Ethan drove the ax deeper into the debris. Rage consumed him. Strong, putrid and nearly blinding, it pulsed from his spine to his fingertips and into the head of the ax as he tore the mountain apart. Every blackened board and every brittle nail, every grim reminder of Le-Farge, had to be plowed back into the earth where it would erode into the soil and even do some good.

Birds cawed as Ethan worked. A buzzard circled over the ridge, but he refused to follow its sweeping arc with his eyes. The sun peaked in the noon sky, but he didn't stop to eat the meal Jayne had left for him. Instead he guzzled water from the well and hurried back to his task.

The debris pile was nearly level now. Using a shovel and hoe, he spread the dross throughout the meadow. Before he knew it, he reached the rocks marking Dawson's grave. Looking down, Ethan took in the green grass growing between the stones and a scattering of orange poppies reaching for the blue sky. Yellow sunshine warmed his shoulders, and he paused to take in both the vastness of the earth and the smallness of a single human life.

The grave might have been Laura's resting spot,

or Jayne's, or his own. He closed his eyes, wishing with every breath that he'd hear his wife's horse coming down the trail. He counted to ten, then twenty, but nothing happened.

There was no breeze, no sound, no sense of time or space or life of any kind. Then, in that long, unearthly quiet, he heard first one gunshot, and then another and another, ringing across the land like thunder coming before a storm.

Chapter Nineteen

As long as she lived, Jayne would remember lifting Priscilla Chandler's wedding dress out of the old-fashioned cedar chest. The dress had yellowed with age and it needed a good pressing, but the wrinkles only made her mother seem closer. A quiet joy filled Jayne's soul as the older woman reached across time to bless her daughter's marriage and the baby in her womb.

Feeling both lonely for her mother and joyous, Jayne held the dress up to the sunlight pouring through the bedroom window. "It's beautiful," she said.

"I knew your mother well," Priscilla replied. "I always thought she poured her love into wedding dresses because someone had broken her heart."

"My father died when I was three. She married again, but her second husband wasn't a good man. I don't think she trusted anyone ever again."

"That's a shame," said Priscilla. "It's not easy to start over, but it's worth the effort, don't you think?"

"I definitely do."

She had started over today by making this trip to the Chandler ranch and so had Ethan. Longing swelled in her chest. Since her husband had given her this moment, she wanted to return the consideration by arriving home sooner than he expected. Moving with familiar precision, she took Amy's measurements, sketched the dress and sat down for a quick lunch with Priscilla and her daughter.

The three women talked about the wedding.

"At least two of my friends are getting married next year," Amy said. "They both want special dresses, but the seamstress in Midas says fancy things take too much time, and she doesn't like to do them. Do you think you could sew for my friends?"

"I'd love to," Jayne replied.

Priscilla chimed in. "The town's growing every year. If you want the business, we'll pass the word and you won't know what to do with all the work."

A slow smile spread across Jayne's face as she imagined the pleasure of sewing for new brides in Midas. "I'd like that," she said. "Maybe wedding dresses only. I'll be busy with Ethan and the baby."

"He seems like a good man," Priscilla said. "I'm glad to see him happy."

"We're good for each other," Jayne replied. "I'm happy, too."

A pure and honest contentment poured from her heart. She had everything a woman could want—a loving husband, a baby on the way, friends and meaningful work for her hands. She could hardly wait to get home, just to tell Ethan how much she loved him.

"I have to go," she said when the dishes were done. "Ethan will be worried."

"Of course, he will," said Priscilla. "All men worry from time to time. Tell him Luther and I are expecting you two for Sunday supper sometime."

Jayne bid the two women farewell, climbed on Buck and headed for home.

An hour later she was glad she had taken the precaution of leaving early. The ride was more uphill than downhill and the gelding's pace slowed with each weary step. The shadows in the forest were thickening with each passing minute.

"Come on, Buck. It's not much farther."

As she leaned forward to pat the horse's neck, a shimmer of gray caught her eye. The flash had come from the trees a few paces ahead of her. It was too pale to be a shadow and too dull to be a ray of sun.

Her skin prickled as she scanned the sides of the trail where pine branches formed a net of sorts. Turning the gelding, she peered down the road she had just taken and waited for muted hoofbeats or the stirring of a bird, but she didn't see a thing.

With a breath to steady her nerves, she nudged the gelding into a faster walk.

"Hold it right there, Jayne." The dry voice drifted through the pines like smoke.

Every instinct told her to make a run for it, but LeFarge had picked the spot well. Steep slopes marked both sides of the trail and the path stayed straight for several yards. If she bolted, he'd have plenty of time to aim and fire before she vanished around the bend.

Acid churned in her stomach. Ethan was waiting for her, and he'd be worried sick. She couldn't let him down. She had to escape before LeFarge shot her dead or dragged her home with a gun pressed against her temple.

Trust God and stay strong.

Her mother's advice rang clear and true, and Jayne knew what she had to do. If she couldn't outrun the outlaw, she'd have to bluff him.

Squaring her shoulders, she peered straight into the forest until she spotted him between two Jeffrey pines. His duster hung like a rag from his scrawny shoulders, and his skin was the color of damp flour. Even his horse was gray, a dappled nag that looked as exhausted as he did. Only his orange hair, dirty and unkempt beneath his dusty hat, convinced Jayne that the ghost in front of her was human and not a specter rising from the grave.

"What do you want?" she demanded.

"You already know what I want."

He guided his horse between the two Jeffreys and rode up next to her, putting them face to face. The stench of his breath filled her nose. Nearly gagging, she forced herself to look into his eyes. The blue irises were glittery with fever, and the whites were covered with a sickly pink film.

The man was ill and possibly delirious with fever. Her only hope was to play to his greed. "You want the money Hank Dawson stole," she said evenly,

"It's in a bank in Los Angeles. I'll give you his will and a letter."

"It's a little late for the truth, isn't it, Jayne? You didn't tell me about the bank account before, and I have to wonder what else you're keeping from me."

"Nothing. Hank left me with the train tickets. That's all."

He cocked the hammer of his gun and aimed it at her face. She had to buy time. "Okay," she said calmly. "You're right. There's more money."

"Where is it?"

"You'll kill me if I tell you."

"I'll kill you if you don't," he said, stroking the trigger.

"It's hidden," she said. "You can have it all, but I want something in return."

"You're in no position to bargain."

"If you promise to take the money and never come back, I'll take you right to the spot where I buried it and I won't go to the authorities." Of course she would, but later, when Ethan and the baby were safe.

"You've already been to the law." The gun dipped from her face to her chest as if it were too heavy for him. "Where's the goddamned money?"

Jayne squared her shoulders. "What assurance do I have that you won't shoot?"

"Absolutely none," he replied. "But you can be damn sure that I *will* shoot if you don't tell me everything."

LeFarge was a buzzard who survived on the carrion of the lives he ruined. As long as she didn't roll over and play dead, she and Ethan had a fighting chance.

Sitting straighter in the saddle, she turned the gelding down the trail. "Let's get going. It'll take awhile to do the digging."

LeFarge rode close enough to fog the air with his body odor. Her skin crawled, but she kept the gelding to a walk. As long as the outlaw held her hostage, he'd have the advantage over Ethan. No matter the cost, she had to escape before they reached the ranch.

Using only her eyes, she scanned the sides of the road for a hidden trail. Behind her, LeFarge coughed hard, spit on the ground and let loose with a string of obscenities. She had never heard such foul words or been called such vile names.

With each rumble in the man's chest, she imagined the thunder of his gun. As the sky darkened, arrows of light knifed between the trees. Time was running out. Desperate to find a hidden path, she craned her neck to look down the last steep slope.

"What are you looking at?" LeFarge growled.

"There's a shortcut."

With a coarse laugh, he said, "I'm in no hurry. We've got all night, and I intend to enjoy myself...with you."

Terror pulsed in Jayne's blood. Whispering a prayer for God's help and mercy, she spotted a deer trail jackknifing down a steep slope.

Staring straight down the road to keep LeFarge from guessing her plan, she slid her hand into her pocket and gripped Ethan's gun. Ten slow paces later, the gelding emerged into bright sunshine while

LeFarge was still shadowed by trees. She yanked the gun free, aimed it wildly behind her and fired one desperate shot.

"What the *hell!*"

Snapping the reins, she kicked the gelding hard. The startled animal bolted into the trees just as a bullet whizzed past her ear. Branches cracked in her wake and the gelding's labored breath matched her own. Pine needles whacked her in the face. Grit filled her nose and eyes, blinding her and making her gasp.

When the gelding coiled to control the slide, she lost her grip on the reins. Tangling her fingers in the mane, she fought to keep her balance as the animal plunged down the hill. With each stride, it gathered momentum until its hindquarters shimmied. A panicked squeal tore from the horse's throat as it splayed its forelegs, sending Jayne flying over its head.

She knew, even before she heard the second bullet, before it pierced her flesh and left a trail of blood, that she and the baby weren't going to make it home to Ethan. All she could do was trust God and stay strong, hope for the best and whisper a prayer.

Please, God.

"Dammit!"

LeFarge rammed his Colt back into the holster. The fool woman had nearly taken off his left ear with the potshot. From the top of the trail, he saw her twisted body lying between a boulder and a lightning-scarred tree. He was too far away to see if she was breathing, but she'd hit her head and he could smell blood in the air. If she wasn't dead yet, she would be soon. Timonius prided himself on being a good shot and he had been aiming to kill.

"Oh, hell!" he muttered.

She hadn't told him where she had hidden the money. Ethan Trent's ranch was a big place, and Timonius didn't care for the idea of another wild-goose chase. He would need a bargaining chip to get the rancher to talk. Dead or alive, Jayne Dawson had given him what he needed. Looking down at her body, he made a note of the tree and the rock. He was banking on Trent being fool enough to trade the money for a shred of hope.

With a grimace, he hocked up a mouthful of spit, let it fly and headed down the hill to claim what was rightfully his.

Who among you walks in darkness and has no light?

First spoken by a crazy old man seeing visions of a tortured future, the Bible verse echoed in the depths of Ethan's soul as surely as the three shots had blasted from the forest.

His heart turned to ice, hard and blue, the color of his wife's eyes. He couldn't breathe. If Jayne was dead, he wanted to die. If she was alive, he had to find her. Was she hurt? Had LeFarge taken her hostage? He didn't know. He had only the chilling certainty that his wife was in grave danger.

Frozen or not, he knew what he had to do. He strode into the barn, snatched up his rifle and listened for a cry, a shout, some sign to guide him.

Loose and ready, his finger rested on the trigger

as he scanned the edge of the forest. A flock of sparrows took flight. Pine branches swayed without reason. He heard the staccato call of chipmunks and the whisper of a breeze. And then he saw LeFarge emerge from the forest on a gray horse with bulging eyes.

The animal looked ready to collapse and LeFarge didn't look much better. Ethan wanted to shoot the man on sight, but he couldn't do anything until he found Jayne.

With the rifle aimed at the outlaw, he edged out of the barn and looked into the man's silvery eyes. It was like touching frozen metal with wet skin. LeFarge had the power to tear him into pieces.

"Where is she?" Ethan demanded.

"Give me the money and you'll get her back."

Ethan narrowed his eyes. What lies had Jayne told? For all his worrying, not once had they played the "what if" game. It had been too painful to imagine LeFarge in their midst, and now Jayne's life depended on Ethan's ability to guess what she had told the outlaw. He needed more information.

"What did you do with her?" he said forcefully.

"The money or the woman. You pick." The old man settled back in his saddle. Ethan saw the gun in his hand, but LeFarge didn't make a move to shoot. That hesitation told him that he had something the man wanted.

"What makes you think she's that important to me?"

The outlaw glared at Ethan. "Don't play games

with me, Mr. Trent. That money is mine and I want it back. Now, where is it buried?''

A clue. Jayne had told him something. She had to be alive. Staring hard at the outlaw, Ethan took a chance. "It's buried in the garden."

"Then you better start digging up your bean plants if you want to see her alive."

Hope warmed his frozen heart like a beam of sunlight, but he pushed it out of his mind. He couldn't afford the distraction as he weighed his options. Perhaps it would be best to give LeFarge the illusion that Jayne's lie about the money was the truth.

"I'll get a shovel."

But as he stepped toward the barn, Jayne's horse emerged limping from the forest, riderless and streaked with blood. With a burning certainty that turned his heart to a bloody pulp, Ethan knew his wife was dead or dying.

LeFarge looked at the animal with a smirk. "I guess I hit her after all." With a smooth sweep of his arm, he raised his gun, pulled back the hammer and took aim.

As the outlaw's empty gray eyes focused on him, Ethan saw his own death as plainly as he saw the setting sun. His whole life had come to this one moment. He could live well or die like a coward. He could let LeFarge take him or he could fight. He could die right now or he could risk living without Jayne.

With sweat on his brow and his hands as cold as they had ever been, Ethan knew what he had to do.

LeFarge seemed to know it, too. Ethan saw the

misery of sickness in the man's eyes, the pity of a
wasted life, the guilt and shame of lying, stealing and
even murder, and he knew LeFarge was facing the
same choice he was.

The outlaw's shoulders sagged ever so slightly and
his eyes dimmed. Before the man could change his
mind, Ethan aimed at his chest and fired.

The gray horse bucked in a frenzy, causing Le-
Farge to slump forward and fall to the ground in a
heap. The sulfur smell of gunpowder hung in the air.
With his nose burning, Ethan lowered the Winchester
and stared at the man who had taken everything from
him. He saw the last twitch of his fingers and heard
his last rasping breath. His eyes stayed open, staring
blindly at the heavens, and in that moment Ethan
begged for mercy.

Please, God, let her be alive…

With blood rushing to his brain, he ran into the
barn and jumped bareback on the roan. The sun was
huge and red, a fire burning in the sky, and he raced
through the meadow at a gallop. He didn't know if
Jayne had survived or if he was looking for a body,
but he had to have answers.

When he reached the crest, he slowed the horse.

"Jayne!"

Silence sliced at his hope, but then a ray of sun
glinted off a metal object lying in the middle of the
road. It could have been anything, a scrap of metal
from a wagon, a broken tool, but as he rode closer,
he saw his six-shooter lying in the dirt. Hopping
down from the roan, he snatched it up and opened
the cylinder.

Jayne had gotten off a single shot. Her fight had begun on this spot, but it hadn't ended here. Ethan scanned the forest below him. Twilight turned it into a bottomless canyon, but between the trees he saw a jagged trail marked by patches of dirt.

Gripping the reins, he led the roan down the steep hill. Another glint of light caught his eye and he skidded toward it. The flash disappeared with the changed angle of his line of sight, but he spotted his wife's sewing bag. It had been torn nearly in half and the contents were strewn among the trees.

"Jayne!"

He heard nothing, but as he searched for her, he found other clues. Hoofprints marked the earth where pine needles had been pushed aside. Shattered tree branches dangled like broken arms. The odors of sap, sweat and blood hung in the dusky air. He sensed her heart beating as if it were his own, and then he saw her hat, a glove and finally her crumpled body lying askew at the base of a lightning-scarred tree.

Dropping the reins, Ethan ran to her, skidding down the trail until he was kneeling at her side. He saw that she had pulled both arms tight across her belly. Mulch clung to her cheeks and neck. He saw blood in her hair, and her skin had turned pearlescent in the dying light.

With his heart pounding, he pressed two fingers against her throat and felt for a pulse. Heat flowed through his fingertips, but he couldn't tell if it was Jayne's warmth filling him or his own hope draining away. He pressed his ear against her chest and held his breath. He felt it then, the steady beat of her heart looking for his.

Hope flickered like a match and he spoke her name. ''Jayne…''

But still she didn't make a sound.

Shaking inside, Ethan surveyed her wounds. A purple lump had risen on her temple and he saw a bloody scalp wound. Tree branches had shredded one sleeve of her jacket and gouged her arm. As he straightened her elbow, he saw where LeFarge had left his mark. A single bullet had pierced her shoulder.

As gently as he could, he probed the wound. Thick blood rimmed the hole, but it wasn't oozing or sucking air. The shot had passed clean through. The injury was serious but it wouldn't kill her. It was the lump on her head that made his gut clench.

''Sweetheart, wake up,'' he pleaded.

Still she didn't make a sound.

He had to get her to the cabin where she would be warm and he could tend to her wounds and tell her to wake up. Scooping her into his arms, he took heart at the warmth of her cheek against his chest and then trudged down the mountain with the roan following in his wake.

With each step, he listened for a moan from Jayne's lips, a whisper of life, but he heard nothing. The coppery scent of her blood filled his nose. A head injury, a miscarriage, bleeding to death. He had to get her home where he could tend to her wounds, as she had tended to his, both seen and unseen.

Let her live, let her live, let her live.

* * *

By the time he pushed through the cabin door, the sky had turned from pale blue to a purple expanse crowded with shining stars. After placing his wife on the bed, he peeled off her jacket and loosened her skirt much as he had done all those weeks ago. Trying to be gentle, he removed her blouse and cleaned the shoulder wound with whiskey, talking to her while he worked.

When he finished bandaging her shoulder, he looked again at the gash on her forehead. The blood had dried, but she needed stitches. Mostly, though, she needed to wake up.

He didn't have any smelling salts, so he dampened a rag with cold water and wiped at her cheeks and forehead. She needed a doctor, but he didn't dare leave her. Nor could he see jouncing her in a wagon all the way to town on a moonless night.

Having done his best, Ethan pulled a chair to the side of their bed where he rubbed her hands and talked to her as if she were answering back. He told her about the last moments of LeFarge's life and the bleakness of his death. Then he whispered that he loved her and needed her and begged her to open her eyes.

She didn't stir, but he could imagine her telling him to stand tall and live well. He could feel her speaking deep in his soul, in the same place where Laura and the children lived, and he knew with certainty that some things in life couldn't be taken away.

Now…this very moment.

No one could take this sliver of time away from

him. Nothing could erase Jayne from his heart, not even death.

Forever…a time yet to come.

Nothing could make him doubt the promise that someday he would see all the people he loved again, in heaven—a place full of love, laughter and unspeakable joy.

Ethan looked up at the silver heart hanging near the bed. He had put the mirror away when they returned from Midas as man and wife, but Jayne had hung it back on the wall. "Laura and I would have been good friends," she had said.

The gesture had touched Ethan deeply and the sight of the fire reflecting in the silver glass warmed him now. As he dropped his chin to his chest, he prayed. Words didn't come to him, but vivid pictures from his life filled his mind with color and light.

He saw Laura smiling at him with dovish eyes, and then one by one, William, Josh and Katie each waved at him. The four of them were in the yard of their Missouri home. Laura was cutting back a rosebush, the boys were rough-housing and his baby daughter was hanging on to her mother's skirt and teetering on wobbly legs. It was a glorious, ordinary day.

The picture changed then. Ethan saw himself on the ranch, walking down the path from the corral to the cabin. Jayne was pumping water at the well. Smiling, she offered him a brimming cup. He took it and drank.

"Come with me," she said.

As he took her hand, she led him to a spot of

shade where he saw a wicker basket. Nestled in yellow flannel was a golden-haired girl with her mother's eyes.

Ethan nearly wept at the pictures in his mind. Heaven touched earth when a man truly loved. He was sure of it. It was "now" and "forever" that counted, not tomorrow or later or someday. The in-between times could drive a man crazy, but love was worth the risk. With love came hope.

Hope is a rope. Tie a knot and hang on.

Closing his eyes, he rested his head on his wife's chest, grabbed that rope and hung on with all his might. God willing, he'd never again have to bury someone he loved, but if the worst happened, he knew he'd survive. As long as he stayed in the small glow where time and eternity touched, he was at peace.

Her shoulder throbbed with each beat of her heart, pulling her back to consciousness. With the dull pain in her torso came the memory of LeFarge and her ride through the forest. Her head hurt, too, and it felt wonderful. She was alive. Gloriously alive.

As the fog in her mind cleared, she remembered Ethan telling her that LeFarge was dead. Relief flowed from her head to her toes and her bones felt light against the bed. Her hand drifted down to her belly where she felt a hardness that told her the baby was safe, too.

Glancing down the length of the mattress, she focused her bleary eyes on her husband. Seated in a chair, he was slumped at her knees with his head cradled on his forearms. She could only begin to imagine the terror he'd experienced when he found her. She touched his temple. "Ethan?"

He jerked awake. Joy filled his eyes as he grabbed her hand and kissed her fingertips. "You scared the living daylights out of me," he said.

A fresh stab of pain radiated from the hole in her shoulder. She wanted to sleep, but she needed to talk about what had happened. "Are you all right? When I saw LeFarge, I was so worried about you."

"I'm fine," he said, squeezing her fingers.

"It had to be awful for you, but I had to go. Can you understand?"

A soft chuckle shook her husband's shoulders. "I do, and I love you for it. You're a strong woman. I'm just thankful God made you too stubborn to die."

"I wasn't being stubborn—"

"Of course not," he agreed. "You're strong-minded."

"I am."

"So am I. We're going to live this life as best as we can. We're going to cherish every day and enjoy every minute we have together." Ethan caressed her cheek. "I feel good, and it happened even before you opened your eyes just now."

"LeFarge is dead, isn't he?"

"Yes, but it's more than that." He told her about seeing her bloody horse, the defeat in the old man's eyes, about finding her and finally about the peace he'd made with the inevitable uncertainty of life.

"No matter what happens tomorrow, we have today and we have the promise of heaven," he said. "A man can't ask for more than that."

Tipping her head, she gazed into his brown eyes where she saw the loaminess of fertile earth. He moved one hand so that it rested on her belly where the baby was safe and stirring, and with the other he smoothed her hair away from her face.

"Lie with me," she said.

He stretched on the bed, then rolled onto his side so that she was cradled against the length of him. As he pressed his lips to the nape of her neck, he shifted his hand so that his palm covered the baby. Her tummy jumped and the hum in his throat told her that he, too, had felt the wonder of new life.

"I hope we have a little girl who's as strong-minded as her mother," he said.

"And three boys who grow up to be just like their father."

Gratitude for her husband, this child, the children that were yet to come, for life itself, flooded through her. With their hearts beating in perfect time, Jayne and her husband took joy in the hope of a new day.

Epilogue

∞⨯∞

Midas Community Church
Seven years later, 1892

Being a pastor brought John Leaf many pleasures, but without a doubt, he liked christening babies best of all. Standing tall in the pulpit, he made his voice boom in the crowded church. "Ladies and gentlemen, we are gathered here today for a very special occasion. Ethan and Jayne Trent stand before you for the dedication of their fourth child, John Robert."

The red-faced bundle of joy let out a squall that inspired ripples of laughter from the congregation. Glancing at the child, the Reverend smiled, too. A crying baby always got the same reaction from its parents. Just as he expected, Jayne jiggled the baby serenely while Ethan stood at her side looking as helpless as a first-time father.

John had to hide a grin. Ethan was far from inexperienced when it came to children. The evidence was squirming in the front row of the church.

The oldest, Louisa, was seven years old, and the boys were already calling her Lulu and making cow eyes behind her back. She had her mother's golden hair, and though Ethan wasn't her blood father, she was the daughter of his heart.

Next to Lulu stood the two boys. Ethan Jr., called E.J. for short, was five years old. He had his father's eyes and the promise of his broad shoulders. He also had an impish streak that he had no doubt inherited from the Trent side of the family.

Stephen, barely three years old, had more of his mother in him. With his new little brother shrieking at the top of his lungs, Stephen did the only sensible thing a boy could do. He covered his ears and groaned.

"Cut that out!" squealed Lulu.

As E.J. jammed his hands in his pockets, Ethan Sr. gave him a look that promised a talking-to after church. Lulu glared at her brothers as if they were lower than skunks, and Jayne Trent stood in front of the congregation with a screaming baby and a smile that lit up the sky.

The Reverend cleared his throat. "Ladies and—"

"Eeeeek!" shrieked Lulu.

John hid a smile as the girl flung a bullfrog out of her pocket. It landed in the second row, right on top of Mrs. Handley's head. The poor woman screamed and knocked a small orchard of wax fruit off her new hat. The baby wailed even louder, and Hildy Reynolds took it upon herself to pound out "Onward Christian Soldiers" on the piano. Mercifully, the frog found the center aisle and hopped out the door.

It might have been an awkward moment for another preacher, but John Leaf liked to stir things up now and then. He glanced at Ethan just as the man bent to whisper in his wife's ear. After she nodded, he scowled down his nose at all three kids and curled his index finger, motioning for them to come to the front of the church.

The two boys took their places with the mournful expressions of children who knew they were both loved and in trouble, while Lulu stood primly next to her mother. Ethan gripped each boy by a shoulder and gave his daughter a look that said she had a few things to explain as well. Smiling, Ethan glanced at his wife and then nodded for John to continue.

As the congregation sang the last verse of the old hymn, the baby's crying turned to a gurgle. Reverend Leaf cleared his throat and began again. "As I was saying, we are here today to celebrate the miracle of love."

* * * * *

PICK UP A HARLEQUIN HISTORICAL
AND DISCOVER EXCITING AND EMOTIONAL
LOVE STORIES SET IN THE OLD WEST!

On sale July 2004

TEXAS BRIDE by Carol Finch

Join the fun when a brooding Texas Ranger
reluctantly escorts a spirited beauty on a
hair-raising adventure across the Texas frontier!

WEST OF HEAVEN by Victoria Bylin

When a desperate young widow is pursued by
a dangerous bandit, she finds shelter and love
in the arms of a grief-stricken rancher.

On sale August 2004

THE HORSEMAN by Jillian Hart

A lonely horseman eager to start a family
jumps at the chance to marry a beautiful
young woman. But could his new bride be
harboring a secret?

THE MERCENARY'S KISS by Pam Crooks

Desperate to find her kidnapped son, a
single mother enlists the help of a hardened
mercenary. Can they rescue her child before
it's too late?

Visit us at www.eHarlequin.com

HARLEQUIN HISTORICALS®

FALL IN LOVE WITH
THESE HANDSOME HEROES
FROM HARLEQUIN HISTORICALS

On sale September 2004

THE PROPOSITION
by Kate Bridges

Sergeant Major Travis Reid
Honorable Mountie of the Northwest

WHIRLWIND WEDDING
by Debra Cowan

Jericho Blue
Texas Ranger out for outlaws

On sale October 2004

ONE STARRY CHRISTMAS
by Carolyn Davidson/Carol Finch/Carolyn Banning

Three heart-stopping heroes
for your Christmas stocking!

THE ONE MONTH MARRIAGE
by Judith Stacy

Brandon Sayer
Businessman with a mission

www.eHarlequin.com
HARLEQUIN HISTORICALS®

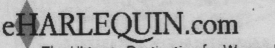

Savor the breathtaking
romances and thrilling adventures
of Harlequin Historicals

On sale September 2004

THE KNIGHT'S REDEMPTION by Joanne Rock

A young Welshwoman tricks Roarke Barret into marriage
in order to break her family's curse—of spinsterhood.
But Ariana Glamorgan never expects to fall for the
handsome Englishman who is now her husband....

PRINCESS OF FORTUNE by Miranda Jarrett

Captain Lord Thomas Greaves is assigned to guard Italian
princess Isabella di Fortunaro. Sparks fly and passions flare
between the battle-weary captain and the spoiled, beautiful
lady. Can love cross all boundaries?

On sale October 2004

HIGHLAND ROGUE by Deborah Hale

To save her sister from a fortune hunter, Claire Talbot offers
herself as a more tempting target. But can she forget the
feelings she once had for Ewan Geddes, a charming
Highlander who once worked on her father's estate?

THE PENNILESS BRIDE by Nicola Cornick

Home from the Peninsula War, Rob Selbourne discovers
he must marry a chimney sweep's daughter to
fulfill his grandfather's eccentric will. Will Rob
find true happiness in the arms of
the lovely Jemima?